Mystery of the Fallen

C. Lee Tocci

Laurel Canyon Publishing
North Hollywood, California

This is a work of fiction.
Names, characters and incidents are either the product of the author's
imagination or are used fictitiously.
Any resemblance to actual persons, living or dead,
is entirely coincidental.

'Let us swear an oath,
And all bind ourselves by mutual imprecations
not to abandon this plan but to do this thing.'
Then sware they all together and bound themselves
by mutual imprecations upon it.

The Book Enoch 6:4-6

Prologue

The number one thing that practically nobody knows about me:

My real name is Mystery.

Everyone calls me Misty and I've managed to make everyone, including my school, think my name is Melissa.

Mystery Hill. My mother has a weird sense of humor.

The number two thing that most people don't know about me: I have a problem with boys.

Don't get me wrong. It's not like I don't like boys. I do. I always have. But just not in the mooning, talk-about-them-all-the-time, pretend-I'm-not-looking-when-they're-look-ing-at-me kind of way. I always thought I was cooler than that. You know, more subtle. They were just boys, nothing special. Like girls, only different. Nothing to get excited about.

Until my sixteenth summer. And then, it wasn't all boys that became interesting, just two of them.

I know everyone's first love seems cataclysmic, but mine really was. All I wanted was my first real kiss.

But what I got was apocalyptic chaos.

Pitiful. That is so me.

Chapter One

Finally.

I held it reverently, cradling it with both hands. It was so small, yet so powerful. I tested its heft. It was lightweight, yet surprisingly dense. I stroked it gently, I had suffered through so much to possess it. I didn't want to risk crushing it or even scratching it.

My own cell phone. I finally had my own cell phone. If you didn't count that obscure community of Mennonites up in Lebanon, I had to have been the oldest person in New Hampshire without a cell phone. I was sixteen years old! I'd be seventeen in four months! How could I have survived this long without one?

"Lemme see! Lemme see!" My three-year old sister, Tiffany stretched to grab at the phone but she was strapped tightly into the car seat and all she could do was swing her arms at me in vain.

"See?" I flashed her a quick glimpse of the screen before turning the phone back so I could work it. I knew how to use it. Half the kids in my high school had this same phone, but this one was mine and there were calls I had to make.

"Mom!" Tiff had a voice that could ground planes. "Misty won't lemme see!"

"Tiffany, you have your own toys." Mom was using her Wisdom of Solomon voice. "Let Misty play with her toy and you can play with yours."

Yeah. Right. Toy.

The backseat looked like the returns desk at Toys R Us: broken and grimy hunks of plastic everywhere. While Mom tried to distract Tiff with a headless Barbie doll, I huddled into the corner, punched in a number and stuck a finger in one ear.

The phone rang twice before it picked up.

"Hello?" My best friend Kat sounded tentative. She didn't recognize the number.

"Guess who finally got a cell phone?" I asked.

"Misty?" Kat knew my voice right away.

I nodded as if Kat could see me.

"FINALLY!" she yelled so loud, my parents in the front seat could hear despite Tiff's tantrum. "Where are you?"

I looked out the window. "Maryland, I think. Though we might be in New Jersey by now. We left Ocean Isle yesterday and stayed in Maryland last night. We stopped after breakfast at the phone store. We're about halfway home."

"You'll be home today?" Kat didn't wait for me to answer. "Good! I've been so bored. There's been no one here to talk to except the Tucker Twins. And I want to hear all about Cade."

Cade. She said the name. The name that no one had dared to speak for the past forty-eight hours. Not since that afternoon, two days ago, when I had to say good-bye to him on the beach. We had always known that summers end and so will summer romances, but if I'd thought about it all, I'd thought we would be different. That somehow we would never have to part. But we did. I took a deep breath to hold back the misery.

"Misty? Misty?" Kat's voice scratched in my ear. "Are you still there? Did I lose you?"

"I'm still here." I pulled myself together. "I can't talk now."

"Your parents there?"

"Yeah." The word was heavy with meaning, all of which I knew that Kat would understand.

"Crap. You finally get a cell phone, and we still can't talk. What time will you be home tonight?"

"Not 'til late. We'll have to talk tomorrow morning."

"But school starts tomorrow!" Kat was in flat despair, but perked up quickly. "Go down to the bus stop early, okay? We can talk then."

"Right." I smiled as I hung up. Kat has been my best friend since forever. She's sometimes funny, sometimes goofy but mostly she's just been there, through both the happy and the crappy times.

But there wasn't a chance that Kat was going to get down to the bus stop early. She could barely make it on time as it was. But maybe the lure of gossip would drag her out of bed. I hoped so. I needed to talk to someone about Cade. Not my parents. They thought it was just a summer thing. They didn't understand that you really can fall in love forever when you're only sixteen.

My phone beeped. Kat had texted me. Well, maybe we couldn't talk, but that didn't mean we couldn't chat.

By the time we reached New Hampshire, my thumbs were killing me. I think I'd developed carpal tunnel.

There was one thing weird that happened on that long and boring ride home. I didn't pay much attention to it at the time, but it stuck in the back of head and I remembered it later.

It was after we left the phone store in Maryland. I was too engrossed in my new phone to pay much attention. I knew why Mom and Dad had broken down and finally bought it for me. I really had been trying not to sulk in the backseat, but I was so miserable and all I did for the first half of the trip was stare out the window and think about Cade. I don't remember seeing one thing as we drove; I just stared like a zombie.

"Hmm," My father had said, looking out his rear view mirror as we pulled out of the parking lot. "There's that car again."

I was only listening with half an ear, too busy plugging the phone into the power port in the back and getting it fired up.

"What car?" Mom had asked.

"I've been seeing it off and on, not long after we got on the highway in North Carolina."

Mom squirmed around to look out the rear window.

"Oh, my!" she said. "That one?"

The tone of her voice made me turn in my seat. A sleek black car that looked like a mini-stealth bomber on four wheels was two cars behind us as we pulled up on to the entrance ramp.

"Hard to miss it." Dad said, a note of worry in his voice. "Not exactly a car you see every day."

I turned back to play with my phone, but rolled down the window first.

"Misty," Mom said, still looking out the back. "Close the window. You'll blow us all to pieces."

"Sorry, Mom," I said as I rolled the window back up. "There was a fly back here buzzing around. I wanted to get it out."

There were two more times that I heard my Dad say something like "There it is again," but I didn't give it much thought. There's no way some weird sports car could have anything to do with me, right?

Chapter Two

I waited at the bottom of our street in the drizzly rain. I had known that Kat would never get there early, even though I'd called her once and texted her three times.

I checked my watch. I'd have to start down the street to the bus stop if I was going to make it on time. Kat would have to catch up. She'd get there at the very last second. Like she always did. I began walking toward the bus stop, slowly.

"MISTYYYYYYYYYYYY!" Kat's voice echoed all over the neighborhood, bouncing off the sides of the houses, waking anyone who had any intention of sleeping in past seven twenty in the morning.

She came careening down Fisher Place, her winter parka unzipped and flapping around her like bat wings. Her clothes were baggy in shades of fluorescents. She looked manic, but it was an image she had honed for years. Teachers didn't know how to take her, which is precisely why she dressed and acted the way she did. My heart might be broken, but she still made me smile.

She barely slowed down as she barreled into me, grabbing me in a bear hug as she hit me. I braced my legs and held my ground as she spun around me like a tether ball.

"Look at you!" Kat yelled so loud that, even though the bus stop was still a hundred feet away, everyone turned to stare.

I looked down at her. This was weird because the last time I saw Kat, two months ago, we were the almost the same height.

Kat looked me up and down like I was some kind of alien. "What happened to you?"

"I grew," I mumbled. Four inches. In one summer.

"Pissa!" It was Kat's favorite expression, useful in a variety of situations.

"It's no big deal." I hunched my shoulders. "My mother said she did the same thing at my age. She hit a growth spurt when she was sixteen and shot up almost overnight."

"Are you taller than her now?" Kat stood close to measure herself against me. I pulled at the sleeves on my raincoat, but it didn't really help. Mom and I had to go out and buy all new clothes before we got back from summer vacation, but we'd forgotten to get a new raincoat and my blue-green slicker, which was new last spring, crawled up my arms and pulled on my shoulders.

"No," I shrugged and rain dripped down my neck. "She's still an inch taller than me. She's five eleven and I'm only five ten."

"Only?" Kat rolled her eyes. We'd been taking the same bus together since first grade, the same as everyone else at the bus stop. Seemed like nobody moved in or out of Wicassett. By New Hampshire standards, Wicassett wasn't a small town, but after the fabulous summer I'd had, Wiscasset suddenly seemed like a backwoods wasteland, practically primeval.

The bus pulled up and we had to sprint to catch it. As usual, the Tucker twins were the first to board. They skipped backwards as the door swung out and open and then clambered onto the bus.

"Morning, Charlie!" Kat and I greeted the bus driver in unison as we had practically every morning since first grade.

Our street wasn't the first stop on the bus route. Technically there was one stop before ours, at the end of Harrison Ave, but since it was all strip malls and industrial parks in that neighborhood, we were used to always being the first ones on, which explained why the twins stopped short in the middle of the aisle.

There was someone already on the bus. And he was sitting in the back row. In the same seat that the Tucker Twins had always claimed as their own.

"Oomph," Kat grunted as she plowed into Chad Tucker's back. "Why'd you st---"

She got no further. Even though we both leaned to the left at the same time, I could still see the new kid right over Kat's head.

My first impression of him was both heat and ice. His eyes stared back at us, cold and hard, but I was hit by a searing aura that pulsed from him and scorched my skin like a blast from a flame. He was dark. Clusters of black curls cast shadows over his face and dusky eyes glittered from the murk. His jacket was black leather that hung open, showing a black tee-shirt that clung tightly to a lean chest. Faded blue jeans were the only color he wore and even they seemed to darken into the shadows. Danger throbbed from him like a black strobe light.

I'd seen gorgeous guys before, but there was something about this one that went beyond good looking. He was mesmerizing. Like the way you'd expect a cobra to be before it struck.

"Step in and sit down," yelled Charlie. Years of experience made us obey by reflex. Ty Tucker tensed like some psycho terrier and headed down the aisle, intending to oust the usurper from their throne, but Chad, always the wiser of the two, grabbed his shoulder, jerked him back, shoving him into a nearby seat.

Kat wriggled onto the bench seat and I slid in beside her. The new kid's eyes seemed to burn into the back of my head. I wanted to turn and look at him, but it would be too weird. Kat had no such reservations. She twisted around with her back to the window so she could stare at him while she supposedly talked to me.

"Pissa!" Kat bellowed over the growl of the engine as the bus groaned forward. I was grateful for the noise, because it almost drowned out her next words. "He is SO hot!"

"Be cool!" I leaned to hiss in her ear. "Don't look at him."

With all the subtlety of a third-grader, Kat pointedly faced me while peering out of the corner of her eye.

"What's he doing now?" I whispered.

"How can I tell if I'm not looking at him?"

I answered her with a glare.

She slid her eyes back in his direction. "He's staring at us!"

"He is not!" I shot back as I involuntarily turned to look. I caught his eyes for a millisecond that lasted a million years before ripping my gaze away.

He wasn't staring at us. He was staring at me. Definitely at me. His eyes were like searing black needles that pinned me like a bug to a board. I had to force myself to breathe.

The bus rattled to a stop and the kids from Country Club Condos poured on. I sighed in relief. A dozen kids got on the bus, mostly juniors and seniors. And three of them were cheerleaders. The girls bubbled onto the bus, bumping into the boys whenever they could. I used the distraction to turn around, supposedly to look at them as they took their seats, but really to check out the new kid.

He was still staring. Even if a body in the aisle blocked his view, when it moved, he'd still be staring right at me, as if the others didn't exist and he could see right through them. I twisted around and blindly faced the front. The heat on the back of my neck felt like a sunburn. I could almost feel the rain in my hair sizzling off. The bus roared and rattled forward.

"He's still looking at us!" Kat was blatantly gleeful. She loved drama. With the bus half full, her staring wasn't as noticeable, especially since everyone else was staring and mumbling about the new kid as well.

And because he kept staring at me, all the other kids started looking at me too. And they weren't admiring my frizzy hair or my too small raincoat. The cheerleaders eyed me up and down, as if to wonder if I was going to be some kind of competition to their powderpuff domination of the male population. But I didn't think it was admiration that made the new kid stare at me the way he did.

His glare seemed almost homicidal.

I shook my head as I turned back to stare out the front of the bus, trying to make myself believe that I was just being melodramatic but I felt the heat on the back of my neck and I knew, without looking, that he was still staring at me. Kat babbled excitedly in my ear, but if I could hear her over the roar of the bus, I couldn't make out a word she said. It was as if she were just another piston or carburetor or some other engine part cranking loudly. All I was aware of was his gaze boring into the back of my neck. Beyond the roar, I could almost hear a wordless whisper in my head.

What are you?

I shook my head. Not *"Who are you?"* but *"What are you?"* Which was weird, because if I had the nerve, that's what I would be asking him. *"What are you? And why are you here?"*

A million years later, and all too soon, the bus rattled to a stop in the school driveway. Charlie cut the engine and there was that strange millisecond of silence when everyone who'd been yelling to be heard over the roar of the bus suddenly stops. Then, with groans and muttering, the chatter started again as everyone reached for their backpacks and scrambled for the door.

Kat was still talking as she stood up, looking down at me as I sat, not moving, staring straight ahead. I wasn't going to get up until the new kid passed. I don't know why, I just didn't want him behind me anymore. I felt like I wasn't going to be able to really breathe until he was away from me. She nudged my arm with her backpack. I knew she wanted me to move, everyone else was passing us by. This broke one of those strange rules that the people on the front of the bus always got off first and the ones in the back waited. But Kat could have cracked my head open with her biology book and I wouldn't have moved. I wasn't budging.

It started to get quieter as the other kids poured off the bus. You could actually hear the rain beating lightly on the roof. Kat plopped back down, glancing from me to the rear of the bus and back to me again. I didn't need to look, I knew he was coming down the aisle. I hugged my backpack closer to my chest and waited.

He stopped. Right behind me. I could feel him standing there, like a bonfire when the fire has died down but the center timber is still glowing, black and glittering, hotter than the flame itself. I waited.

"Let's go!" Charlie's voice echoed through the near empty bus. I could see his face in that big mirror that he used to watch us while he was driving. He never turned to look into the bus; we knew that if he ever did, there'd be big trouble. A glance and a bark were always enough.

Except for today. I clenched my teeth and gripped my bag and stared straight ahead. I was not moving first.

"C'mon!" Kat hissed, caught between excitement at being in the middle of a dramatic moment and worried about being late for homeroom. "What's your problem?"

She pushed at me and I snapped a glare at her. She pulled back as if she'd been burnt and then sulked back into her seat.

Another million years went past and nobody spoke. Not Charlie. Not Kat. And certainly not me. The bus should have been getting cooler with all the warm bodies gone, but it was turning into a sauna. Moisture dripped off my brow but it wasn't from the rain.

"After you."

His voice was low and throbbing with a faint accent that I couldn't even begin to place. Unable to stop it, my head turned slowly as if all by itself, to stare up at him.

His eyes. They were dark, but I couldn't tell if they were black or the darkest blue I'd ever seen. They glittered down at me, as if he found my stubbornness amusing. I flared defiantly.

"I'm good." I wanted to sound cool and sophisticated, but my voice came out so breathy, I sounded like some brainless groupie who had just bumped into her idol.

The amusement in his eyes finally reached his lips and his mouth curled in a lop-sided smirk. "You think so?" he whispered.

I stood, dropping my backpack to the seat, and folded my arms in front of me, ready to wait him out.

Charlie ended the standoff. "Misty!" he barked at me, and out of habit, I twitched, grabbing the backpack. "Off the bus! Now!"

I held the new kid's stare as I edged into the aisle, Kat right behind me, and walked stiffly off the bus.

The quad was nearly empty by then. Everyone else had hurried inside, either rushing to get to homeroom on time, or maybe just to get out of the drizzling rain. Kat ran ahead, not stopping until she'd reached the overhang. But I dawdled in the rain and glanced back to see Charlie grab the new kid's arm as he went to get off the bus. I don't know what Charlie said, but an aura of fury pulsed from the new kid. For a moment, I was frightened for Charlie. He was an old man, maybe fifty or more, and pseudo-grouchy, but he'd been driving us to school for years and we all liked the cranky old dude.

The moment passed though, and the flare of anger died down. The new kid nodded respectfully and said something I couldn't hear. It seemed to be good enough for Charlie though, and he had a small smile on his face as he closed the door.

We stood in the rain, about twenty feet apart and stared at each other as the bus pulled away. The bell rang and I broke first, heading for the lobby, hurrying to get to homeroom before the second bell.

Kat was at the door and held it open for me as I passed through. I glanced back.

He stood staring in the pouring rain, as still as death. I ran down the hall.

Chapter Three

Second bell rang as I sloshed into homeroom. Ms. Merfeld looked more distracted than annoyed; she saw me dripping wet and probably figured I'd missed the bus. She waved me vaguely to the back of the room.

Great. The only seats left were in the back row, right under the air vent. Notwithstanding an act of God or Student Council, everyone tended to stay all year in the same seat they had from the first day; which meant I could expect freezing cold air dumping down on me all winter and sweltering heat in the warm months. This was because they turned off the heat at night and didn't turn it back on until five minutes before first bell. This corner wouldn't start to warm up for at least another hour.

What a pisser start to the year. My backpack dropped onto the desk with a loud wet splat that made everyone turn. I sat down with a huff and finger-combed some of the rain and snarls from my hair. The vent hummed above me and drowned out Ms. Merfeld's announcements, which was okay since she rarely said anything I hadn't already heard four thousand times before.

Homeroom assignments got divvied up by name and since my name last name was Hill, and Kat's last name was Randolph we've never had the same homeroom. Of course I knew everyone in the room, I'd known most of them since first grade, but that didn't mean I was friends with them. There were a lot of "Jackets" in my part of alphabet. That's what they called the tough kids that smoked in the bathrooms spent most of their time hanging in the hallways, snickering at

14

you when you walked by. Two football jocks, three of the perkier cheerleaders and a half a dozen assorted geeks finished off the roster. I could talk to the geeks, at least they were marginally human, but the rest were as alien as orangutans in the zoo.

"…he should be here shortly and I want you all to be polite."

I had missed the first part of Ms. Merfeld's spiel but I figured it was just the vice principal, Mr. Vanderhorn, coming to make an announcement. Maybe the P.A. system was down. My eyes wandered out the window and I caught myself wondering which homeroom the new kid was in. If he was N-through-S, I know Kat would tell me all about it. I had second period Calculus with Kat. I'd ask her then.

A waft of balmy air sailed into the room, smelling faintly like a sea breeze and reminding me of the best part of my summer vacation. I hugged the memory around me and let it warm me as I reluctantly pulled my eyes from the window and looked at the visitor.

The best part of my summer vacation was standing in the doorway.

My mouth dropped open as I stared at all six foot two inches of him. He stood there, looking gloriously golden and surprisingly dry. His blond hair was licked with silver where the sun had bleached it and his skin was tanned to a bronze so perfect, you could easily believe that he was cast out of pale copper and then decked out in corduroy and denim. A Greek god in blue jeans. As he turned toward the classroom he caught my eye and his eyebrow twitched up. A tiny smile teased a dimple into his cheek.

My hair was a disaster.

Ms. Merfeld, hardly immune to the paragon of beauty that had just walked into her classroom, simpered as she gestured him toward the back of the room. His smirk grew into a grin as he headed straight for the last open seat in homeroom. Next to me.

My hair was a disaster.

"This is Cade Himisanto," Ms Merfeld was saying, although, between the buzz of the heating vent and the humming in my head, she could have been announcing a fire drill. "He just moved to Wicassett last week and I'm sure we'll all extend a warm New England welcome…"

Blah blah blah. She went on and on but none of the babble penetrated. He was headed right for me. Or at least for the seat next to me. He stopped, swung his backpack onto the table and stared down at me, his eyes dancing.

My mouth was bone dry from gaping. I tried to close it, but it would just drop open again in amazement. Finally, coherency scattered the haze and I spoke.

Well actually, I squealed.

"CADE!" I jumped to my feet and launched myself at him, my arms wrapping around his neck. He laughed out loud then, that deep and fabulous chuckle that could thrash away any bad mood. His arms reached around me and I felt my feet leave the ground as he pulled me against him for a brief hug. He set me down quickly, remembering where we were much sooner than I did.

"Cade!" I said again. There were so many things I wanted to say, so many questions I wanted to ask, and all that came out was, "My hair's a disaster!"

He laughed even louder then, a contagious throttle that had the rest of the class snickering as well. Even Ms. Merfeld, fuming with disapproval from the front of the room, bit back a grin.

"Well," she huffed, straightening papers on her desk. "Apparently you already have an *acquaintance* here in Wicassett, Mr. Himisanto."

A wave of laughter rose from the class, which made my face burn. I broke away from him, mortified. "We met this summer," I muttered as I quickly sat down, my eyes on the desk.

"Did we?" He paused as if he was having trouble remembering. "I think you're right. Sometimes I have the most horrible memory."

I looked up at him, torn between indignation at the idea that he might have forgotten even one millisecond of our glorious summer vacation, and grinning because I knew that every memory was as etched into his mind as it was in mine. I decided that, for the moment, it was safer to go with being pissed. I stuck my tongue out at him.

Cade settled down into the seat next to me, almost as close as that last night on the beach when I'd thought that I'd never see him again. Ms. Merfeld went back to her announcements and handouts and I leaned into Cade, inhaling the clean briny scent of the sea that seemed to cling to him even here, fifty miles from the nearest ocean.

"What are you doing here?" It was impossible to whisper, what with the vent roaring above our head, but the buzzing blocked our conversation from the rest of the world and we huddled together in our own private cone of silence.

"Well, my little Misty Blue," he always dropped his voice to a throaty rasp when he called me that. I sighed and edged closer. "The way you went on about Wicassett, you made it sound so amazing, I felt I had to see for myself."

I snorted. (I admit it: I snorted.) I had done nothing but complain all summer about how boring Wicassett was, stuck in what seemed like the middle of the woods. It was ten miles to Manchester, and even though they called Manchester a city, it was just a big town; a bigger, more boring version of Wicassett. But now even Wicassett didn't seem quite so boring. If anything, it suddenly seemed like the most wonderful place on the planet.

"But how can you be here? In high school, I mean." I dropped my voice even lower and looked around to make sure no one was listening. "You told me you were eighteen!"

"Ah, but that was two months ago. This week, I'm seventeen."

I bit my lip as I stared at him. "But, you can't just---"

The bell sounded. Much too soon. Homeroom was only fifteen minutes long and the sounds of scrabbling chairs and shuffling feet penetrated even our little auditory sanctuary.

"What's your first class this morning?" He asked me before I could ask him.

"English Lit," I answered between hope and despair.

He didn't seemed surprised. "A coincidence," he said. One of his arms picked up my backpack while the other draped over my shoulder. "Mine too."

Chapter Four

Last Summer

That summer had started out with all the omens of being a complete disaster. My parents had rented a house near the beach in Ocean Isle. Their friends, the Villanuevas and the Coblyns had rented houses on either side. The Coblyns had no kids and the Villanuevas had a three year old boy, about the same age as my little sister, Tiffany. (Why couldn't I have a normal name like Tiffany?)

My parents had their friends, and Tiffany and Carlos had a built-in babysitter. Me.

The first week of the summer went as miserably as you can imagine. Up and down the beach, packs of kids roamed, heading down to the rocks where they'd congregate. And I, anchored by a pair of three year olds, could only watch as they passed by. By the time my mother or Mrs. Villanueva came out to relieve me, the kids would have disappeared, having headed off to some cool place that I could only dream about and I'd be stuck walking up and down an empty beach full of little kids and old people.

And so it seemed like my summer was doomed and I would spend all eight and a half weeks sitting in the "san bock" which is what Tiff and Carlos called the patch of fine sand near the lifeguard tower.

By day five, I was resigned to my fate. Carlos' parents spoke Spanish to him at home, so his chatter had an added element of bilinguality to the normal toddler gibberish. I entertained myself by interpreting their babbling into social and political debate.

For example:

"Mine!" Tiff yelled as she grabbed the sand shovel from Carlos.

"I using it." Carlos held onto his principals and the handle.

"Mine!" Tiff offered a persuasive counter argument.

Since this discussion didn't seem to be elevating to its highest level, I removed the article of contention. "Tiff," I explained gently. "Carlos is embracing a more socialist view of resource utilization. Since he is directly engaged in the construction of the sand castle, he feels that his immediate need of the tool overrules your prior right of litigious possession."

Tiff considered my line of reasoning dispassionately as she glared up at me, her fists on her hips. "Mine!" She barked. A woman of few words. At times, she could be quite succinct.

"Carlos," I explained. "Tiffany embraces a more capitalist view of property rights. She contends that, since she can trace the chain of ownership of said sand shovel from the manufacturer to the store to her mother and then, since said parental-unit subsequently granted custody of the tool to her, her rights prevail in this situation."

Carlos stared at me, his lower lip jutting angrily. He then pushed both feet through the sand castle, crumbling it into a grainy heap. Tiff immediately responded with an eloquent howl.

"Now Tiff," I lay back on the sand and closed my eyes against the blinding blue sky. "Carlos was simply demonstrating the innate difficulties of maintaining the physical infrastructure of society within a strictly capitalist economy."

And so it went.

I was impressed by Carlos' opinions on Global Warming, and while Tiff didn't dismiss his concerns for the environment, she was skeptical because of the lack of concrete empirical evidence supporting his conclusions.

I was wasting away on the seventh ring of hell, doing anything I could to keep my eight remaining braincells from going Kevorkian on me, when, like a gift from heaven, the cavalry arrived. And it was heralded by a chuckle.

Carlos had almost convinced Tiff that a modified National Health Plan, instituted in phases, might actually be a stimulus to the economy, when a disembodied laugh startled me.

I sat up, brushing the sand from the back of my head, and looked around. There was no one nearby and I didn't think the lifeguard, sitting on his tower thirty feet away and ten feet in the air, could have possibly heard us. I looked up at him, shielding my eyes from the sun's glare that always seemed to be directly behind him whenever I looked his way.

He dropped from the tower, landing on his feet like a cat. When I'd noticed him before, I'd thought he was old, like maybe in his thirties. There was something in the way he held himself that looked older to me, but as he dropped to the ground, he seemed to grow younger and by the time he hit the sand, he looked like a teenager.

And oh, what a complete to-die-for teenager he was. He had a kind of seen-it-all, been-all-over-the-world, nothing-could-ever-surprise-him attitude, but he looked young. And golden.

And hot.

"It would appear…" My personal sun god folded his legs beneath him as he sat himself down on the sand next to me. "…that young Tiffany remains unconvinced of the need for Universal Health Care."

I was having trouble breathing. I tore my eyes away from the vision to stare blindly at the kids. "Well," my mouth answered for me, because my mind was in complete chaos, "she's only three so I think we should cut her some slack."

Everything I said seemed to make him laugh. I smiled back weakly. I was completely over my head. What do you say to an angel that drops from the sky? He told me his name was Cade. I can't remember what we talked about, but he seemed really interested in everything I said and after a while, it got easier to talk normally. He was completely different from any other boy I'd ever met. Even the way spoke was different. He had this melodic drawl when he spoke, not really an accent, it was more of a poetic rhythm to his words. I loved to listen to him and whenever I could get him to say two or three sentences in a row, I went a little orgasmic.

That afternoon shot by and, before I knew it, it was five o'clock and I had to bring the little gremlins back to the house.

"I'll be off duty in an hour." He stared at his feet as he dug his toes aimlessly into the sand. It was kind of cute, like he was nervous or something. As if someone as amazing as him could be nervous talking to *me*. "Perhaps we could get something to eat?"

"Sure." My mouth was suddenly dry and my voice sounded scratchy.

"Shall we meet back here at six?" He stared out at the Atlantic and I wondered if he was watching for drowning people or just avoiding my eyes.

"Cool," was all I could think of to say.

"Cool." He echoed, glancing over at me for a moment before staring back out at the water.

I gathered up kids and buckets and towels and sippy-cups and started leading the pack up to the street.

"Until later." He called to me, tapping the side of his head with a finger in a tiny salute as if he would have tipped his hat to me, if he had been wearing one.

"Later," I answered back, grinning.

And that was the start of the most fabulous summer vacation in the history of mankind.

Chapter Five

So now, on the first day of the fall semester, my summer sun god walked beside me through the corridors of Wicassett High, bringing a golden glow to the dull hallways. Heads turned to stare. Maybe they were looking at Cade, but they could very well have been staring at me. I knew I was beaming like a moron, but I didn't care.

We walked into Mr. Gallagher's English Lit class holding hands. Normally, I'd sit in the one of the middle rows; the Jackets hung out in the back and the know-it-alls sat in the front; but today there were only two seats left next to each other and they were in the back row. Without a word, we both headed for them.

We settled in, our heads together, oblivious to the Jackets who glared at us for invading their territory. I didn't care; if I got my head flushed into a toilet later, so be it. It would be worth it.

Mr. Gallagher hadn't arrived yet when I caught the scent of something that smelled like cinnamon-pine and wet steamy leather. It seemed vaguely familiar and, as I looked up, a wave of heat enveloped me like a blanket.

The tall dark boy from the bus stepped up to Cade's desk. His gaze was stony cold, almost like he wasn't even focusing on him, but just facing his direction. All the chatter in the class faded as everyone turned to stare.

Beneath his tan, Cade paled. His face turned almost as vacant as the new kid's but I could see a muscle throbbing in his neck. He slowly rose to his feet.

They stood facing each other, so different, yet somehow, there was something in the way they held themselves that made them alike. Cade was bright and golden while the other was dark and brooding. They looked to be about the same height, maybe Cade was an inch or so taller, but as I watched, the new kid straightened up and seemed to grow an inch taller than Cade. Then Cade pulled himself up and seemed to rise higher than the new kid. I'd stopped breathing as they stood nose to nose, seeming to grow right in front of my eyes. Then the new kid gave a snort that sounded like a bull about to charge.

"You're in my seat." The new kid's voice was expressionless, but I could hear the shadow of a threat in his words.

I don't know what it was, but I got the feeling that they knew each other and this wasn't the first time they'd gone nose to nose.

"I belong here," Cade shot back between clenched teeth. "You… do not."

I wondered later how it would have turned out if they hadn't been interrupted; it didn't look like either one would have backed down. I couldn't even imagine how ugly it might have gotten if Mr. Gallagher hadn't stepped into the room.

Mr. Gallagher never had a reputation for being the most observant of teachers. Once he started rambling on about his precious Literature, you could blow up a desk and he'd keep on lecturing. Once, an entire class slipped out a first floor window, one at a time, trying to figure out how many kids could leave before he'd notice.

That class got down to four students before he had looked around, puzzled. But he didn't stop lecturing and a week later, they moved his classroom to the second floor.

Today though, Mr. Gallagher was a little more aware of his surroundings. He got as far as his desk, dropped his briefcase and an armful of books before looking around, baffled as to why it was so quiet and why everyone was turned to the back of the room.

"What's this about?" He bristled as much as a meek little man like Mr. Gallagher could bristle.

"He doesn't belong here," the new kid said, holding Cade's eye for a moment before turning to face Mr. Gallagher. "I'm signed up for this class and he isn't."

I bristled, wanting to tell him to shut up and sit down and stop picking fights, that there were plenty of seats, but as I looked around, I saw that all the seats were filled. For probably the first time in the history of Wiscasset High, English Lit was completely filled.

Mr. Gallagher huffed as he went back to his desk and lifted a file folder out of his briefcase. "And your name is?"

"Danel Stark, sir." The new kid's voice turned deceptively respectful. "I just moved here from Egypt."

Egypt? I didn't know what an Egyptian accent sounded like, but it sounded more European.

Mr. Gallagher harrumphed as he read the roster. He didn't look up as he asked Cade, "And you are?"

"Cade Himisanto." The fury in Cade's face as he glared at Danel leaked into his voice.

Mr. Gallagher harrumphed again, this time more sharply. "Well Mr. Himisanto, I don't see you on the roster and since this class is filled, you'll have to leave. I suggest you head down to the office and find out which class you're supposed to be in."

Cade held Danel's gaze for another long beat before glancing down at me. "I'll wait for you in the hallway after your class," he whispered. Then he picked up his backpack with an angry swipe and stormed out the door, thumping shoulders with Danel as he passed.

Now the only open seat in the room was the one that Cade had just vacated and Danel smugly settled himself into it, placing his messenger bag of books onto the floor between us. Then he turned and gave me a wink and a half smile.

Furious, I turned to stare at the front of the room. Did he honestly think that I was going to be *nice* to him? After what he just did to Cade? I sat fuming, not listening to a word Mr. Gallagher said.

Danel didn't seem put off by my attitude. From the corner of my eye, I saw him lean back, satisfied. I tried to focus on the lecture, but I was too conscious of Danel beside me, so when one of the other students dropped a couple of pieces of paper on my desk, I twitched, startled.

It was just the semester outline, two copies. I was supposed to hand one to Danel, but I wasn't feeling cooperative. I picked up both copies and shuffled them together, as if it was a two-page handout and I hadn't got around to reading the second page yet. I stared at the papers, not seeing them, very aware of the person beside me.

"Can I have it?" he asked with that strangely fascinating accent.

Maybe it was Egyptian, but it sounded more like British, with perhaps a little Italian mixed in. Or was it German? Since I was so absorbed in placing his accent, I actually did a pretty good job of ignoring what he'd said.

"Can I have a copy?" he asked again, his hand reaching forward, inches from mine. I thought about saying no, telling him to go get his own, but after a minute I snapped the second sheet into his hand.

My heart sank even further as I read the outline. Could this get any worse? Not only wasn't I going to have English Lit with Cade, not only was I stuck next to a rude pretty-boy bully, but this semester, Mr. Gallagher was going Elizabethan. Three plays by Shakespeare, two poems by Christopher

Marlow and a play by John Lyle. I'd been hoping for the Great Gatsby or even Jane Austen. I hated this really old stuff. Half the words don't mean the same thing they do today and the other half are spelled wrong. It would be like spending an entire semester deciphering the scribbles of a three-year-old. I sighed.

"It's not that bad." Danel's voice carried so only I could hear it. "Once you get the hang of the language, it's actually pretty good stuff."

For a minute, I wondered if he'd known what I was thinking, but then I figured that he'd probably had the same first reaction I did and was trying to look on the bright side. Or maybe he was just trying to get on my good side.

As if that could happen.

I didn't say a word to him for the rest of the class. I wouldn't even look at him. And when the bell rang, I was out of my seat and out of the classroom in a heartbeat.

Cade was waiting for me in the hallway.

Chapter Six

"So, Morning Mist," Cade draped his arm possess-ively over my shoulder, calling me by the nickname he had given me over the summer. His attitude was almost too casual as his eyes flicked up and down the hall. "How was English Lit?"

I snuggled against his chest, reveling in the contact. I don't know how the fresh scent of the ocean could still cling to him, but smelling it, I felt all the crap fade away.

"Not bad, not great," I said. And at that moment I meant it. I was with Cade and anything that happened ten minutes ago was suddenly, completely unimportant.

Danel strutted out of the classroom, smirking as he caught Cade's eye. Cade immediately swept me around, placing himself between Danel and me. Their eyes locked for a long minute before Danel moved off, strolling down the hall without looking back.

I watched Cade as he stared after Danel, still looking even after he had turned the corner.

"Who is he?" I whispered.

Cade seemed surprised by my question. "Who?" he asked blankly.

"Danel." I said. Cade looked puzzled, but I wasn't buying it. "Don't give me that, I can tell you know him from before. Who is he? What's going on?"

Cade pulled me closer. "Nothing," he said as he led me down the hallway, in the opposite direction that Danel had walked. "No. He is *less* than nothing. An insect who thinks he is a tiger. A gnat. Beneath your consideration. Ignore him."

Part of me was pissed off at the way Cade blew off my question, but it felt so right with his arm around me, and it had only been a few hours ago that I'd thought that I'd never see him again, I decided not to push it for now and just enjoy the moment.

But I didn't forget.

Calculus was next and this time, Cade was in my class for real. I'm pretty good at math, but I do need to pay attention and take notes. It was a good thing Mr. Hart was just reviewing last year's Algebra basics because I don't think two words sunk in. When I wasn't staring at Cade, I was watching how all the others girls were checking him out.

Kat was the worst. I could tell by the way she bounded into the room that she was bursting with gossip, probably about Danel, but when she saw me sitting with Cade, his arm around my shoulders, her eyes got so big, she looked like some anime morph character.

"Cade, this is my friend Kat." I couldn't help but gloat as I introduced him. Kat stared back, speechless. "Kat ... Cade."

"I am most pleased to meet you, Kat." Cade smiled at Kat, which made her even less coherent. He bit back a chuckle.

Kat wasn't the coolest of people, in fact, at times she was a little dorky, but I was used to her. I got the feeling that Cade was being nice to her just because she was my friend, which made me like Cade even more. If that were possible.

Mr. Hart cleared his throat and we all turned back toward the front of the room, but my brain was nowhere near math world; Cade had moved his leg so it was touching mine and I didn't want to so much as twitch for fear he'd move it away.

Gym was next.

Here, in the backwoods of New Hampshire, Phys. Ed. was not co-ed. Kat and I had signed up for Archery and I had to keep hushing her since Ms. Bushnell, our Phys. Ed. Teacher, kept glaring at us for whispering. When finally Ms. Bushnell got through her safety babble and started to hand out equipment, Kat pounced.

"Tell me!" she said as she completely ignored all of Ms. Bushnell's instructions and proceeded to string the bow backwards. "What's he doing here? Did you know he was coming?"

"No!" I answered the easiest question first. "I had no idea he was here." I looked around to make sure that no one else was close enough to overhear us.

Everyone else was just holding their bows, the strings dangling. A couple of girls were pretending to go fishing while Bernadette Costello and Linda Kessell, two of the meanest of the Jacket Girls, were using theirs as whips to lash out at the bare legs of anyone stupid enough to get too near them.

"I thought you said he was older." Kat was a bulldog when it came to gossip. "What's he doing in high school? Has he really moved here? 'Cause of you? That is so romantic!"

"I was completely surprised to see him when he showed up here in Wicassett, especially at the high school, because he's, um, I mean, I thought he was older, but I guess I was wrong."

"You've barely told me anything about what happened last summer." Kat was oblivious to the rest of the class. "Did you make out? How far did you go? Did you go all the way?"

"NO!" Appalled, I was much louder than I meant to be and half the class turned to look. I dropped my voice to a hissing whisper, "Jeez, Kat! It wasn't like that. You watch way too much T.V. We just, you know, hung out."

I didn't want to make a big deal out of it, but it had taken Cade weeks before he'd even touched me. I didn't want to admit it, but it had bothered me all summer. There'd been plenty of chances for him to kiss me; it just never seemed to happen.

Kat read my face. "You think he's gay?"

"NO!" My reaction was knee-jerk, but then I took a long minute to think about it. "No," I said again at last, "not gay. Definitely not gay, but---"

I didn't finish the sentence because I couldn't finish the thought. There was something about Cade that was just a little out of sync. I didn't think he was gay, but he wasn't an average guy either. I got lost thinking about it.

"Do you think---?" The rest of Kat's question got cut off as Ms. Bushnell's voice bellowed across the gym.

"KATHERINE ANN RANDOLPH!"

Another drawback of living in a small town your entire life: the teachers knew all your names. And your parents' names and the names of every brother or sister or cousin that had ever gone to the school.

Ms. Bushnell's sneakers slapped angrily as she pounded across the laminated floor. She snatched Kat's mis-strung bow out of her hands and waved it in her face.

"Didn't you hear what I said?" she roared.

The honest answer would have been, *no, of course not, I was busy talking,* but Kat had enough sense to say nothing. She looked down at her feet as if she were feeling chastised, but I knew Kat and I knew she couldn't care less if a gym teacher yelled at her. Me, I would have been quaking like a cell phone on vibrate. When Ms. Bushnell told Kat to go sit on the sidelines for the rest of the class, I was the only one to see her tiny shrug as she strolled over to the bleachers.

The rest of the class was pretty nothing. Ms. Bushnell used Kat as an example of how not to string a bow; how not to pay attention; how not to treat the archery equipment with the respect you should treat any weapon… blah, blah, blah. Me, I just watched Kelly Bell (aka KellyBelly) who was always the most perfect student in the world and I just did whatever she did.

32

But mostly I spent thinking about Cade and wondering why we hadn't kissed yet. Was there something wrong with me?

Or was there something wrong him?

Chapter Seven

Last Summer

It was the third week of summer vacation.

Nine and a half days. That's how long we'd been hanging out together.

Nine days, six hours. I can't tell you how many minutes.

I'm not psycho.

Actually, that's not completely accurate. That summer, I was a little psycho. As soon as I'd get back to my bedroom, I would lie across my bed and calculate, to the minute, how long it had been since I'd met Cade, and how many minutes we'd spent together and everything we'd done and everything he'd said and every expression on his face.

But when we were together, time seemed meaningless. Five minutes could be five hours. It was impossible to keep track. It seemed like two seconds ago, the sun was directly overhead and before I knew it, the sky was turning purple and the moon was rising over the ocean.

We were walking on the sand. The sun had dropped behind the houses, but the weather was still hot and sticky. I knew in a couple of hours it would be cooler and I'd need the tee shirt that was back at the cottage, but, for the moment, all was good and I wasn't going to risk going back home and getting dragged into the house for the night. I didn't have to be back until nine o'clock and I didn't care if I froze to death, I was going to savor every second.

"So…" I was feeling brave. Cade knew just about everything about me and I knew practically nothing about him, "…are you staying with your parents this summer?"

Cade cocked his head as he glanced at me. "No," was all he said.

I waited for more. When he didn't speak again I wondered if I'd pissed him off, but he was still smiling; a secretive, mysterious smile that made me crazy. He didn't intend to answer, but I wasn't going to be put off that easy.

"Then where are your parents? Are they around?"

"No."

Now I was getting pissed off, but Cade was grinning even wider. He was toying with me. I framed the next question so he couldn't answer with a yes or no.

"Where do you stay at night then?"

"With friends."

Ha! A real answer!

"Where? Can I meet them?"

Shoot, I blew it. A yes or no question. I let out a loud sigh as I waited for the no.

But Cade was quiet for a half a minute and I held my breath expectantly.

"Definitely not," he said at last. "You really wouldn't get along with them."

"Well, I don't have to marry them. I just want to meet them."

"No."

The smile had left his voice. I shot a peek over at his face. He was staring out towards the beacon light that glowed out at the end of the rocky breakwater. Suddenly, he seemed a million miles away. When I edged near to him, trying to close the gap, my arm bumped his and I trembled as I realized that this was the first time we'd actually touched.

I know it sounds lame, but it really did feel like electricity shooting through me. My blood buzzed through my veins and I could feel myself face heat up. One look at Cade, and I knew he had felt something too.

He had stopped dead still on the sand, his eyes still looking ahead but not focusing. I stepped in front of him and faced him, my eyes forcing his to look at me.

It took a long minute. Slowly his gaze drew back from the distance and he looked at me. Really looked at me. I got the feeling that no one had ever really seen me before, not the way he was seeing me in that moment. The real me. The deep down me. Not Misty the daughter. Not Misty the sister. Not Misty the dweeb who lived at the end of Camden Place. But the real Misty. Mystery Elizabeth Hill. I felt naked and vulnerable. But I wasn't scared. I was exhilarated in a way I'd never dreamed of before.

And I think I was seeing Cade in a way that he had never been seen before either. I didn't know his secrets, his parents, his friends or even where he'd been a month ago. But I knew a part of him that went deeper than dates and facts.

We didn't speak. We didn't move. We just stared. I didn't say a word because I didn't know what to say. I wasn't sure what I wanted, but I knew I wanted to touch him again. His chest was bare and smooth and golden. The warmth drew me closer and I stepped toward him, my hands raised, wanting nothing more than to touch his cheek, his neck, his shoulders.

I didn't blink. I know I didn't blink. But one second his face was inches from my fingers and the next, he was eight feet away, strolling on the beach. He stopped and turned as if he was puzzled as to why I was just standing there. He was acting like that last moment had never occurred.

I was confused. Had it happened? Did I imagine the whole thing? How could he have moved so fast? I looked down at the ground, but the sand was fine and dry and his prints were impossible to distinguish from the thousands of other bare feet that had walked the beach that day.

"Misty?" There was a question in his voice, as if he were wondering why I had stopped. Casual, but perhaps too casual.

I tried to shake off my funk. I stepped forward carefully as if the sand beneath by feet might liquefy at any moment.

"Cade?" There were a million questions in my head and my voice quavered up and down an octave.

"Are you cold?"

I searched his face. If he was trying to avoid the issue, he'd have to come up with something better than that.

"No." My voice sounded wispy and was almost drowned by the crash of the waves. "Of course not, the night's still warm."

"Then why are you shivering?" There was a soft note in his voice, concern so genuine that it disarmed me. How could he not see what he his touch had done to me? Was still doing to me? I wasn't shivering but I was trembling. I took another step toward him and my hand rose again, almost as if it were being pulled by a string and I was being reeled in. Cade stared at it, strangely pale in the rising moonlight, his gaze as transfixed as mine.

"Hey, Cade!

The sound of a strange voice broke the spell. We both started and while I ground my teeth in frustration, there was a faint ring of relief as well. I wondered if Cade felt it too. I turned back to Cade, wanting to recapture that moment, but he had already turned to the guy running towards us from up on the dunes.

The new guy was real good looking. Tall, buff and tanned. No way near as gorgeous as Cade, but he was still a nine, going on ten. He skidded down the dunes, his bare feet leaving a trail of fine sand hanging in the air behind him. I felt a stab of jealously as he plowed into Cade, grabbing his arm to slow his descent. How come he was allowed to touch Cade and I wasn't?

"Shelly's been looking everywhere for you. Where have you been disappearing to lately?" He stepped around Cade and then acted like he hadn't noticed me before, which I didn't believe for a moment. "Oh, hello! Is this what's got you M.I.A lately? Shelly's going to spit fish when she sees her."

"No she will not because she is not going to meet her." Cade said as he walked away from the newcomer. "Come along, Misty."

I stood where I was, torn between the need to be near Cade and the chance to find out more about him. Curiosity won out. I wanted to know more about his friends and where he went when he wasn't with me. And about fish-spitting Shelly.

"Hi!" I stabbed my hand out at the new guy, a bright smile on my face. "My name is Misty."

He grinned as he looked me up and down. I was wearing my bathing suit and the look on his face made me wish that I had gone back for that T-shirt. He shook my hand slowly, his thumb doing something weird to my palm that creeped me out. I pulled my hand back as soon as I could. His grin widened.

"I am Rojo, king of the Mo-Jo." He gave a little hip thrust action as he said this.

It was now official. Rojo completely creeped me out. But it wasn't enough to make me run away. My smile grew tighter and I wanted to wipe my hand clean, but I couldn't figure out how to do it without being rude, so I just crossed my arms tightly across my chest.

"Are you Cade's roommate?" Behind me, I felt Cade step closer. My fingers, which had been gripping my elbows, slackened and the knot in my stomach that I hadn't even noticed until then, eased slightly. I leaned back towards his warmth.

"Roommates?" Rojo barked out a loud laugh. "You might say that. We all crash with Shelly at The Shack. You want to come up and check it out?"

"Yeah. Sure. Thanks." I shot a look over at Cade. He was fuming mad, but I was safe; his anger was aimed at Rojo. As Rojo turned and headed up the dune, I followed.

"Misty, wait." Even though Cade's voice was soft, I could easily hear him above the surf. I turned back to face him. He just looked at me and shook his head.

"C'mon," I wheedled. "I just want to see who you hang out with."

"I hang out with you." The moon was rising behind him and I couldn't see his face, only a black silhouette framed with a silver glow. His voice dropped to a whisper, husky, like he hadn't used it for centuries. Or maybe it was just the words that he had never spoken before. "When I'm not with you, I don't exist."

I froze. That's when I knew that he had felt it too. I felt like a yoyo on a string and once more I was being pulled back toward Cade. I knew he could see my face, paper white in the moonlight, but I needed to see his, to look into his eyes and go back into that moment when I knew him better than I knew myself. My hand reached out again as I stepped toward him.

With my whole being so focused on Cade, I'd forgotten about Rojo. A hand gripped my arm and I let out a squeak as I was jerked back.

"C'mon, sweet doll. The gang's gonna be thrilled to meet you."

The tug on my arm had pulled me off balance and I fell back, landing hard, jarring me up my spine and scraping my palms on the harsh dunes grass. Before I could even start whining, something whistled past my ear. I turned to look.

39

Cade was no longer behind me. It didn't seem possible that he could move that fast, but he now stood in front of me, facing up the dune, his hands clutched into fists and his entire body tight with an anger barely held in check.

Of Rojo, there was no sign. As I pulled myself to my feet and brushed off the sand imbedded in my palms and knees, I looked around the beach for him. I couldn't imagine where he could have gone that fast. A millisecond ago he was tugging on my arm and now he was nowhere in sight. At least not until I moved a step to the right and looked further up the dunes.

Rojo was flat on his back, forty feet away, almost at the top of the dune. Had Cade hit him? And if he had, could Rojo have possibly been thrown that far? As I watched, Rojo groaned and rolled himself to his feet, rubbing his jaw. In the moonlight, I couldn't tell if it was bruised, but I was betting that he'd have some interesting colors on his face by morning. As he looked down at us he muttered curses that I will never repeat, and then with one last glare, disappeared over the dune and toward the house.

Cade wouldn't turn to look at me, so I stepped around to face him. For a moment, there was so much anger in his face that I almost couldn't recognize him, but then he met my eyes and the fury passed. He didn't smile, but his eyes softened into a deep aqua blue. I felt myself being pulled into the ocean of his eyes. I wanted to drown there.

He moved first. His eyes dropped to my hands and he reached out toward them. I didn't dare move. I wanted so much for him to touch me that I was afraid I'd wreck it if I so much as twitched. When his fingers finally touched my wrist, I thought I would implode. The surge of energy that I'd felt before was back, twenty times stronger. His fingertips lightly sketched my scraped palms and even the faint pain of the scratches pulsed joyous through me. He was barely holding one of my hands and I thought I was going to pass out.

"Misty?" Cade's voice was like hot honey, and I felt myself swaying under its spell.

I couldn't speak, I didn't want to rouse myself to force my mouth to work.

"Misty?" Cade was a little more urgent this time, the passion tinged with concern and a hint of laughter. I was so fascinated by his voice, I didn't pay attention to his words. "Are you breathing?"

Slowly, his words penetrated. *What a ridiculous question,* I thought. *Of course I'm breathing.* But then I realized that I had been holding my breath since his hand had first started to reach for mine. He started to draw his hand away, so I grabbed it with both of mine.

"Don't let go," I whispered. The world darkened and I felt his arms around me as I sunk to the ground in a dead faint.

The night air was cool but the soft sand under my back was still warm from the afternoon's sun. I blinked up at the moon until my mind pulled itself back together. Then I remembered what had happened.

I jerked myself up on to my elbows and looked around, my panic not fading until I saw Cade sitting on the sand a couple of feet away, his arms crossed on his knees, his chin resting on his arms. He glanced away from the moonlight flickering on the waves to shoot me a small, pinched smile. I reached out for him, anxious to close the gap between us, but he leaned away.

"I don't think that is a good idea," he said softly. "You seem to have trouble breathing when I touch you."

"No," I said as firmly as I could. "I just forgot to breathe. It'll be better next time."

"Next time?" Cade smiled crookedly.

"No retreat. I won't allow it." I rolled to my knees and squirmed over to within inches of him. "We just need to practice."

I moved slowly. I know knew that Cade could move a lot faster than I could, so I wasn't going to catch him if he didn't want me to. I reached out and gently captured one of his hands with mine and slowly drew it to my cheek. I remembered to breathe this time as his thumb gently glided along my chin. I closed my eyes when his fingertips traced my eyelids. The night was getting cooler but we were getting warmer. I could smell the ocean and felt the sea breeze rustle my hair. I leaned toward him, my lips parted. I wanted this more than anything else I'd ever wanted in my life. Time stopped. The earth stopped. I waited for my first real kiss.

"It's late. I should take you home."

His hand disappeared and I felt like I'd been dowsed with a wave. I had to remind myself to breathe again. I opened my eyes and saw Cade standing above me, one hand extended. The smile was gone from his eyes. He had put up a wall and I didn't understand it. But at least he was offering me his hand. I grabbed at it like a drowning sailor and he pulled me to my feet.

Stubbornly, I held on to it and we walked back to my parents' cottage, silently, hand in hand. It hadn't been a perfect evening. My butt hurt, my hands stung and I hadn't been kissed, but maybe we could change at least part of that when we got to the door.

"I shall see you tomorrow." he said as he gently tried to draw his hand free.

I wouldn't let go, but instead, pulled myself closer to him. That was the first time I noticed that I was having a growth spurt; I suddenly felt taller and my face seemed like it was closer to his.

"Good night." My voice sounded breathy like someone on TV. The night was cool and I leaned into his warmth. I stared into his eyes and he stared back, like a deer in headlights. A very hungry deer. I wasn't going to close my eyes this time because every time I did, he backed off. So we just stood, inches apart from each other and breathed in each other's breath.

"Misty? Is that you?" My mother's voice jarred the night. "You're late! It's almost nine thirty."

I sighed. At that moment, I'd have given anything to have been an orphan.

Cade's crooked smile was back. He tapped my cheek with his fingers before drawing away into the night. I stood in the pool of light cast from the windows and watched as Cade disappeared into the shadows.

"Tomorrow," his voice promised from the darkness.

I couldn't answer. I just stared into the night for what seemed like forever. It wasn't until I was absolutely certain that I wasn't going to see him again before morning that I turned and went into the cottage.

But, being psycho, I didn't wash my cheek that night, but lay across my bed stroking the spot where his fingers had touched me.

Chapter Eight

The rest of the first day of school was a roller coaster. When I was with Cade, everything was perfect. But when I had class without him, I spent the entire time worrying why we hadn't kissed yet. Then, when I had a class with Danel, I scowled and ignored him. By the time the final bell rang at 2:50, my stomach was a huge knot.

I left Civics in a huff, having endured Danel's eyes boring into the back of my head the entire class, and headed for the driveway where the buses lined up.

Typical Fall day in New England: the morning rain was long gone and it was now warm and sunny. The sky was a bright crisp blue with a flock of white clouds milling around the horizon. The trees had started to turn orange and red and yellow. Geese passed in a vee overhead, heading south. It was one of those perfect moments and the only thing that could have made it better would be if Cade were with me.

I shifted my backpack from one shoulder to the other while I waited on the pavement, curious to see which bus Cade would get on. One of few pluses about being taller than most people was that I could see over everyone's heads as they poured out of the building and headed for the parking lot. Most of the kids were loading onto the buses, only a dozen or so seniors had their own cars. The swarm had trickled down to a handful of dawdlers who sprinted for the buses, but still no sign of Cade.

"Misty, you coming?" Kat called out the window.

I didn't even turn to look at her as I nodded and climbed the steps. One last look, no sign of Cade, and the door slammed shut. I shouldered my pack and headed down the aisle as the bus lurched forward. I fell into the seat beside Kat, my eyes still scanning the parking lot.

"New guy's missing." Kat sounded like an on-location reporter for the 6 pm news.

I cocked my head at her, puzzled by what she meant, but her eyes were on the back of the bus. I twisted around to see that the Tucker Twins were once more in possession of the last row of seats. Of Danel, there was no sign.

"I wonder if…" I said under my breath, not wanting to finish the thought. But the thought finished itself and I couldn't help but think that perhaps Cade's disappearance was linked to Danel's.

"OMG! You should have seen the Beast in Biology!" It was catch-up time and Kat had three periods worth of gossip to relate. "She was throwing herself at the new guy, Danel, like he was some kind of rock star. And he was all, like, get out of my face, but she kept at him until he turned and looked at her like she was some kind of bug or something, but while that finally made her shut up, she's still, like, following him around and drooling. She was so pathetic. It was awesome!"

Bernadette "The Beast" Costello was the nastiest of the Jackets. If tormenting fellow students was an intra-mural sport, she'd have three varsity letters. Ever since the first day of seventh grade, she'd made a hobby out of making me miserable. (Of course, I had shown up for the first day of school with knee socks and a plaid skirt – my mother had insisted – but that was four years ago. You'd think she'd have moved on by now, but no.) She'd been horrible to Kat since even before that, so we both felt an unholy glee in watching her suffer.

My cellphone vibrated in my pocket. I didn't recognize the phone number, it said *Unknown Caller : New York City*. I didn't know anyone in New York City. I flipped it open to answer, figuring it would be a wrong number.

"Hello?" I kind of yelled. I hadn't used it enough to know how loud I had to be and the bus was noisy.

"Hello to you, my Morning Mist," replied my favorite voice in the world with a muffled hiccup of laughter.

"CADE!" This time, I really yelled. The entire bus went silent for a millisecond before doing a collective eyeroll and going back to talking.

Be cool, Misty, I thought to myself. *Be cool.* "I waited for you after school in the parking lot, where were you?"

Okay, not cool. That sounded too needy. Need to recoop.

"Listen, Misty," Cade ignored my question, the smile leaving his voice. "I need to leave you for a few days. Nothing of concern, but there are a few things I need to attend to."

My heart fell apart. It was over. I knew it. I'd been too obvious. Too pathetic. I was the nerd version of Bernadette Costello. Death, take me now.

Be cool, Misty. Don't let them see you cry. "Do you have to go?"

That sounded whiny, even to me. New depths of patheticness. I needed to act fast. My eyes whipped around the bus, trying to find some guy I could pretend to like so no one would know that I was being dumped. Ty was a definite no. Maybe Chad.

"It shouldn't be more than a few days, Misty, I promise." Cade sounded so sincere.

"Will you call me?" Dear Lord in heaven, could I sound any more pitiful?

"I may not be able to." Cade sounded distracted. "I mean, I will if I can, but if I don't, it just means that I may be someplace that... I can't."

"Why not? Where are you going that you can't get a signal? The backwoods of Maine? The middle of the Atlantic Ocean?"

"I have to leave now, Misty." His voice told me he was practically gone already. "I'll call you as soon as I can."

The cellphone went silent in my ear. I kind of wished for that click and dialtone that you hear on T.V. when someone hangs up. Something to fill the void that happens when the person you're talking to is just not there anymore.

I closed the phone slowly. Kat, perhaps showing the budding vestiges of tact, said nothing as I stared blindly. After a second, I shook my head as if that could change all the thoughts bouncing around inside it.

"No biggie." I said brightly. "Cade's got to go away for a few days. Weird, but not deadly."

I hoped.

I spent the rest of the ride thinking about all the strange things about that call. First, how long has Cade had a cellphone? I never saw him with one at the beach and he never mentioned one. He always seemed like one of those rustic techno-virgin granolas. You know, the kind of guy that lived simply and didn't believe in all the latest toys and gadgets. It was one of the many things that I liked about him. And how'd he get my number? I'd have given it to him if he'd asked, but he hadn't. And why the New York City phone number? And where was he planning to go that he knew he wasn't going to get a signal?

And most important, was he really coming back?

The bus rattled to a stop. Since Danel wasn't there, our stop was first. I stood up quickly, anxious to get away from Kat's prying silence.

"Hey Misty!" Kat called as I sprinted down the steps. I strode a couple of yards from the bus before stopping and turning, just enough to let her know that I really needed to walk alone. "Um, what's our Calculus homework?"

I couldn't stop a half-grin. Kat never remembered that stuff and she never wrote it down either. I don't know why I even bothered to answer, she'd call me after dinner and ask again. "Chapters one and two, odd number questions."

"Right." I could see that Kat was still sizing me up, trying to figure out if she should grill me. Tact won out and she nodded. "Talk to you later."

"Later." I answered as she turned left and headed down the street to her house. I turned right and slowly walked toward home.

I needed to speak to Cade again. More than I needed to breathe, I needed to talk to him. But I also needed a reason to call him. I didn't want a replay of that last pathetic conversation. I racked my brain.

Calculus!

I flipped open my phone and did a call-back of the last number. I'd ask about Calculus homework. The phone rang twice then went to voicemail. My chest hurt as I listened to the mechanical voice telling me to leave a message. He hadn't even programmed a voicemail greeting. I waited until almost the end of the greeting before snapping the phone shut.

Two rings. One ring meant that his phone was shut off or he was on another call. Four rings meant he couldn't get to his phone in time. But two rings meant that it rang, he saw the number and then sent me to voicemail. On purpose.

He didn't want to talk to me.

I tried to think of a rational reason why he didn't pick up. The only one that came to mind was the obvious.

It was over. He was dumping me. Wicassett had sucked out whatever love he might have felt for me. In less than one day, Wicassett had destroyed everything. I hated this town, the high school, my house, my life, everything.

I was stopped dead in the street and waited for the misery to kill me. It had to. No one could live with this kind of pain.

"Stop being melodramatic," I spoke aloud. "Maybe there's another reason he can't talk to you. Maybe he's in a meeting or getting pulled over by a cop or something."

There had to be a million reasons why he couldn't take my call. Of course, the only one I could think of was that he was dumping me, but it might be something else. I pulled out the phone and hit redial.

Two rings again, and then nothing. I waited in despair for the voicemail greeting, but it didn't happen. I looked at the phone. Weird. The call was still connected. I pressed the phone against one ear and stuck my finger in the other. I could hear rustling, like a phone being slid into a pocket.

I'm sure somewhere on the planet, Dr. Phil or Dear Abby or some other etiquette guru would advise that a polite person should hang up now, but screw that. I listened.

"She's persistent, isn't she?" The voice was faint, muffled through fabric, but there was no mistaking that accent. Wherever Cade was, Danel was with him.

Cade answered, his voice deeper and louder, I figured the phone was in his chest pocket, since his words, cold and biting, had a bass vibrato to them. "She is no concern of yours. She's no one's concern but my own."

"You know it's not that easy," Danel sounded smooth, soothing. "Just go talk to Sam. Explain it to him. Set his mind at ease. He's worried."

Cade snorted. "You make him sound like a benevolent uncle."

Danel gave a short laugh. "The original Saint Nick."

"I haven't seen Sam in ages."

"He's noticed. It's one of the reasons why he's worried."

The rustling got louder, as if Cade were striding angrily. "I want nothing to do with Sam or any of his lot. I never have."

"Hold your tongue!" Danel's voice was louder now, not from yelling, but from being closer to Cade. They must have been standing nose to nose for his voice to sound as loud and deep as Cade's did. "Never say that. Not out loud. Don't even think it. You know what would happen if it got back to him."

"On Gabriel's Head, Danel!" Cade's exasperation was edged with a brittle tension. "We're in Wicassett, New Hampshire. The savannahs of Botswana are less remote than this town. And Sam Jaza is not omnipotent, despite what he tries to make everyone believe."

Yet Cade was whispering, as if this Sam Jaza dude were standing twenty feet away.

"He's powerful enough to take you down if you cross him." Danel spoke the words softly, without hostility, and yet the threat was deafening. I shivered and pressed the phone tighter to my ear. "Cade, you know I'm not the enemy. The only reason I'm here is to get you to listen to reason, to nip this thing in the bud before it gets too big. Just go to Sam. Tell him the words he wants to hear, that your allegiance is to him and that this girl is nothing to you."

"What a hypocrite!" Cade spoke much louder now. "For Sam to be telling anyone not to get involved with women!"

"It's not lust that Sam objects to. Actually, he quite encourages it, the more the better." I thought I heard a note of disgust in Danel's voice. "It's love that he won't permit. It divides loyalties and that is what he will not tolerate."

The rustling grew louder again. I could almost see Cade striding, tension punctuating every step. After a few minutes, I could hear his pace lessen until the rustling slowed to a stop.

It was Danel who spoke again. "If you won't do it for you own sake, then do it for the girl. You don't want to bring her to Sam's notice."

"Sam would never waste his energy on an obscure young girl!" The fear in Cade's voice contradicted his own statement.

"You're right." Danel didn't sound very reassuring. "He'd send someone else to handle it. He was planning to send Azaz weeks ago, but I talked him out of it. I told him you were just having a summer fling. But when you moved up here a few days ago, he ripped me in two, as if you're acting like a fool was somehow my fault."

"He knows that I'm in New Hampshire?" Cade sounded even more worried. "Is he watching me that closely?"

"He always keeps an eye on his *prodigals*," Danel answered, irony in his voice. "You should know that. None of us are allowed to stray too far."

Again the rustling. Pacing, but slower, as if Cade were digesting all this.

"Just go to him, Cade," Danel sounded faint, as if he were speaking from a distance. "Tell him what he wants to hear. It's what we all do. It's what we all must do."

"This was not the way it was supposed to."

"I know."

"Sam Jaza is---"

"Don't say it. It won't help and it'll probably come back to bite you."

"I don't want to leave." Cade sounded uncertain. "What if Sam sends someone here while I'm away?"

"Do you want me to hang around until you get back? Keep an eye on things?"

Silence for a long moment.

"Yes."

Rustling sounds and the muffling of fabric stopped.

"Don't call her again." Danel said softly. "She'll just ask questions you can't answer. Unless you want to lie to her, just let it drop. When you get back you can---"

The phone went silent. Not the silence of two people not speaking, but the silence of a lost connection. I looked at the phone. Call Ended. I stood in the street, staring into nothing.

What did it all mean? Who was Sam Jaza? And why did he have this hold over Cade and Danel? I had so many questions, but if Cade wasn't in school tomorrow, who would I ask?

I'd have to wait for Cade to come back, because there was no way I was going to ask Danel.

Chapter Nine

I stood at the end of the street, waiting for Kat. We'd always meet there and then walk the last hundred feet down to the bus stop together. I'd be on time and she'd be late. It's always been that way. Today however, I was very early. I hadn't slept well the night before and I'd been up since four a.m.

It had been tough, but I hadn't called Cade again. I started to dial about eighteen times, but then I'd snap the phone shut before it could connect. If he could call me, he would, I told myself that over and over. But what I didn't want to think about was whether he *wanted* to call me.

"Hey Misty!" Ty Tucker called out as he and Chad sprinted down the hill.

"You'll miss the bus, waiting for her," Chad said.

Ty hip checked me as he passed.

"Ty! Knock it off! We're juniors! Stop acting like a third grader!"

Practically every day, Ty would bump into me whenever he passed, whether it was on the street or in the hallway or at the mall. Mom said it was because he liked me, but I think it was because he was emotionally stunted geek. I liked Chad better. He was cool, even if they were both into comic books and science fiction TV series.

They headed down to the stop while I impatiently shifted from one foot to the other. One more minute. Sixty seconds and then I'd have to go without her.

"MIIIISTYYYYY!" I was just starting down the street when I heard her call. She was running full out, trying to put on her jacket while holding onto her backpack. She looked demented with everything flapping all over the place. She caught up and passed me, not even breaking stride. The bus was pulling up and we both had to run flat out.

"Why are you two always the last ones?" Charlie grinned as he closed the door behind me.

"It's Misty!" Kat wailed before I had a chance to speak. "She always keeps me waiting."

It was the same joke that she'd made a hundred times before and Charlie still chuckled. Everyone knew the truth, it wasn't even worth arguing about, but Kat was a favorite of Charlie's and she always made him laugh.

Danel was already in his seat at the back of the bus. He glanced at me casually before looking out the window, but I wasn't fooled; I could tell he was very aware of everything I was doing. I slid into the seat before Kat so that I could lean against the window and watch him.

I wasn't flinching today. Every word I'd heard yesterday played in my head as I stared at him, trying to figure out what was going on and how he fit into Cade's life. And mine.

Kat was not to be denied. As quietly as I could on a roaring bus, I filled her in on the conversation that I had eavesdropped on. Her face was still except for her eyes that flicked at every detail until I had finished.

She leaned back and stared out the window. "Sounds like they've got the same probation officer," she said at last.

"What?" I hadn't thought of that.

"Yeah, they both have to report to this guy 'Sam' who keeps track of their movements and gets mad if they leave town."

"But, why would a probation officer want to stop someone from falling in love? And why would he send someone to 'handle' me?"

"He does sound a little psycho." Kat dropped her voice melodramatically. "Maybe he's some kind of perverted probation officer who gets obsessive with his offenders." I could tell Kat liked this idea a lot.

I didn't. It didn't seem to fit. I looked over at Danel and suddenly felt chilled to the bone.

He was staring at me, glaring with that same focused rage of yesterday. There was no way he could have heard what we were saying but I couldn't think of any other reason for that kind of intensity.

I was determined not to turn away. A fly buzzed around my head but I ignored it. I met his glare and waited.

The bus was as noisy as ever, but I couldn't hear a sound. Kat held her breath as she looked from Danel to me and back to Danel.

The bus rattled to a stop in front of the Quad. Charlie cut the engines and opened the door.

This time I wasn't going to wait to be the last one off. I stood up quickly, pushing past Kat as I headed down the aisle and off the bus. Kat ran behind me breathless as I strode up to the front doors.

"Hey, Misty!" There was no mistaking Danel's accent.

For a millisecond, I toyed with idea of pretending I hadn't heard him, but curiosity won out. I hefted my backpack onto my shoulders, crossed my arms across my chest and turned to face him.

"Walk you to class?" Danel flashed me a warm smile.

Walk me to class? This guy was schizoid. One second, he's ignoring me, the next, he's homicidal, and then he's charming. Charming in a retro-fifties kind of weird way. I had a flash of alarm; if this Sam guy was his Probation Officer, then what had he done? Maybe he was a teenage serial murderer or a rapist.

"No thanks." My arms hugged my chest even tighter before turning and hurrying into the foyer.

"See you in English Lit!" He called as the doors slammed behind me.

Great. English Lit was fourth period today. That gave me a short three hour reprieve from dealing with him.

I walked slowly down the hall, stalling in front of the door to Homeroom. Linda Kessell elbowed me as she pushed past. I followed her in and stood staring at the last row.

It was empty. It hadn't really hit me until that moment that Cade wasn't here. And that he wasn't going to be here. As I walked blindly to the back, I realized that I had been holding on to the hope that his going had been all a mistake. Or a joke. I dropped my backpack under the desk and plopped into the seat, too miserable to even notice the cold air blasting down on my head.

Ms. Merfeld stood up, did her normal, morning, finger-pointing headcount. She only glanced down to the roster once or twice before she stopped, one digit hovering in my direction. She glanced down at the roster again before continuing.

"Does anyone know where would Mr. Himisanto be this morning?" The question was supposed to be directed to the entire class, but she was staring at me.

The class snickered. Linda Kessell turned in her chair and sneered, "Yeah, Hill. Where's your new love snack?"

Love snack? Where does she get this crap?

Ms. Merfeld snapped a glare at Linda, which was ignored, before turning back to me.

I shrugged. "Out of town, I think. Family stuff." I tried to make it seem like I didn't care, that it really wasn't any of my business, but after yesterday's performance, I doubted that anyone bought it.

"An auspicious start to the school year, I'm sure," Ms. Merfeld muttered.

I didn't hurry out of homeroom. I was in no rush to get to Spanish, or anywhere else on the planet. I hooked my backpack over my wrist and let it bang against my shins as I headed out into the hallway.

Next to the water cooler, the Jacket girls were congregating. Linda Kessell glanced over at me as she whispered to Bernadette Costello. Four or five other Jackets hovered around them. I turned and walked the other way.

The only hallway to Spanish class was past the water cooler. I was going to have to go out the west door, cut around the back of the building, and hope the door by the Biology lab wasn't locked. If I got there fast enough, I could get in before Mr. Bodovitch, the Biology teacher, snuck back in after his cigarette. He almost always had a butt between classes and today I was depending on it. The hallway traffic was already starting to thin out as I headed for the west corridor exit.

I stopped in my tracks. A half a dozen guys stood around the west exit. Jackets. And they all turned to stare at me.

I froze like a possum.

This was weird. Normally, Jacket guys only picked on the other boys; they'd leer and make snide comments to girls, but they never really bothered them. Only the Jacket girls messed with other girls. Today however, something was very different. It was almost as if the smell of violence was pouring down the hallway like a tsunami of bile. I turned quickly and headed back the other way.

A hand reached out, grabbed my arm, and slammed me against a wall. I didn't even see where it came from. My head cracked against hard plaster and for a second, everything went white. Nearly blind, I felt myself being shoved through a whining door.

I stumbled as I was pushed into the Boys Room. Ricky Murphy was peeing into a trough along the wall. He glanced at me, annoyed for a moment, until he saw who was behind me. He didn't even zip himself as he ran out of the room.

I shook my head clear and turned to see Gary Kasanjian standing in front of the door. Gary had an unusual status at the school: both a Jock and a Jacket. His size and his innate desire to inflict pain made him a linebacker on the football team. The same qualities ensured his status among the Jackets. What was strange was his picking on me. Even though I'd heard rumors about how he liked to hurt the girls he dated, there always seemed to be a gaggle of willing cheerleaders to satisfy him. I'd never heard of him bothering any girl who wasn't throwing herself at him.

I backed up as he stepped toward me. I had never been in the Boys room before. It stank of urine and chemicals. Normally I would never have gone anywhere near the urinal-trough with all the unidentifiable floating things in it, but at that moment, I couldn't spare it a thought. Edging away from Gary, the back of my legs hit the trough and I teetered off balance, my shoulders leaning back another eight inches to press against the wall. Gary grinned as he stepped closer.

The door opened and a half a dozen other Jacket boys moved in. They were laughing wildly, almost giggling girlishly. It went beyond odd; the whole thing was nightmarish in the same way that things don't make sense in a dream, they were just terrifying.

Gary gripped the collar of my shirt while his other hand reached to grab the hair above my neck. He jerked my head back as he pulled me closer.

"Well, didn't you grow up all pretty this summer." It wasn't a question. It wasn't even a statement. It was a threat and my legs turned to rubber beneath me. His hand tugged harder at my hair and I yelped in pain. I wanted to ask him why he was doing this, but some instinct told me to shut up. I bit my lip to keep from crying out again.

"That's enough." The accented voice didn't seem as out of place as the tone was. It was so calm and commonplace, as if he were speaking to a waiter about ground pepper on his salad. Gary's grip slackened slightly and I was able to turn my head.

Danel stepped out of one of the stalls. I hadn't noticed anyone in there earlier, but then I hadn't really been paying attention. When Gary let go of me to face Danel, I slid out of Gary's reach. I rubbed the bruise on my forehead as I watched Gary and Danel go nose to nose.

Danel was tall, well over six feet, but Gary was huge and towered over him by four inches and at least fifty pounds. Danel didn't seem worried, though. He just stared at Gary like he was some out-of-season mosquito: mildly curious, but not concerned.

"What? You want a piece? We'll save you some." Gary's laugh was forced as he turned to the other Jackets, looking for support.

Bravado had deserted the rest of the boys. Their faces had gone pale; their eyes wide. Two of them pushed their way back out the door and disappeared into the hallway. The others just shifted their weight back and forth, uncertain what to do next. For the moment, I was forgotten. My first instinct was to crawl to the door and follow the two defectors, but I stayed put; partly because I was too terrified to move, but partly because I was curious as to what was going to happen next.

"You have someplace else to be." Danel's voice was monotone, as if he were giving instructions to a hypnotized patient. He stared only at Gary, but it was the other Jackets who nodded blankly. "You should leave now."

The Jackets dissolved. That's the best way I can describe it. They shook their heads, as if they were shaking off a drug, then they looked at each other a little confused, almost frightened, wondering what they were doing there. First one and then the others shoved their way out the door.

Except for Gary. He might have been made of tougher stuff, but he didn't seem so tough with his backup gone. His face had dropped when the other guys had bailed, but now, as he turned to Danel, his hands clenched into fists.

Danel stood as still as a brick wall, the smallest smile on one cheek, and waited. Gary huffed and clenched, leaned in and huffed again. But in the end, he turned away. I'd never seen Gary back down before and he didn't do it gracefully. He broke from Danel's gaze to glare over at me.

"Don't think you're getting off," he sneered. "I'll catch up with you later."

His arm cocked back to crack me in the head, but faster than I could register, Danel moved.

Gary's weight was forward and Danel gave, what seemed to me to be, the slightest tap with his boot against Gary's shin. At the same time, he gave Gary a nudge on the arm. All of the momentum Gary had focused on me was now off balance and he slammed face-first into door before crashing out into the hallway. I got one quick glimpse of blood and astonishment on his face before the door closed shut, leaving Danel and I alone in the Boys Room. We stared at each other without speaking.

But it's never completely silent in a school lavatory. Somewhere in the building, there's always a toilet flushing and the sound echoes through the pipes. It reminded me of waves on a beach. I stood, not moving, and listened. For some reason, I couldn't think of what to do next.

Finally, I took a step towards the sinks, but for some reason, my legs wouldn't work and I began to sink to the floor.

Danel moved forward to catch me. He grabbed me with both hands and, I wobbled, trying to reach a wall to steady myself but somehow, I ended up leaning into his chest.

"Are you okay?" There was even less emotion now than when he had spoken to Gary.

I nodded, but I was lying. My body was shaking uncontrollably. I tried to remember what we'd learned in Health Class about shock. Was I supposed to put my head between my legs? Drink fluids? Wrap myself in a blanket? I couldn't remember. I just leaned into Danel and waited for the spasms to pass.

Danel up close smelled even better than from a distance. It was leather and pine and cinnamon, a little bit like apple cider. It reminded me of Christmas. I closed my eyes and tried to decipher the scent.

My eyes flew open. Everything was wrong. I was missing Spanish class. I was in the Boys Room. And I was cuddling with Danel. Cade hadn't been gone twenty-four hours yet, and I was cuddling with Danel. I jerked away quickly.

Too quickly. The room spun. I braced myself against the urinal, not even caring what kind of gross stuff I was touching. Danel released me as soon as I had started to pull away and now he looked at me with that same detached gaze that he had stared at Gary.

"Take a minute to cool off," he said. "Then wash up. You've got blood on your face."

I stumbled over to the sink, washed my hands then looked up at my reflection. My hair was wild, my face was white and the small cut on my forehead wasn't nearly as alarming as the lump around it. I was going to have a nasty bruise and I hoped that it didn't turn my eyes black and blue. I splashed my face and then used my cupped hands to drink some water. I leaned against the sink and, with my face still dripping, I stared past my reflection to see Danel, watching me passively.

"What just happened?" I asked, my voice barely a whisper.

Danel didn't answer.

"I mean, with those boys. I've known them most of my life. They're jerks, but they're not…" I let the sentence die. I didn't want to say it.

"Don't make a deal of it," Danel said quietly. "They're probably almost as shocked about it as you are."

"Don't make a deal of it?" My voice rose as anger kicked in. "They almost… They were going to…" I could barely say it, "…rape me."

Bile rose in my throat as I said the word. I spun around and vomited my breakfast into the sink. I stared down at undigested Cheerios as I ran the water. Cupping my hands again, I washed my mouth out and once more splashed my cheeks. This time I grabbed a handful of paper towels and dried my face, rubbing at the drops of water and blood on my blouse.

"Don't make a deal of it," Danel said again. "Come on, I'll walk you to class."

This time, I didn't turn him down. He opened the door, glanced up and down the hall for a moment, before holding it open for me.

I really needed more time to pull myself together, but obviously, I wasn't going to get it. I took a deep breath, checked the mirror, finger-combed my hair and then headed out. Danel followed, pausing only to bend down and pick up my backpack where it had fallen in the hallway.

As I took it back from him, I saw a movement behind him. A moment before the hall had been empty, but now it wasn't.

A stranger leaned quietly against the wall and stared. I don't know why he looked so out of place. Wicassett wasn't such a small town that a stranger was unheard of, but this one didn't fit. He looked too old to be a high school student, but too young to be a teacher. He wore jeans and a plain green tee-shirt, which should have been completely normal, but it wasn't. Not only did his clothes look brand new, they looked like he'd just put them on minutes ago. There wasn't a wrinkle or even a fold in anything. His hair was brown, not a curl out of place. His face was handsome, but distant and plastic. He looked like a mannequin. Until he smiled.

Then he looked creepy.

Danel, turning to see what I was looking at, froze. He stepped between us, for a moment blocking my view of the stranger. Looking to Danel's face, I was stunned. If I thought his expression on the bus yesterday morning had been murderous, it was nothing compared to the venom that poured out today. I peeked over his shoulder, expecting to see the stranger, if not dead on the floor, at least in full retreat.

The stranger met Danel's stare and just smiled wider. And creepier. The hall, which should have been chilled by the autumn, boiled with tension. I waited.

Danel moved first. An arm on my shoulder, he pushed me roughly down the hall. He didn't pause as we turned the corner, but he shot one last, vicious look back. I looked too.

The stranger was gone.

If the stranger had made it out the west entrance, he'd done it fast. And silently. I tried to lag a bit to try and figure out where he'd gone, but Danel was relentless and I was shoved along like a grocery cart.

The halls were empty and before I could catch my breath, we were standing in front of the door to Mr. Pavao's Spanish class.

"I'll meet you here after class," Danel whispered in my ear, one hand on the doorknob. "Wait for me. Don't go anywhere without me."

With one swift movement, Danel opened the door, shoved me inside and closed the door after me.

I stood there, gaping, with insane hair and water stains on my blouse. The entire class stared at me. Mr. Pavao scowled. I edged toward the nearest open seat, hoping to avoid any more attention, but no such luck.

"And where have you been, Ms.---" Mr. Pavao made a play at looking at the attendance roster, as if he didn't know my name. "---Hill?"

Normally, I'd have had a well-planned semi-plausible excuse ready long before I'd even touched the doorknob. But not this time. There were dozens of good stories I could have used. It was the first day of this class, I could have said *Sorry. Scheduling issues.* It was the first class of the morning. I could have said *Sorry. Missed the bus.* But no. Without thinking I blurted out:

"Sorry. Woman problems."

The class roared. My face burned. It was probably as red as Mr. Pavao's face as he turned away quickly and didn't look at me again for the rest of the class. I settled into a chair and stared at the desk until I could pull myself together.

I felt eyes on me and turned to see Ricky Murphy, the kid who had run out of the Boys room, staring at me, his eyes wide. We both turned away quickly and that's when I saw Joey Sussman, one of the Jackets that had been with Gary. He looked pale, almost green, like he was going to vomit at any minute. He stared fixedly at the front of the room, pretending not to notice me. Trying too hard. I could tell he was very aware of me, and I could also see that he was scared sick.

Everything was going too fast and nothing was making sense. Why would a bunch of boys, admittedly jerks, but not criminal, suddenly turn on me like they did? Was Joey afraid of getting in trouble over this, or was he afraid of Danel? Or was he afraid of something else?

And what about Danel?

"Don't make a deal of it" he'd said.

I should be at the Principal's office, or even at the police station, filing a report, but Danel shoved me into class before I even had a chance to think.

My head swam for the rest of the class. Mr. Pavao could have been teaching Swahili for all I knew.

If the rest of this school year went like the first two days were going, I was so going to fail.

Assuming I survived.

Chapter Ten

Danel was nowhere to be seen. The hallways were swarming with kids and buzzing with chatter. Then the looks started. Whisper, whisper, look at me, look away, whisper, whisper. Ricky Murphy had a circle of people around him, and by the way he was waving his arms, I'm guessing the story was already out. And out of control.

There wasn't a Jacket in sight. I didn't know how I felt about that. Joey Sussman had torn out of Spanish and disappeared.

Someone pushed past me, barely brushing me, but the scrape on my arm flared, jogging me out of my funk.

Chemistry was next, but I started walking the other way, towards the principal's office. It's what I should have done earlier. And if it was going to be all over the school, then it would be better if I told someone first, before one of the teachers read about it on FaceBook.

Hallway traffic was thinning out as I stood in front of the door to the Office. Now that it was time to go in, I stopped to think. When they'd covered this kind of thing in Health Class, I'd always thought that it was beyond lame that the girl would be too scared to ask for help, but now that it was me, I wasn't so sure. It wasn't fear of the boys. Much. It was fear of what everyone would say. And what would they do. And what they would tell my parents.

My parents. Oh, God. What a mess it would be if they told my parents. My mother would go freak. And even my father, normally normal, would over-react.

The Nurse's Office was beside the Principal's office. Maybe I should go in there. I wondered if could talk the nurse into not calling my parents.

The hallway was almost empty now. The sound of footsteps echoed into silence as doors closed into the classrooms. I was moving to the door of the Nurse's Office, my hand reaching for the knob, when an arm came out of nowhere and grabbed me.

It was too much like what had happened earlier. I let out a scream.

A hand quickly covered my face, choking off the sound.

"Shh!" Danel hissed in my ear. His arm slid around my waist as he herded me away from the offices. "What are you doing? I told you to wait for me."

"I was attacked. I need to report it." I twisted to free myself from his grip, but he held tight. "Let me go!"

We turned a corner, out of view of the offices. He led me up the stairs. When we reached the landing between floors, I managed to spin loose from his grip, but he quickly pinned me against the wall. He leaned in, his arms on either side, barring escape. I thought about kneeing him in the crotch or biting his arm, but I wanted to hear what he had to say.

"Don't make a big deal of this."

"You're repeating yourself," I snapped. "And it is a big deal. Maybe Gary's done this to other girls that were too afraid to report it. And maybe he'll do it again unless someone does something. Did you ever think of that? Do you know how I'll feel if I hear that he's done this to someone else? I'd feel like I was responsible; that I could have stopped it, but I didn't."

Danel's arms dropped to his side as he stepped back. "It won't happen again. I'll make sure of that."

There was a strange certainty to Danel's words and for some reason, I believed him. I thought back to that moment in the Boys' room and remembered how he seemed to suck all the violence out of those boys with just a few words. I stared into his eyes, trying to add this piece to all the other strange pieces that made up the mystery of Danel and Cade.

"Ms. Hill?" Principal DeVeau's voice jarred me out of the spell of Danel's eyes. I turned to look at her as she stood at the foot of the stairs, her arms crossed in front of her. "I'd like to speak to you in my office. Now."

Ms. DeVeau was rarely seen in the hallways. She was always in her office holding meetings or off attending seminars or whatever it was that school principals did. That she had roused herself out of her lair to come in search of me meant only one thing: she'd heard the rumor. At that moment, I was almost more afraid of Ms. DeVeau than I was of Gary Kasanjian.

Danel quickly stepped away from me. Ms. DeVeau's glare followed him as he headed up the stairs, but she couldn't see him when he stopped on the landing above me.

He shot me one last look before he disappeared into the second floor. I knew what that look meant. I just wasn't sure what I should do about it.

A deep sigh escaped me. I hadn't even been aware that I'd been holding my breath. I started down the stairs and followed Ms. DeVeau into her office.

I had never been in the Principal's Office before. I don't know anyone who had. It was usually the vice principal, Mr. Vanderhorn, who dealt with all the problem kids. He was good at it too. He'd been a fullback in college, almost went pro, and now he used all his bulk to scare the crap out of high school students. Rumor had it that even Gary Kasanjian was almost afraid of him.

But Ms. DeVeau was even scarier, because she never dealt with any of us. The only time we ever saw her was when we'd occasionally catch a glimpse of her walking to her car in the Teacher's Lot.

She motioned me to a chair as she walked around to her side of the desk. As I sat on the edge of the seat, I looked at all the framed certificates on the walls. There must have been two dozen of them. If she hung them there to intimidate people, she really didn't need to work that hard.

She cleared her throat. In the quiet of the room, it sounded like someone grinding the gears of a car. I flinched.

"Excuse me?" I asked.

"I haven't said anything," she said as she sat back in her chair. "Yet."

I squirmed and twitched. She steepled her fingers together in front of her chest. I opened my mouth to speak, but nothing came out.

"Is there anything you'd like to discuss, Misty?" Ms. DeVeau's voice dropped to a gentle but insistent pitch. I wondered if this was one of the things they taught principals when they went to all those conferences.

I shrugged. Now that I was here, I didn't know how to begin. I hunched back down into the chair and stared at my feet.

"I've received some unsettling reports from several of the teachers." I looked up to find her staring at me, unblinking. "And Mr. Pavao tells me that you arrived late for Spanish class, with cuts and bruises."

"It's no big deal." Why did I say that? Because Danel told me to? I straightened in the chair, took a deep breath and let the words spurt out. "Gary Kasanjian and some of other boys roughed me up a bit, but nothing happened."

"Nothing happened," she echoed and then let it drop there.

"You, know. Nothing major. I mean, it might have got out of hand, but Danel broke it up. It's cool now. No biggie."

"Danel?" The question was sharper. "Danel Stark? One of the new students?"

"Yeah, turns out he was in the Boys Room at the time and he kind of broke it up."

"What were you doing in the Boys Lav?"

I sniffed. "Well, I wasn't there by choice, if that's what you're asking."

Ms. DeVeau leaned back in her chair and tapped her fingertips together, all the time watching me. I don't know why I couldn't look at her, I didn't do anything wrong, except maybe not come directly to the principal's office as soon as it happened, but I shouldn't be feeling guilty.

But I was. It didn't make sense, but I was feeling like this was all my fault, which was stupid. But that didn't mean that I still didn't feel it. My eyes were getting wet. I wiped them with my fingers, but then my fingers were all wet. A box of tissue appeared and moved toward me as I was wiping my fingers on my jeans.

"Sergeant Huebner will be here shortly..."

I looked up then, horrified, but she continued as if she didn't notice.

"...You'll need to file a pol---"

"NO!" The word burst from me, a lot louder than I intended. "I mean, I don't need to. It wasn't a big deal. Nothing really happened."

"This time."

The silence got longer. I wanted to tell her, no it won't happen again because Danel said it wouldn't. But that sounded lame, even to me, so I went back to staring at my shoes.

"How are you going to feel if they try it again to someone else, only the next time, there's no one around to stop them?

You could have prevented it, if you had only done the right thing."

Great. The old do-the-right-thing-or-else-writhe-in-guilt-the-rest-of-your-life speech. The fact that I'd said just about the same thing to Danel ten minutes earlier didn't make me feel better.

"It's just that..." I didn't know what bothered me most, so I went with the easiest. "I don't want my parents to know. They'd majorly over-react and I wouldn't be allowed out of the house until I was twenty-seven."

"They're going to see the bruises. They're going to wonder what happened."

"No they won't. I'm a complete klutz. No wall or door is safe from me. Mom says I'd trip over a good intention if it were within a hundred feet of me." This was true. Since my stupid growth spurt, sometimes my body was longer than I expected and I tended to bump into everything.

"We have to notify your parents of the incident, but the details you share with the police officer and your guidance counselor will remain confidential."

Brilliant. Ms. DeVeau had no idea how impossible it was to keep details from my mother. I swear in a former life, she taught interrogation techniques to the Nazis.

There was a knock on the door and Sergeant Huebner stepped in. I tried to melt into the chair. I'd seen him around town, but I don't think I'd actually spoken to him since my fourth grade field trip to the police station. The kids called him Sergeant Hubby, but never to his face.

It actually went better then I expected. Sergeant Huebner didn't act like it was some horrific crime, but he didn't blow the whole thing off either. I told him what happened. He asked some questions, real calm, like we were talking about something that happened to someone else. I was just starting to chill when he asked me for the names of the boys that had been there.

I stiffened. I'd already named Gary Kasanjian but I balked at naming the others.

"Um, I don't remember." I whispered.

I don't know if all adults have mastered the art of long uncomfortable silences, but these two were definitely pros. I didn't look up until I heard paper rustling. Sergeant Huebner was holding a sheet of paper with ten names written on it. He held it in front of my face.

"Are these the boys?"

They'd worked fast. I have no idea how they managed to get these names, but they were almost dead on.

"Not Trong. I didn't see Trong." I answered quickly. It was easier to un-name people than it was to name them. "And Barry and Fletch. I think they were hanging in the hall at first, but they didn't come into the Boys' Room."

I stopped. By naming the guys who weren't there, I had inadvertently named the ones that were. I tried to recoop. "The rest, um, I'm not sure."

Sergeant Huebner sighed as if he was disappointed. I felt like a jerk, but that wasn't nearly as bad as being singled out by the Jackets as a rat.

Ms. DeVeau stood up. "If you'll wait here one moment, Ms. Hill, I'd like to speak with Sergeant Huebner privately."

The two of them stepped out, leaving me alone in the office. I pulled a tissue out of the box and proceeded to shred it into lint. Then I studied the diplomas on the wall. She actually had her High School diploma up there from Portsmouth High School, as well as her B.S., her Masters and her PhD. The rest were impressive looking certificate programs. Blah, blah, blah. I pulled out a second tissue and was brushing the shredded bits into it when the door opened and they both stepped back in.

"Sergeant Huebner will take you over to St. Joseph's now," Ms. DeVeau said as she crossed back behind her desk. As she sat down, she picked up a file folder and flipped through it. "I'll contact your parents. They'll meet you there."

"Saint J's?" I pulled my fingers through my hair as if ripping it all out might change something. "I don't need to go to the hospital. I told you. Nothing happened."

"And we believe you." No she didn't. "But we need to have you checked out. It's Standard Procedure."

Her attention was on the papers in front of her. I was dismissed. I stood up like a robot with no will of my own. A slave to Standard Procedure. I wanted to scream. To pick up her desk and tip it over, tumbling all her precious files onto the floor.

I compromised. I tipped the Kleenex full of shredded tissue onto the carpet before I turned and followed Sergeant Huebner into the hallway.

I slouched as I walked beside the officer, my hair falling over my face, but it was no use. Even though the hall was empty, every classroom had a thin window lite in the door and there's nothing like a dark blue uniform passing by to drag everyone's attention. I hoped that they all thought I was being arrested. That would be much cooler than the truth, but I doubted it. If Ricky Murphy had been blabbing enough for the teachers to hear about it, I'm sure every student in Wicassett High knew about it too.

It was actually a relief to get out into the parking lot. Sergeant Huebner held open the front passenger door. That was better than getting in the back. I peeked over the seat, past the metal grating. It's true. The backseats of police cars have no door handles. I was glad I was in the front; the way I was feeling at the moment, being trapped in the back seat with no door handles would have completely freaked me out.

It's a thirty minute ride to St. Joseph's in Manchester, most of it highway. It was silent for the first five minutes and it was bothering me, so I blurted out what was on the top of my mind.

"Nothing happened, you know."

Sergeant Huebner didn't look at me. After a minute or so, his eyes still on the road, he replied, "You were bullied. You were bruised. You were threatened with rape." He glanced over at me for a second before looking back to the road. "You were frightened. That is not nothing."

I almost lost it then. I think it was the fact that he understood that the worst part had been the fear was what got to me. I groped in my backpack, hoping that some long forgotten Kleenex had been left in one of the pockets.

Sergeant Huebner reached over and popped open the glove compartment, pulling out a small package of tissues. They scratched like paper towels, but I didn't care. I blew my nose and pulled myself back together.

"I'm okay." I sniffed at last. "Danel stopped it before it got out of hand. It's no big deal. I'm okay."

"Danel Stark?" The tension in Sergeant Huebner's voice made me stiffen. "I wanted to ask you about that. How well do you know Danel Stark?"

"Just barely. He's new. I met him yesterday. We've got a few classes together. We ride the same bus. That's all."

The cruiser was slowing, stuck behind a tour bus that was crawling along Route 16, letting the leaf gawkers have a good look at the foliage. Route 16 is only one lane in each direction and traffic was backing up. Sergeant Huebner flicked on the flashing lights for a moment. The bus pulled over and we passed, along with the other dozen cars that had been stuck behind it. Sergeant Huebner gave the bus driver a dirty look as we passed. You could see the driver cringe. That was kind of cool. We sped back up again and silence settled back in.

"Why?" I asked at last.

"How about Cade Himisanto?" Sergeant Huebner ignored my question. "How well do you know Cade?"

"Pretty well." I paused for a second, surprised that Sergeant Huebner had linked them together. "We met down in North Carolina this summer. He was a lifeguard on the beach. We hung out all summer." And we never kissed. And now he's disappeared.

Sergeant Huebner seemed like he wanted to say more, but didn't.

"Why?" I asked again. "Because they're both new?"

"There's that." He chewed his lip. When he spoke again, it was like he had made a big decision. "That, and the fact that neither of them seem to have existed before they moved to Wicassett."

"Yes they did! Well, I don't know about Danel, but Cade was a lifeguard on the beach in Ocean Isle all summer! And I don't think that was his first summer there either!"

"There was no lifeguard at Ocean Isle this summer." Sergeant Huebner's voice was calm despite the nonsense he was speaking. "I contacted the chief of police there. He remembered Cade, but only as a stranger who liked to sit on the lifeguard tower and act like a lifeguard. There hasn't been a lifeguard on that beach for a couple of years. Budget cuts."

"But that doesn't make sense! Why would Cade hang out every day on the lifeguard tower if he didn't have to? And why wouldn't someone stop him, or at least say something?"

"That does seem a bit odd. But what's even odder is that the police chief only knew about Cade through word-of-mouth. Seems like every time he patrolled the beach, the mystery lifeguard would disappear. If he'd seen him on the tower, he'd have chased him off, but he never caught him there."

My mouth opened and closed a couple of times as I started to argue, but nothing came out. I was on that beach almost every day this summer and I tried to remember a moment when I was with Cade when the police chief's jeep would cruise by.

I couldn't remember one time. I remembered Cade. I remembered the jeep going by. It was weird though, I couldn't remember one time they happened together. I never noticed it before, but it was always *I'm going for a soda. You want one?* or some other completely reasonable errand and Cade would disappear.

And then the jeep would pass.

"Yeah, but…" I tried to come up with something, but nothing was there.

"They both have valid Social Security numbers which show them as being seventeen years old, but there is no record of them at their previous schools or ever having existed before."

"Well, maybe they were both home-schooled."

"No parents. No relatives. And no one's ever heard of them at their prior addresses."

We were pulling into the city and the traffic started to absorb more of Sergeant Huebner's attention. I leaned back against the vinyl seat, my head spinning.

"Do you always check out every new kid that moves to Wicassett?"

"Only the ones that arrive without notice, without family." He didn't look at me. "And then appear to focus all their attention on one of our citizens."

"It's no big thing, you know, with Cade and me." I said quickly. "I mean, it is a big thing, but it's not surprising that he moved here, because, you know, we're a … thing."

"Were you expecting him?"

My mouth opened, ready to lie, but then I snapped it shut and thought about it for a minute.

"No." I said at last. "He surprised me, but that doesn't mean anything. He probably just didn't know how much he was going to miss me after the summer was over."

It sounded good to me. I watched Sergeant Huebner to see how it sounded to him.

We were stopped at a light. He turned to give me his full attention. "And Danel Stark? How long have you known him?"

I shrugged. "Danel? I just met him yesterday. I don't even really like him very much. He and Cade don't get on well. I think---"

I cut myself off. I wasn't supposed to know that Danel and Cade knew each other from before, and that they shared some other secrets as well. I certainly didn't want to tell that to Sergeant Huebner. Not right then, anyway.

The light turned green. The cruiser pulled forward.

"You think what?"

I scrabbled for a good cover and made a quick decision to go with something that was also true.

"Danel kind of creeped me out at first." I said with a shrug. "He was kind of scary. And then when he got into Cade's face, I thought he was a bit of a jerk, but after this morning, I don't know. Maybe he's cool."

We were pulling into the hospital driveway. There were a couple of parking spots right near the door marked for emergency vehicles and Sergeant Huebner pulled into one. He shifted into park and then faced me, his face as serious as death.

"Go with your first instinct." His voice was brusque as he snapped off the ignition and pulled out the key. "I haven't got a shred of evidence, but I've been a cop for sixteen years and my gut is telling me that there's something seriously wrong with Danel Stark. I'm not your father, Misty, and you don't have to listen to a word I say, but my advice is, stay as far away from that boy as you can."

Three hours ago, I had no intention of getting any closer to Danel Stark than was absolutely necessary, but this seemed so unfair that it rankled. I'm not normally a defiant kid, but there was something about this that really pushed my buttons.

"Why? Just because of your feeling?"

"Wicassett is a small town, Misty, and just because you don't see the police on campus every day, doesn't mean we don't keep a close eye on what happens at the high school. We've never had anything close to this morning's incident. Why now? Within forty-eight hours of arriving, Danel Stark has managed, not only to join the Jackets, but the reports I'm getting is that he's taking a leadership role. We're worried that a high school clique is turning into a gang. It doesn't take much to push it from a relatively harmless group of kids into a pack of criminals. Believe me, we're going to do whatever we have to to nip this in the bud."

My head was reeling. "But.... Danel's the one who stopped it. Before it got out of hand. He stopped them."

Sergeant Huebner spoke the words just as I thought them.

"With barely a word. They stopped their attack and they all left, and all Stark had to say was *that's enough*."

I raised my hands to drag my fingers through my hair, but my palm brushed the bruise on my forehead. Pain flared. My hands snapped them back like they had grabbed an open flame.

"But why?"

"Exactly. Why would he order them to attack you, only to come to your rescue at the last moment." Sergeant Huebner opened his door and got out.

I jumped when his door closed even though he hadn't slammed it that hard. I tried to pull my thoughts together as he walked around the car to open my door, but the door opened much too soon and my head was still a roller coaster.

"I don't know what kind of game Stark and this Cade boy are playing, but I'm not going to allow it in my town. And my advice to you is that you steer clear of both these boys."

Chapter Eleven

Sergeant Huebner reached in to help me out of the cruiser, which by now wasn't just an act of courtesy, but almost a necessity. I was so dazed by what he'd said, my fingers were trembling. He led me into the Emergency Room and sat me in a chair while he went up to the desk.

I don't care how gentle and sweet a doctor talks, there's nothing pleasant about lying on a vinyl platform, your back sticking to plastic and your feet in stirrups. Thankfully, the doctor made it just a quick look and then let me get back into my own clothes. Whatever she was looking for, she could tell almost immediately that it wasn't there. By the time I got dressed and walked back out to the waiting area, my parents had arrived.

Mom swept down on me like a palm tree in a tornado. She's tall and pencil thin and hyper. Under normal conditions, she can get herself worked up into a frenzy over practically nothing. Today, it was frenzy times ten. I didn't know what they'd told her, but she wrapped me up in her arms, pulled me close, and then grabbed my shoulders to push me away again. She stared into my eyes, looking for, I don't know what. Then she pulled me back in again, slamming me against her chest.

"Oh, thank God, you're alright!" She bellowed full volume right next to my head. I wanted to rub my ear, but my arms were pinned at my side.

This was so embarrassing. Everyone in the waiting room was staring. I squirmed free.

"I'm fine, Mom. Nothing happened. Really."

Dad stepped up, pale and harried and gave me a quick hug. Dad's normally the calm anchor in Mom's tempest, so it was out of character for him to be freaking. Somehow, his quiet panic upset me more than anything else.

"It was just some guys, goofing off." I dropped my voice so that the rest of the people in the waiting room wouldn't hear. "Everyone's making a big deal, but it's nothing."

"We're pulling you out of that school!" Mom was going just where I had hoped she wouldn't. At full volume. "We're sending you to Ignatius!"

My heart stopped. Saint Ignatius was an all-girls prep school, twenty miles away. I didn't have a ton of friends, but I didn't want to lose the ones I had. And having to travel an hour or so each way to school would stink.

And then, of course, there was Cade. How lousy would Junior year be without him?

I think Dad read the panic on my face. He placed his hand on my shoulder and the rollercoaster in my head began to slow down. Dad always had that ability to bring calm into turmoil. "We'll discuss this later."

Mom herded me towards the front door while Dad did the paperwork thing at the Admissions Desk. I stopped to thank Sergeant Huebner as I passed. He was chatting with a nurse behind the counter, but he stepped away as we approached.

"Remember what I said, Misty," he said. "Better to be safe than sorry."

"Right. Thanks. I'll keep that in mind." I said as I pushed Mom out the door.

"What did he mean, Misty?" She slowed from her normal breakneck stride. "Sorry about what?"

"He's just being a cop, Mom." I would have dragged her along, but I didn't know where they'd parked the car. "He just wants me to be careful, is all."

Dad joined us and we walked to car, not speaking much until we were all settled in.

"You can just drop me at the top of Maple Street," I told Dad as I buckled up. "I can walk from there. I should be able to make it back in time for English Lit."

"You're not going back to that school!" Mom was in high gear. "Ever!"

"But Mom! I can't just run away. Even if you send me to another school, we live in this town. I'll see everyone sooner or later and the longer it goes, the harder it'll be!" I was fighting a losing battle and I knew it. Logical argument is a lost cause against Mom's passion.

Reinforcements appeared unexpectedly. "Misty's right," said Dad quietly. "The sooner she gets back into her normal routine, the better it will be for everyone."

Dad didn't step in between my and Mom's battles very often, but when he did, Mom usually would actually stop and listen.

Mom swiveled in her seat to stare at Dad. She looked liked she wanted to argue, but then clamped her mouth shut as she changed her mind. Then she turned to look at me in the back seat. I didn't realize I was holding my breath until she finally nodded. The air left my lungs in a whistle as she turned to stare out the front window.

It was quiet for a while. Mom tried a few of the "so how's school going" ploys, but my mind was a million miles away and after a few minutes, she let it drop.

I don't know what was harder to get a handle on. That Cade wasn't what he appeared to be, or that today's entire attack and rescue might have been engineered by Danel. I dug into my backpack and pulled out my phone. I hadn't tried Cade's number in nearly 24 hours; I was past due. I needed to talk to him, to hear him explain all these things away. I needed him to be here, but just hearing his voice would be enough to make everything right again.

I could hear the phone ring once before it went to the anonymous voice mail message. As I snapped the phone shut, I could see my mother's eyes in the rear view mirror. She shot Dad a meaningful glance. I didn't care. I needed answers.

The trip back to Wicassett seemed a lot shorter than the ride to Manchester. Dad pulled over to the curb before he turned to look at me. "Are you sure you don't want us to drop you at the door?"

My hand was already on the handle. "No, I'm good." I said as I pushed open the door and got out. "I'll see you tonight. Thanks."

As I slammed the door, I heard my mother call, "I love you!" I turned to look back into the car and saw Dad mouth the words "me too" before he pulled the car away from the curb.

I didn't watch them pull away. I was too busy thinking about what was ahead of me. School. Whispers in the hallways. Sideways glances. English Lit. And Danel.

I pulled myself up tall and walked down Maple Street to the high school. Maybe I couldn't get hold of Cade, but I knew where Danel was. I was going to ask him some questions and he was going to give me answers.

Or else.

Chapter Twelve

I was being overly optimistic when I said I could make it back in time for English Lit. Strictly speaking, I could have made the last ten minutes of class, but there was no way I was walking in there, bruised, bandaged and forty minutes late. I'd wait for the bell and then join Kat in the cafeteria for lunch and act like nothing happened.

It would blow over. I kept telling myself that. Like that time in eighth grade when my pants split in the back on the way to school and I didn't notice it until second period and everyone knew that I wore plain white underwear and I wanted to die but I didn't.

Technically, this was a much bigger deal than the notorious split jeans incident, but I was hoping that if I could live that down, I could live this down too. But at the moment, I had the problem of what to do with myself for the ten minutes before the bell rang for lunch.

There's something really eerie about walking through the halls of a high school when everyone else is in class. Even though I had a perfectly good excuse, I was edgy. I kept waiting for someone to call out *Hey, you! Why aren't you in class?* I tried to walk quietly, but even the tread of my sneakers sounded loud as it echoed down the hallways.

I'd hide in the bathroom, I decided. I'd sit on the toilet with the door locked and send a long text message to Cade, telling him everything that happened. Even if his leaving was a break-up and he was avoiding my calls, he'd have to respond when he read what happened this morning.

It was a decisive course of action and it immediately made me feel better. I had no way of knowing if Cade could receive the message, but at least I was doing something. Besides standing by myself in an empty hallway. I headed for the Girls Room.

As I turned the corner, I slowed down. The Girls Room was almost directly across from the Boys Room where I'd been attacked only hours before. I took a deep breath and kept walking. I couldn't let this get to me.

The smell of cigarette smoke stopped me again right outside the lav door. Great. That meant that some of the Jacket girls were skipping class and smoking in the bathroom. So much for sanctuary.

"I still say she needs a swirly." It was so quiet in the hall, I could clearly hear Linda Kessell's sulky whine coming through the vent above the door.

I was guessing they weren't talking about chipping in to buy someone a soft-serve ice cream.

"I vote that we drag her into the Boyth Room and give it to her in the urinal." That had to be Jessie Faulkner; she's had a lisp since first grade.

It was definite now. They were talking about dunking someone's head in the toilet, a favorite pastime among the Jackets. And given the morning's events, it wasn't hard to guess who they were talking about. My stomach felt queasy.

"And I say," Bernadette Costello's voice had the edge of authority in it, "that we do just what Danel told us to do and lay off. He said he'd take care of it."

"Like he took care of Gary?" Jessie's voice was shrill as I heard her slam one of the lav doors. "He's been expelled for three weeks. And we're playing Salem next Sunday."

Jessie was more of a cheerleader than a Jacket, but since she was Gary's favorite punching bag, she was tolerated by the tougher kids. That didn't mean they'd listen to her, though.

"Shove it, Jess." Bernadette said. "Danel says to back off. We'll just watch and see what he does."

There was some rustling noise, like they were thinking about leaving. I started to edge away from the door, but Jessie's next words held me there.

"And why, all of a sudden, is everyone doing whatever this new guy, Danel, says? Who died and made him king?"

It was dead quiet in the lav until Bernadette finally broke the silence. "Good question, Jess. I'll let him know you were asking. Do you want me to tell Danel that you don't think we should be listening to him? That some dumb pompom is wondering who died and made him king?"

I could feel the chill of Bernadette's threat right through the door.

"Well, do you?"

"No," Jessie answered, low and sullen.

"What?" I could feel Bernadette getting right into Jessie's face.

"No," Jessie said again, louder and even more sullen.

"I didn't think so."

I decided not to push my luck any further. I headed down the hall and into the stairwell. There was a little space under the stairs where Mr. Castian, the janitor, kept a locked trunk full of cleaning supplies. I sat on the trunk and hugged my knees against my chest.

So Sergeant Huebner was right. In less than two days, Danel was now the leader of the Jackets. I don't know if they officially considered him their leader. I'd never heard of them ever having an official leader, but it was obvious that he was now firmly in control.

I uncurled myself and started to text a message to Cade but I didn't know where to start. I must have punched in a dozen different opening sentences, but then deleted them. They either sounded pitiful, complaining, or incoherent.

Then the bell rang and I ended up quickly texting him "miss u" and left it at that. Within seconds the stairwell was full of stomping feet. I slipped out and joined the herd heading to the cafeteria.

Kat and I weren't cool enough to have a regular table, but we did tend to find open seats over by lockers, away from the windows. She was already there when I walked into the lunchroom. She saw me and stood, waving her arms as if I were on the other side of a football field. So much for a subtle entrance.

"What happened?" Kat demanded even before I could sit down. The kids at the nearby tables were all looking. They turned away when they saw me glance at them, but they were all too quiet. They pretended to be focused on their meals, but I could tell they were listening for what I was going to say next.

"Nothing happened," I said, for maybe for the fortieth time today. "Gary was just being a jerk, but it got stopped before it got out of hand. Everyone's just making a big deal out of nothing."

I spoke a little louder than I needed to and Kat, getting the clue, looked around once before nodding. As I put my pack on the chair, Kat pulled out a bill from her pocket. "Get me lunch and I'll hold our seats."

"Sure." It was weird how grateful I was for this small slice of normalcy. There wasn't much to choose from on the cafeteria line and we both knew what the other liked. It was always the first one at the table who held the seats while the second one to arrive ran to get the food. Tuna sandwich, granola bar and chocolate milk for me. Two slices of pizza, a piece of fruit and a diet soda for Kat. There were looks and nudges when I was in line, but at least my underwear wasn't showing so I knew I could live through it.

There was no one else at the table when I got back to it, which was a bit weird since we normally had to share since the lunch room was always crowded. The looks from the other tables had eased off and I felt my stomach unwind a bit.

"Okay," Kat's voice dropped to a whisper and she leaned in so that no one else could hear. "Show time is over. So what's the real scoop?"

I would have unloaded on her then, but we were suddenly invaded by the Wicassett High equivalent of Men In Black. The Tucker Twins dropped their packs on the two seats next to us and noisily sat down.

"No sweat." Chad announced with a swagger. "We've got your back."

I exchanged a baffled look with Kat before turning to the boys. They were scoping out the room with intense glares, sort of like Secret Service agents who've had too much sugar.

"What," Kat asked for both of us, "are you talking about?"

"Rumor has it that the Jackets are ripped and they're looking to take you down." Ty sounded like he'd been watching too much CSI Miami.

Chad laughed. "Hey, that's pretty good! 'The Jackets are ripped.' Funny."

Ty grinned back, but he was not going to be distracted. "That's right. So Chad and I are volunteering to be your bodyguards. You know, escort you to and from class and to the bus and stuff."

This was really goofy, but it was kind of sweet too. I didn't know what to say.

Now, it might be fair to tell you a little bit about the Tucker Twins:

We've always called Ty and Chad Tucker "The Twins," but not because they share a birthday. They live at the top of the hill at the end of Fisher Place. There was only one slight condition that made them not-really-twins.

They weren't related.

Ty Tucker lived with his parents and two younger sisters at 23 Fisher Place, while Chad Tucker lived across the street with his parents and a dog at 24 Fisher Place. They declared themselves twin brothers at the age of seven and no one bothered to argue. It was always a laugh whenever we got a new teacher and they introduced themselves as twin brothers. Ty was short, plump, with pale Irish/Scottish freckled skin and red hair while Chad was tall, lanky and with the dark skin and black hair of an African-American. They'd perfected the art of staring innocently at people who stood, slack-jawed, trying to figure out how they could be twins.

We played together when we were little kids, but around seventh grade, we stopped. No particular reason. They started getting into comics books and video games, while Kat and I started putting on makeup and talking about clothes and stuff.

And today, they've decided they're going to be my bodyguards.

"Oh, c'mon guys." I picked at the crust of the sandwich, flicking the crumbs around the plastic tray. "Is this really necessary?"

"You haven't been here for the past three hours!" Kat leaned in and dropped her voice to an urgent hush. She was joining the Twins in their covert operations attitude. "It's all over the school. The Jackets are pissed. They're out for blood. Yours!"

"And what does Danel say?"

This stopped Kat in her tracks. She shot a puzzled look at the boys.

"Danel?" Kat asked as she turned back to me. "What's he got to do with it?"

So I filled them in on what I'd overheard in the girls room, "...and it was Danel who stopped Gary and the rest of the guys this morning. He barely said one word, and they all bailed."

"You think the new kid, Danel, is now leader of the Jackets?" Chad asked.

"Not only me," I said quietly. "Sergeant Huebner thinks so too."

As I told them what Sergeant Huebner had said, I realized that I was avoiding mentioning his suspicions about Cade.

"I think we need to find out more about this Danel guy." Ty was still in Secret Agent mode. "I think we need to do a little recon."

Kat rolled her eyes. "Recon?"

"We should tail him after school," said Ty. "See where he lives. Where he goes. Known associates. Stuff like that."

"It'll be pretty obvious if we get off at his bus stop," Kat said. "I think he might catch on."

"Then, we'll follow the bus," Chad had a cocky grin on his face, "and tail him when he gets off."

"With what? Skateboards?" Kat's sarcasm was pardonable; it was a pretty dumb idea. "Or maybe we can just run after the bus, real fast."

"We'll be in a car." Ty explained like he was talking to a three-year-old.

"Two problems with that idea." I said. "No car. No driver's license."

Evidently, Ty and Chad had been waiting for this moment. They'd probably rehearsed it for hours, because with identical movements, they both reached into their pockets and then slapped their hands down on the table. When they pulled them away, their faces grinned up at us on two brand new, freshly laminated, New Hampshire driver's licenses.

"You guys got your licenses?" Kat was in awe. "When?"

"We took Driver's Ed over the summer." Chad's smile was smug. "Took our test three weeks ago."

"And aced it!" added Ty.

All of a sudden, Ty and Chad seemed slightly less geeky.

"But we don't have a car." I said, chewing my lip.

"I'll borrow Dad's tomorrow," said Chad. "He told me that if I get up early enough to drive him to the train station, he'd let me borrow it for the day."

I liked the idea of finding out more about Danel. He was my only connection to Cade. The others stared at me, waiting for me to say something.

"Okay," I said at last. "Tomorrow, we'll need to be out before the buses, so we'll have to cut last period. We'll meet behind the field house."

Kat grinned. She loved cutting classes. Given any excuse, she'd be anywhere else. Chad and Ty hesitated before nodding. They were like me and never skipped out. Too chicken.

But Junior year was being a year of all kinds of firsts for me.

Chapter Thirteen

Calculus was dismal. I kept remembering yesterday's class when Cade had been there, but at least today I was able to focus on Mr. Hart's lecture. I kept my head down and took notes, ignoring the whispers around me.

Last period was Civics and I braced myself to having to deal with Danel.

But he wasn't there.

This spooked me even more than if he'd been there. I hadn't seen Danel since this morning when he'd left me in the stairwell. For the first time, I wondered where he'd gone to when I'd been in Spanish class. He hadn't met me like he planned to, right after class, and it had seemed important enough to him that he'd been pissed at me for not waiting for him. I hadn't seen him at lunch. Had he cut the rest of the day? Maybe he was following up on something. Maybe he was talking to the creepy guy in the hallway.

My pencil froze over the scribbles that I'd been etching in my notebook. Until that moment, I'd completely forgotten about the creepy mannequin guy. I hadn't mentioned him to Sergeant Huebner, or Principal LeBeau or even Kat and the Twins.

With half an ear listening to Ms. Cisco, I started to sketch the face of the creepy guy. Normally, I'm not very artistic, but occasionally, when I don't pay attention, my fingers come out with something sloppy but identifiable. I looked down at the paper. The big nasty grin was dwarfing the entire face. It was so out of proportion, it was unrecognizable. I shook my head as I turned to a fresh page and tried to recall what his face looked like before he smiled that big creepy grin. The small nasty smile. With the vinyl sheen to his skin. Like he'd just been squeezed out of a tube and freshly molded, but nothing had set yet. Like he'd just got out of some kind of miracle plastic surgery and he had a brand new face. A face he wasn't used to working yet. Almost alien. I looked down at my notepad and let out a small screech.

The entire class turned to look at me. Ms. Cisco stopped mid-sentence. For a half a moment, she was annoyed, but then you could see her face soften into concern.

"Are you alright, dear?" she asked gently.

She must be thinking this was some kind of aftershock reaction. I nodded my head mutely, my hands covering the sketch that I had made. She gave me a motherly smile before going back to discuss the Supreme Court system and stuff like that.

It was stupid to be afraid of a picture, especially one that I'd sketched myself, but I really had to force myself to spread my fingers and look at the face again.

It wasn't a good picture, but it was recognizable. It looked enough like the creepy guy in the hall to be able to say, hey, that's the creepy guy in the hall, but that wasn't what was worrying me. It was the smile. I recognized the small nasty smile.

It was Rojo from Shelly's Shack.

I closed my eyes. It must be my imagination. The guy in the hall creeped me out and Rojo creeped me out, so I mixed the two faces together. But the more I tried to tell myself that, the more convinced I became that they were one in the same.

Even though they really didn't look that much alike.

I did a quick sketch of Rojo next to the creepy mannequin guy. I had to stop myself from shading it in too much. It's what I always did in Art class. I never knew when enough was enough and I'd end up overdrawing it and ruining the entire picture. I forced myself to stop. I even used my left hand to take the pencil out from my right hand. Then I stared at the sketches.

The shape of the heads was different. The hair was different. But the eyes were very similar. And the smiles, the creepy smiles, were exactly the same.

In complete violation of all school rules, I pulled out my cellphone. Hidden on my lap, I texted a message to Cade.

Rojo 'is in Wicassett. I need you. Now.

Chapter Fourteen

Last Summer

It was four weeks, two days into my summer vacation.

Three weeks, four days since Cade and I started hanging out. (Give or take a few hours.)

I woke up with the dawn, scrambled into my swimsuit, threw a tee shirt over it because the morning was still cool and headed for the beach.

Today was going to be a perfect, wonderful, awesome day. Mom and Mrs. Villanueva were taking the kids to Playland and then to Chuck E. Cheese for lunch. I was going to have an entire day free from toddlers. I was going to have an entire day free for Cade.

On a typical morning, I'd start down for the beach between eight and nine o'clock, herding kids and hauling gear, and Cade would already be sitting on his lifeguard tower. Sometimes he'd be staring at the spot where we'd emerge from, waiting until he caught his first glimpse, and then his face would break out into this huge grin that I could see from a hundred yards away. He'd jump down from his tower, soft as a cat, and trot over to us. He'd take all the gear from me, managing to tuck it all under one arm so he'd have the other arm free to put around my shoulders. Ever since that night on the beach in front of Shelly's Shack, Cade would drape his arm around my shoulders every time he could. And every time, the magic was still there.

Only now I remembered to breathe.

The kids loved him and the four-way conversations we sometimes had made me laugh so hard, my face would hurt. He'd take their comments very literally and then respond back with exaggerated formality.

As I climbed the street side of the dune, I remembered that one time, five days ago, when, as we approached the beach and he had just stared out to sea and pretended not to notice us. For a moment, I had felt crushed, thinking that he didn't want to hang out anymore, but when we finally got to the "san bock," I looked up and saw that he was smirking. He knew exactly what I was feeling and was doing it on purpose. So I did the same thing. I set up the kids, sat down on the sand and completely ignored him. I had actually brought a paperback to the beach with me that morning, so I buried my nose in the book.

The little kids were puzzled. They called out to Cade, but I hushed them, telling them not to talk to strangers. This confused them even more, but when Cade winked at them, they settled down to play in the sand.

I didn't actually read a word of the book, I was much too aware of Cade on the tower behind me. After about five minutes, (which seemed like five hours) I heard a light thump as he leapt to the ground. I didn't move as I heard him approach. He settled down next to me on the sand. I could feel the warmth of his body within inches of mine and I gritted my teeth as I fought against the pull.

"Is that a good book?" he asked. His voice was soft and warm and I felt myself weakening. I leaned into the book and reread the same line four times.

"Must be," he answered himself. "She hasn't turned a page in five minutes."

I bit my lip. I wasn't about to turn the page *now*, so I just moved my eyes to the next page. He leaned closer as if to read over my shoulder.

"Mmmmm."

I didn't know what that meant. Was he musing about my reading choice, humming in my ear, or just enjoying the smell of my shoulder? Maybe all three. I felt his breath on my neck and was very close to dissolving. I gripped the book tighter to keep my fingers from shaking. When it looked like I couldn't hold out for another moment, help came from an unexpected quarter.

"We're not supposed to talk to strangers," Tiff announced with the kind of authority only a three year old can pull off .

Cade gave a crack of laughter and fell backwards, his hand skimming my shoulders and sending tremors down my back. He rolled to his feet, laughing, lifted Tiff in the air and spun her around. Tiff squealed with joy.

Then he placed her back on her feet. "You are absolutely correct, young miss," he said with a bow. "Please allow me to introduce myself. My name is Cade Himasanto." He took her hand, and shook it with a gentle solemnity. "And what would your name be?"

Tiff, always ready to play, entered the game with both feet. "My name is Tiffany Hill, but you can call me Tiffy."

"I'm pleased to meet you, Tiffy. And what is your friend's name?"

"Carlos."

"How do you do, Carlos?"

Carlos was having trouble following the game. His brow wrinkled as Cade took his hand and shook it. He scowled briefly before going back to pushing his plastic dump truck through the sand. With a crooked half smile, Cade turned toward me.

"And may I introduce myself to you?" he asked softly, his eyes glittering. "Or perhaps we've met before?"

"Have we?" I was going for nonchalant, but I was having trouble breathing again.

He reached for my hand, but instead of the casual handshake that he'd given Tiff and Carlos, he raised it to his mouth. When his lips brushed my knuckles, the world began to spin.

"Misty?" The humor was back in Cade's voice. "Misty. Breathe."

Oh yeah. Easy for him to say.

After that, he never tried ignoring me again. Later, he told me that ignoring me for thirty seconds was the second toughest thing he'd ever been through in his life.

"Really?" I asked. "What was the first?"

"Being ignored by you."

Breathe, Misty. Breathe.

I was grinning as I recalled this and crested the dune, getting my first glimpse of the beach, the sea, the rising sun and the lifeguard tower.

Which was empty.

I stood staring at the vacant chair, unreasonably baffled. I don't know why I expected Cade to always be there. It was a little after seven, more than an hour earlier than when I normally arrived. Maybe he didn't start until eight. I walked slowly over to the tower, my mind running through all kinds of scenarios as to how I would greet him. Would he come from down the beach? Even now, was he a speck in the distance that I could watch approach? I sat down in the sand and stared down past the breakwater. It would be fun to watch him walk slowly towards me, making out his features one at a time. I wondered when he'd recognize me sitting here. Would it be after I saw him? Would I be able to tell from his body, even from a mile away, that he'd seen me? I wrapped my arms around my knees and waited, anticipation practically an ache in my chest.

Patience is not one of my stronger points.

I could tell by the sun, that it wasn't even seven thirty yet. I'd been waiting at least ten minutes, or was it ten hours? I stood up, brushed the sand from my legs, and made a decision.

I'd go find Cade. I knew where Shelly's Shack was. I'd track him down and surprise him. This was even better than waiting. Better, because I didn't do the waiting thing very well.

With a grin on my face and unreasonably high expectations in my head, I made my way down the beach.

Chapter Fifteen

The beach is pretty empty in the early morning. Just a couple of joggers and a few gypsy dogs. As I walked the mile and a half down to where I thought Shelly's Shack was, I kept scanning the beach for Cade. It was getting close to eight o'clock and I really expected to see him walking towards his lifeguard tower, but I made it all the way to the dune where we'd met Rojo with no sign of Cade. I stood for a moment on the beach, scuffing my feet in the sand before starting up the path that led over the dunes to the house beyond.

I don't know what I was expecting to see when I first saw Shelly's Shack. Almost all the beachfront houses were new, two or more stories high, with sliding glass doors and balconies, decks and boardwalks. Shelly's Shack had all that and then some.

Even in full light of the morning, I could see what looked like a million twinkling lights, still glowing white, draping the handrails, hanging from the terraces and running like waterfalls along the walls. Two wooden walkways, raised high above the ground, led from the beach to the patio and framed a huge clover shaped swimming pool. Four whirlpool tubs churned in the dimples of the clover, steam rising like sea reeds, dissolving into the morning chill.

I wondered if I might be at the wrong house. In the soft morning light, it was so beautiful, it seemed almost magical. I stood at the top of the dune and stared, reluctant to intrude. I looked back out to the beach, trying to remember the night that we'd met Rojo. I was pretty sure that this was the same spot, but somehow, I couldn't see Cade living in such an elegant place. He was so down to earth and this place was so unreal, it seemed like it belonged in the movies. Or Disneyworld. I glanced up and down the beach one last time, checking for a glimpse of Cade before I started down the boardwalk.

Even though I was trying to walk quietly, my bare feet thrummed like tom-toms on the wood slats of the walkway. A movement caught my eye and I looked down at the pool. What I thought had been a pile of towels left heaped on a lounge chair was actually a person sleeping. A woman's tanned arm plopped out, her fingers banging against the concrete. I froze, but neither the towels nor the arm moved again. As I looked closer, I saw that a lot of the lumps of towels were actually people sleeping, some on lounge chairs, but a few were sprawled on the concrete deck, towels piled on top of their heads as well as under them. They didn't look comfortable. If it weren't for the occasional groan or twitch, I'd have thought they were all corpses.

I continued on toward the house, walking close to the railings so my footsteps wouldn't echo so loudly.

The main door was propped open by a large sea stone and the screen door was ajar, letting in insects, windblown leaves and me. I stood with one foot inside the room and one on the deck and looked around.

It was amazing how a room could look so elegant and yet so trashed at the same time. There was no way this was a summer rental house. The artwork on the walls looked like museum pieces. They glowed in focused beams of light from recessed ceiling lamps. Fresh floral arrangements sat on marble coffee tables and a half dozen designer couches were placed invitingly around the room.

And on these elegant couches were the disheveled forms of more half-naked sleepers. Bottles, glass, trash, dishes and towels littered the room. The stench of cigarettes, stale alcohol, perspiration and vomit made my stomach roil, but I could smell something else as well, something fusty, sweet and herby. Quickly, I stepped back from the door. I might be from a small town in New Hampshire, but I recognized pot when I smelled it and my parents would Kill me (with a capital K) if they ever caught the scent on me.

I clutched the deck rail, my knuckles clenched white as I stared, unseeing, at the still life tableau of the pool.

This is where Cade lived? When he'd leave me at my doorstep in the evening, he'd come back to this pit and spend the rest of the night with his friends, doing who-knew-what?

I shook my head. No, I wasn't that clueless. I knew exactly what he'd be doing when he got back here. My throat closed up, my eyes got teary and my world fell apart. I clung to the railing like it was my only friend.

"Well, look what the cat dragged in."

The voice was soft, almost purring, but I hadn't heard anyone approach and I let out a screech that should have awoken the dead. I did hear an annoyed groan from inside, but that quickly faded back into sleep. I turned to see Rojo standing at the other end of the deck, looking like something out of an old James Bond film. He had a black satin robe that hung open, revealing matching black satin pajama bottoms and a tanned and cut sets of abs. In one hand, he held a drink and he swirled it idly, the ice cubes clinking against the glass. He was smiling. The small creepy smile that changed into the big creepy smile. Instinctively, I stepped back.

"Sorry," I muttered as I headed for the boardwalk. "I was looking for Cade. I'll catch up with him later."

"Were your ears burning? We've been talking about you."

That slowed down my retreat. How lame am I? Every instinct told me to get out of there, but I was curious; I wanted to know what Cade had been saying about me.

"C'mon in." He cocked his head back toward the door and gave me a crocodile smile. "Everyone's been dying to meet you."

"Um, maybe another time. I think they're sleeping right now." Or passed out. It was all semantic.

"Cade's upstairs. I'll take you to his room."

I wavered. I couldn't reconcile the Cade I knew with a Cade that would live in what seemed like a really elegant crack house. I needed to see for myself if he were here. But even more, I wanted to see that he wasn't here. That this was all some horrible mistake and there was some other Cade that spent his nights in this… lair of lechery.

"Hey Cade!" Rojo bellowed up to a balcony above us, completely disregarding all the dozers on the deck and in the living room. "Got company!"

I crooked my neck trying to see up to whatever balcony he was yelling to, but there was no movement above. Rojo ticked his head to one side as if telling me to follow him and then went back into the house. I dithered for a moment, trying to decide between escaping to the beach with my tail between my legs or confronting Cade in person at the scene of the crime.

To tell you the truth, I'm more of a turn and run personality, but part of me couldn't believe that Cade was in there and I had to see for myself. Curiosity won out and I followed Rojo into the Shack.

Tiptoeing between the couches, I could see more evidence of debauchery. There were bodies on the floor, some of them naked. Flecks of white dust were scattered suspiciously on the coffee tables around exotic devices that looked like elaborate incense burners, but I bet weren't.

Rojo stood at the base of the stairway, smirking at me. I knew I was acting like some naïve New Hampshire hick, but I was in way over my head. I forced my eyes up, away from the bodies and away from Rojo, so I was looking directly at the kitchen service window and saw Shelly appear there before she could make her entrance.

She moved slowly and quietly, hoping, I think, to check me out before I noticed her. When she caught me staring, a hint of annoyance flickered in her eyes, and maybe something nastier, but then a smooth smile glided quickly onto her face.

"And this must be Cade's little Morning Mist that we've heard so much about." Her voice was a seductive hum but the words jarred me. That was Cade's nickname for me and that meant that Shelly must have heard it from Cade. My stomach dropped.

My mouth dropped as well when she stepped out of the kitchen and I saw her in her full glory. It's not unusual at the beach to spend the entire day in your bathing suit. In fact, except for the occasional tee shirt to ward off the evening chill or protect sunburned shoulders, everyone tended to do that. It wasn't Shelly's bathing suit, so much, but what was inside it.

Shelly was very tall, nearly 6 foot, and bone-thin, except for her breasts, which were enormous, much too large for her frame. She wore the tiniest gold lamé rhinestone studded bikini that barely covered her and seemed more indecent than if she'd been naked. What she lacked in clothes, she made up for with accessories. Bejeweled hoops hung from her ears, bangles glittered on her wrists and gold lame sandals with six inch heels completed the effect. She was stunning and sexy at the same time.

But she was older too. Maybe my parent's age. Too old to be hanging out with college-aged kids, maybe she was somebody's aunt, but I doubted it. She walked like a tiger and screamed predator with every step.

"I was, just, um, looking for Cade." I stumbled over the words.

"I'm taking her up to his room." Rojo seemed to find some secret joke in this that Shelly shared.

"Well, run along then." Shelly was both gracious and sarcastic. "Maybe I'll be up in a few minutes."

I hurried up the stairs after Rojo, hoping that I wouldn't still be upstairs when she got there.

Cade's room was on the fourth level and my breath was a little ragged by the time we made it to the top landing. As we passed open doors, I peeked in and what I saw was pretty much a repeat of what was downstairs, maybe more skin and less drugs. Rojo was knocking on a door by the time I caught up to him.

"Cade? You up?" Rojo called out as he opened the door.

A sudden burst of fury gave me courage and I pushed past him and into Cade's room, ready to beard the lion in his lair.

His lair was bare. The room, like the others I'd passed, was small, beige and bland. A king sized bed, a wicker chair and a small dresser took up most of the space. Sheer curtains veiled a sliding glass door that led to a balcony that overlooked the pool

But unlike the rest of house, this room was empty. And it looked like it had been that way for a while. The bedspread was smooth and unwrinkled, and the entire room had that stale smell of disuse, as if no one had been in it for weeks.

For a second, I was relieved. He wasn't here. Cade wasn't here. And it didn't look like he'd been there the night before. Maybe he hadn't been there all summer. He wasn't like the people downstairs. He was better than that. Better than Rojo.

Rojo.

I spun around to face Rojo, my anger back but also a little belated alarm.

"He's not here," I snapped.

"Oops." Rojo was smirking.

"Why did you tell me he was? You knew he wasn't here." I tried to force myself to stay angry but fear was starting to make my legs shake.

"My mistake. So sorry." He was leering now. I didn't know what game he was playing, but I wasn't going to stick around to find out. I wanted out of there, but he was blocking the door. I tried to push my way past him, but he stopped me with one hand and shoved me back. I fell onto the bed, caught one glance of the creepy smile and scrambled off the other side. The sliding glass door snagged as I dragged it open. Rojo was openly laughing as he stepped around the bed. I scuttled out onto the balcony, shoving the door shut behind me.

There was no way to lock the door from the outside. I wedged one of the deck chairs under the handle and then looked over the edge. I was four stories up. No way was I jumping. There was another balcony on this level, separated by a slatted wall. I was climbing around the partition when, with one quick yank, the glass door was wrenched open, the deck chair splintering like toothpicks. I clung to the partition, frozen in panic for a millisecond, my breath ripping jaggedly in my chest.

Then I swung myself onto the other balcony and scurried to its sliding door. It was locked. I pounded once or twice against the glass but the draperies on the other side didn't move and I couldn't hear a sound from inside.

A crash behind me and I turned to see the wood partition shatter into kindling as Rojo's hand pushed through it like it was rice paper. In the moment that it took for him to kick out the bottom with his foot, I started over the side. I figured that maybe I could swing myself down to the balcony below and hopefully escape that way. I was halfway over the railing when his hand grabbed the back of my neck and pulled me back like I was a rag doll. He was inhumanly strong. I was no featherweight, but he lifted me up so my feet dangled off the floor. I thrashed and swung my fists at him, but if I made contact with him at all, it was like thumping against a stone wall.

"Not so fast, little girl." Rojo's eyes glittered and his voice was breathy with excitement. He was getting off on this. "All in good time."

I wasn't sure what he meant and I didn't want to find out. I looked up in to his face and screamed "CADE!" as loud as I could.

"How romantic." Rojo leaned his face closer, his creepy smile blocking out the view of the world beyond. I gagged as I tasted his breath in my mouth. "Her last words will be her calling out to her star-crossed lover. I love it."

Then, with his free hand, he reached out and snapped the railing like it was balsa wood. I watched the splinters as they showered down in slow motion.

"Oh dear," Rojo chuckled. "The railings must have rotted out from the sea air. So dangerous."

I froze as he extended his arm to dangle me over the edge. I made a strange stuttering gasping sound as I looked down four stories to the strip of sand and pebbles that separated the first floor wood deck from the concrete pool deck.

Rojo grinned as he looked down over the edge. "You know, a person could break their neck falling from a fourth floor balcony." He sniffed as he considered it. "But then, they might just break their legs. What do you think?"

I don't think that he really wanted my opinion, which was just as well, since I couldn't speak. I wanted to plead with him, ask him why he was doing this, but all that came out was a stuttering gasp.

"Yes, maybe you're right." He spoke like I had actually said something. "But if a person were to land on the concrete deck, that would most likely kill them. Hmm?"

He laughed as he pulled his arm back and for a fraction of a second, I thought he was going to set me back down on the balcony, but he was just winding up to get enough momentum to throw me onto the concrete pool deck.

I arced through the air, my arms waving like I was some psycho human pinwheel. The scream in my throat was stolen by wind and shock. I sailed over the sandy strip, right toward the concrete deck and certain death.

I hit something. Or something hit me. But then I kept dropping. And then I stopped dropping. I waited for death. I waited for the pain. But nothing happened. I opened my eyes.

Cade was here, looking down at me with a concern so furious as to be almost frightening. But I wasn't frightened. Cade was here.

"Oh, Cade." The words came out like a sob. His arms were around me. We were beside the pool. He must have caught me, broken my fall, but wouldn't we both have toppled? I couldn't seem to think properly. All I knew was that before, I had been terrified, and now I was with Cade.

"Oops." I heard Rojo say.

The words were quiet and sarcastic, but they carried down to the pool deck where Cade and I were. We both looked up to see Rojo sneering down at us.

"Cade," I whispered urgently. "He threw me off the balcony! He tried to kill me!"

"It's okay." Cade placed me on my wobbly legs. "I'll take care of him later."

I would have protested, but I was having trouble standing and I needed both his arms to keep from sinking to the ground.

"What are you doing here?" His voice was an angry hiss in my ear as he half carried me toward the boardwalk.

"I was looking for you."

He stopped and turned me to face him. His eyes were so blue, bluer than the summer sky, that I barely heard his words. "I don't come here anymore. I don't belong here and neither do you."

"Hey Cade!" One of the beach chair corpses game back to life. My screams hadn't woken him, but Cade's voice had. Go figure. "We haven't seen you for weeks. Where you been, bro?"

Cade ignored him as he gripped my arms. "You are never to come here again. Do you hear me?"

"You think?" My sarcasm was a knee-jerk reaction. I had no intention of ever coming near this place again.

But I did.

Curiosity dragged me back. Four days later, I crept to the top of the dune and peeked over the ridge. The place was deserted. The pool was drained. The deck furniture, missing. Even though it was mid-July, the hurricane shades were rolled closed. I don't know how Cade had done it, but Shelly's Shack was shut down and no one was there for the rest of the summer.

I didn't expect to see any of them again. Especially Rojo. But sometimes things don't turn out the way you expect.

Chapter Sixteen

Can I be any more of a moron?

I spent the rest of Civics class kicking myself. Occasionally literally.

How could I have sent that text message? How pitiful was I? Rojo creeped me out and tried to kill me and the mannequin guy in the hallway creeped me out. Just because they both creeped me out, didn't mean they were the same guy. I'd have done anything to be able to recall that text message. I could only hope that Cade's cellphone didn't accept texts. Or maybe, wherever he was, he was so far out of range that the message would get lost in cyber-space.

The bell rang and I grabbed my notebook and Civics text. I'd left my backpack in my locker. I'd have to go by and pick it up on the way to the bus.

I'd forgotten I was supposed to wait for my escorts and I hurried down the hall, pushing against the flow as everyone else (who had planned better than I did and had all their stuff with them for final period) headed toward the front entrance and the buses. My locker was on the second floor outside the Chem Lab and the hallway was starting to empty as I quickly spun through the combination lock. I grabbed my bag, slammed the locker shut and was resetting the lock when I sensed someone near by.

I turned and let out a little gasp. Danel stood less than two feet from me, as still as a stone, staring at me with a cold fury.

"How did it go today?" The gentleness of his voice didn't match the anger seething in his eyes. I pushed past him, pleased with myself for not shaking. We were nearly alone in the hall and I wanted to get out to the buses, and other people, as soon as possible.

"Fine," I answered. "No problem."

I walked quickly but he easily matched my stride. I didn't turn, but I could feel him walking beside me.

"What did Officer Huebner have to say?" he asked casually.

He'd only been in town a couple of days but he already knew the name of at least one of the police officers?

"Nothing major." I fell back a half a step so that I could watch his face. His outward composure clashed with the violence in his eyes. "Despite what I kept telling them, they all feared the worst." I decided to add a little jab to see what kind of response I got. "Sergeant Huebner seemed more suspicious about *why* it happened than what actually happened."

We were almost at the foot of the stairs. Danel stepped out in front of me, blocking my way. I hoisted my books and bags closer to my chest and waited for his reaction.

"Suspicious? What do you---"

"Who was that guy in the hallway?" I went on the attack, cutting him off mid-sentence.

"What guy?" The anger disappeared, replaced by wariness.

"The creepy-looking guy who smiled at us." I said, meeting Danel's unblinking gaze.

Danel dropped his voice to that soft insistent level, like the way he had talked to Gary in the Boys Room. "There was no guy in the hallway."

I met his eyes and didn't flinch even though a fly was buzzing around my head. After a long moment, I hoisted my books back up higher in my arms.

"You are so full of crap," I said softly.

For some reason, my words floored him. He looked at me in shock, like I had kicked him in the shins.

111

I pushed past him. I needed to hurry if I was going to make the bus, but as I passed, he reached out and grabbed a piece of paper that was sticking out of my Civics Book. It was the picture I'd drawn of Rojo and the Creepy Hall Guy.

"Hey, knock it off!" I reached to snatch it back but he pushed my hand away. "That's mine. It's none of your business."

If he looked like I'd kicked him the shins before, this time it looked like I kicked him a lot higher. He stared at the picture in amazement and then looked at me. In his face I could see shock and perhaps, it seemed strange but I could have sworn I saw it, fear.

"What... are... you?" The words were almost voiceless and they echoed what I remembered hearing in my head that first morning on the bus. Crap, was it only yesterday?

"It's just a sketch. Give it to me." I leapt to grab at it, but there was no way. He didn't even try to pull it further away; he just stood there, stock still, staring at me.

We were still frozen in a face-off when Kat burst through the double doors followed by the Tucker Twins bristling like bulldogs.

"Misty! There you are! We've been looking for you everywhere!" Kat said with exaggerated cheerfulness. "C'mon, we're going to miss the bus."

Danel ignored them. Our eyes still locked, he slowly brought the sketch down, folded it in half and tucked it into his jacket pocket. I glared at him, but Kat dragged me off.

"Are you out of your mind?" Kat hissed in my ear as I was hustled onto the bus. "You were supposed to wait for us outside Civics. Where'd you go?"

"I forgot my backpack, I had to go to my locker." Why did I suddenly feel like a ten-year-old?

The bus jerked forward before we'd found a seat. The Twins headed for the back row and since the rest of the bus was nearly full, Kat and I ended up there as well.

Danel hadn't made the bus. We'd barely made it ourselves. The only reason it was still waiting for us is because Charlie the bus driver liked Kat.

As I settled into the seat next to Kat, my brain bounced between wondering how Danel gets home when he misses the bus and his reaction to my stupid drawing.

"What in Sam Hill is that?" Ty yelled to be heard over the roar of the bus.

"I think I'm in love!" Chad sounded like he was about to hyperventilate. They were both staring out the rear of the bus.

Kat and I stood up so that we could see out the back of the window. There was a car following the bus. A sleek black sportscar that looked like a mini-stealth bomber on four wheels.

I sat down abruptly, looking ahead blindly, my stomach like lead. I had seen that car before. If it wasn't the same car that I'd seen behind us on the highway in Maryland last week, then it was a car that looked just like it. It was hard to avoid the conclusion that whoever was in that car had followed me back from Ocean Isle. Sergeant Huebner's warning echoed in my brain while Kat and the boys ogled the car.

"What is it?" asked Kat

"It's a Koenigsegg CCX!" Chad sounded so reverent, you'd think he was talking about the Pope or George Lucas.

"Ah." Kat nodded her head as if she knew what he was talking about.

"It's only one of the top ten coolest cars on the planet!" Ty explained, his face so close to window that he steamed the glass.

"And one of the most expensive," added Chad. "That puppy can cost over a million."

"Dollars?" Kat crawled over me to get a better view. "Who would pay that kind of money for a car?"

The boys shot her dual looks of disgust but didn't bother to answer.

By now half the kids on the bus were crowded around the rear windows, trying to catch a glimpse of the car. World class sports cars were not something we normally saw in Wicassett, not even in leaf-peeper season. I stood up again, kneeling on the seat to look above all the heads. I couldn't see anything of the driver; its silhouette was obscured by the blackened glass.

A wave of heat hit me and I slumped back down into the seat. No one could see who was in that car, but I knew who it was as sure as I knew my own name. Even from this distance, I could feel his eyes burning through the back of my neck.

"Danel." I whispered.

Well, that answered the question of how Danel got home when he missed the bus. He just jumped into his million dollar CC-Whatever and drove home. But where had he parked it that he could get to it so quickly? And why, if he owned a million dollar silly car, did he even take the bus?

I already knew that Danel wasn't a typical seventeen year old. But how not-typical he was, I was starting to see that I didn't have a clue.

"He's passing the bus!" Ty yelled out.

Every kid on the bus scurried to the other side to watch the CCX pass. I was the only one left on my side. I'm surprised the bus didn't tip over. With a roar of a couple of dozen cylinders, the car shot past us and disappeared into traffic ahead.

Who was Danel? Or maybe the question should be, what was he?

And if Danel wasn't what he appeared to be, did I have to admit that Cade might not be either? I hugged my backpack to my chest and stared out the window, wishing the rest of my life would go back to moving as slowly as this bus.

Chapter Seventeen

Chad and Ty walked me to my door. This sounds cuter than it was. Actually, they skulked me to my door. Ty would trot ahead and reconnoiter, and then speak into his lapel like he had some kind of microphone hidden there. The fact that he was twelve feet away and we could hear him fine obviously didn't interfere with his M.O.

Kat had tagged along and she started to play as well. By the time we made it to my house, I was relieved, not only to get home after a long, stupid day, but also to leave my three bodyguards on the doorstep.

"Hey!" Chad's eye held a maniacal glint. "You guys want to come over to my place? Let's hack into the NASA network and see if we can keep watch over the neighborhood from an aerial satellite feed."

"You can do that?" Kat can be so gullible sometimes.

"Well, I don't know." Chad admitted, but in no way disheartened. "Want to give it a shot?"

"Sure!" Kat would do anything to avoid going home and having to start her homework. "Want to come, Misty?"

"No, I'm good. You guys go ahead. I'm beat." Beat, and in desperate need of some quiet time to put all the pieces together.

They called out their goodbyes and headed up the hill towards Chad's and Ty's homes. I opened the door as quietly as possible and slipped inside.

"I made an appointment with Doctor Krajeski." My mother's voice rang like the knell of doom from the living room. "But we have to be up early. It's at eight a.m."

I bet you thought this day couldn't get any worse. I knew better.

"I'm not going to a shrink, Mom." I called from the foot of the stairs. "Get over it. It's not going to happen."

"Doctor Phil recommends professional counseling for victims of violence."

"I'm not a victim, Mom."

"Doctor Phil says---"

"Mom. I hate to burst your bubble, but Doctor Phil isn't a real doctor. He's just a guy who stayed in school long after all the rational people graduated and got jobs. I'm not going to a shrink because some slacker on television says so."

There was a long pause.

"That's just the post-traumatic stress talking."

I rolled my eyes and ran up the stairs to my bedroom.

"I'm not going to a shrink. Give it up," I yelled as I slammed the door. I dropped my backpack on the floor and threw myself across my bed.

"We'll discuss this when your father gets home."

Brilliant.

I wish I could say that I had a flash of inspiration that afternoon, but the truth is, I just lay across my bed, trying to dissect all the pieces and getting nowhere. I was willing to give up the idea that Rojo and the creepy hallway guy were one and the same, but what was with Danel's reaction to my sketch? And maybe that wasn't Danel in the CCX car, but my gut told me it was and I couldn't shake that conviction from my head. The creepy hallway guy could have been just coincidence. Danel's white knight rescue could be exactly what it appeared to be. Danel and Cade might have completely valid histories that Officer Huebner just couldn't find. Maybe I was a victim of an over-active imagination.

I just couldn't make myself buy it. Something strange was happening and it revolved around Cade and Danel. And me.

The room was getting dark. I could smell garlic chicken cooking in the kitchen. Usually, Mom had me set the table, but maybe she thought that was too much for someone suffering from post-traumatic stress. I should go down and help, but I was still feeling exhausted, even though I'd spent the last two hours lying across my bed, staring at the ceiling.

I missed Cade. That was the truth. It was worse tonight than when I'd left him on the beach and I thought I'd never see him again. Worse, because now I not only wanted him, I NEEDED him. Everything was wrong when he wasn't there. I grabbed my cellphone and thought about what neurotic, pathetic message I should text to him. I slapped the phone back down on the bedspread. My eyes got teary. I was neck deep in a pity puddle and I wasn't even trying to paddle my way out.

The baleful bay of a dog cut the silence. It fit my mood exactly. I gave myself a mental shake and sat up, wiping my eyes. I dragged myself over to the window and stared out.

It was that time of the night that they used to call the gloaming. The sun had set but it wasn't really dark yet. The streetlights had just come on, but they weren't doing any good. The trees behind the house were dark, but I could still make out the yard.

A basset hound stood in our backyard, facing the woods, its tail pointing. Every ten seconds or so, it would give out a long sorrowful howl. I sighed and grabbed my cell phone.

Chad answered after three rings. "Hey Misty, what's up?" he asked, after swallowing a mouthful.

"Captain Picard's in the backyard."

"He'll come home when he's ready. He knows the way."

"Yeah, but he's howling up a storm."

"He'll stop in a second." Chad mumbled around another mouthful.

"I think he's treed a possum or something. He's been going at it a while."

Chad sighed. "Okay, I'll come get 'em."

He hung up but I knew perfectly well that it would be another hour before he came down the hill, if he came down at all.

I was tired of doing nothing. I grabbed my jacket and headed for the stairs.

"Mom, Captain Picard's treed a possum. I'm going to take him back to Chad's."

"But… well, hurry back. Dinner's almost ready and your Dad will be home soon."

I wasn't in any rush to get back. I knew perfectly well that the dinner conversation would be about the two of them trying to talk me into going to see a psychiatrist. I headed out the door and around the back.

Captain Picard was still at it. It had to be a possum. Anything else would have taken off by now and the dog would either be chasing it through the woods, or proudly strutting around, having scared it off. But a possum will just freeze and not move and unless someone does something, the dog will just keep barking at him all night.

I didn't have a leash so I just grabbed the Captain's collar and gave him a tug. He came readily enough, giving one last "ah-woo" to the woods before letting me drag him toward the street. I let go after a couple of steps. Usually, once you start him going in one direction, the Captain will follow readily enough, but this time he turned around and bolted right back to my yard.

"Oh, c'mon Captain," I muttered as I rolled my eyes and followed him.

The Captain's howls are really annoying and sound more like someone slowly torturing a set of bagpipes than a dog. When I caught up with him again, I looked around for the possum, but couldn't see one. The Captain wasn't pointing up a tree, he was pointing into the woods. I walked over to the edge of the lawn, the Captain at my heels, and peered in.

"The Woods" is a grandiose term for a swath of trees, about a hundred feet wide, that separates the houses on our street from the neighborhood one street over. It's a corridor of "conservation area" that runs about six miles from the state forest in the east, emptying out at Willows Fork at Route 111 (aka Road Kill Junction) to the west. It's only about a mile from my house to the forest. When I was a kid, I'd spent so much time exploring it, I knew it like I knew my own bedroom, so it wasn't the least bit scary stepping into shadows of the trees. I could see the lights from my house as well as the lights from the houses one street over, so it's not like I was being brave walking into the woods.

Just stupid.

Chapter Eighteen

Whatever the Captain had been scenting was gone. I stood still, letting the silence of the trees reestablish itself, but nothing moved. The Captain, bored now, lay at my feet like an ottoman. I let the woods refresh me.

The smell of the woods at night is marvelous. Especially in the fall. The air is crisp and sweet. The aroma of dead leaves turning into mulch might sound disgusting, but it actually smells amazing. Somewhere, someone had lit a fire in their fireplace and the hint of smoke in the air only complemented the faint lingering scent of cinnamon and leather. I inhaled deeply.

The moment shattered. I stiffened and the Captain, aware that something had changed, lumbered to his feet and looked at me expectantly. Warily, I sniffed the air once more. There it was. I might be imaging it, but I didn't think so. Cinnamon and leather. I peered into the shadows, more annoyed than frightened.

"Okay, Danel. Knock it off. I know you're here. C'mon out."

The woods were silent. A faint breeze rustled the branches, jarring free a few leaves that floated softly to the ground. The ever-present insects buzzed around my head, but there was no other movement.

"Jerk," I muttered. Then louder: "I know you're in here, now come on out."

The bugs got worse. I swatted at them, but it didn't seem to help. I don't know what was annoying me more: Danel's playing hide-and-seek in the woods or the insects. There was one solution for both.

"C'mon, Captain." I turned to go back into the house. "If some brainless moron wants to waste his night hiding behind trees, we'll let him."

Since the Captain was no longer howling, I no longer felt the need to walk him home. I was heading back into the house when I caught a movement in the trees. Something light colored and man-shaped.

"Ha!" I turned around and headed right back into the woods. To this day, I don't know why I didn't think Danel was a threat. Maybe because he had stopped Gary. Maybe because he had told the Jacket girls to back off. Maybe for some other reason. But whatever it was, I went stomping into the woods feeling nothing but irritation at his invading my space, and perhaps a little curiosity as to why he was there.

The Captain lost interest and was meandering up the street, bound for home, while I headed for the spot where I'd seen the light colored figure, but by the time I got there, I couldn't see anyone.

"Jerk," I muttered again. I wasn't about to go chasing shadows through the woods at night. I'd probably end up just getting laughed at. I turned to go back to the house once more, when I saw, as clear as day, someone on the path in front of me.

Cade.

His back was to me, walking away. But there was no mistaking him. The blond hair, the broad shoulders. It wasn't just my imagination swayed by loneliness and longings. It was definitely Cade. There in the woods. In front of me on the path.

"CADE!" I ran toward him with only half an eye watching where I was walking. I tripped on a root and caught myself before I fell, but when I looked up, Cade was gone.

But it had been him. I told myself that again and again as I stumbled up the path. The light was fading. I hadn't been this far up the path for a couple of years. I remembered it well enough, but the going was slow. I was almost to the State Forest when I caught sight of him again.

The woods had widened out at this point and I no longer could see street lights or houses, but I didn't even think about that. Joy and relief were giving way to annoyance. What was Cade playing at?

"Cade, knock it off! Wait up!"

He turned and in the near gloom, he twitched his head as if to call me forward. So I followed him into the forest.

I'd camped in the State Forest as a Girl Scout, and when I was twelve, I'd run away from home for five hours and walked among the trees until I got cold and hungry and came back. The forest had never been a scary place to me.

Until tonight.

I got to the clearing where a brush fire, three years ago, had swept out a meadow in the middle of the trees. The skeletons of dead burnt trunks still spiked up in the glen, but they were stark, blackened and naked, their leafless branches letting through the fading twilight. Grass and scrub had grown and filled the void, so there was a knee high carpet of brush blanketing the dell. And there, standing amidst the grass in the dimming light, stood Cade.

Annoyance at this silly game of hide-and-seek fell away as I felt a wave of relief. Cade was here. All the scary stuff would stop now. I stepped off the path and waded through the grass towards him.

"Cade!" I was babbling even before I got within ten yards of him. "Where have you been? I've missed you so much! There's been so much crap happening! I have so much to tell you, but, oh, I'm so glad you're here."

He didn't speak. He didn't even move. This wasn't like him. He usually laughed or at least smiled when we met. It wasn't like he was putting up a wall; it was like part of him wasn't even there. All of my old fears about his not caring any more flooded back and I slowed to a walk, my eyes searching his face for some spark of what I remembered.

"Cade?" I whispered as my hand reached out to touch him. "What is it? What's wrong?"

My fingers went cold when they touched his arm. The electricity that I'd always felt before was gone. It was as if he wasn't even Cade, just a statue that looked like Cade. A mannequin. A façade.

And then he looked at me and smiled.

A very creepy smile.

I screamed. I stumbled backward and the creepy smile grew wider as he stepped toward me. My elbows hit the ground first as I fell and I tried to climb away, crablike. He laughed then, but not Cade's laugh. It was as if some alien had possessed Cade. An evil creepy alien.

"Rojo." Terror made the word breathless and almost silent, but it stopped him in his tracks. He stared down at me, his face an ugly parody of Cade's golden beauty.

"Oh, you are unusual. Not clever. No, not clever. But you are certainly out of the ordinary." The pitch and timber of his voice sounded like Cade's, but it wasn't the same. The rhythm was different, as if Cade were speaking with a strange accent. He reached down and grabbed me by my neck and, lifting me like a glass of wine, he drew me toward his face. "Perhaps that is what he saw in you. Amusing."

A small part of my brain reeled with the implications of what he said, but most of my consciousness was focused on clawing at the fingers around my neck that were slowly tightening, gradually choking me. There was a gleeful look in his eyes as he seemed to savor my fear and pending death.

The night grew darker. My fingers stopped clawing and my arms fell to my side as if no longer part of my body.

Something whistled past like a freight train. The hand released me and I dropped to the ground, my body too unresponsive to reach out and break my own fall. I fell like a rag doll, barely aware of the violence that surrounded me.

I was still alive, but I couldn't seem to move so I just laid there, hacking like a smoker. Breathing seemed to be taking all my energy and for a few moments, I didn't try to do more than keep my face out of the dirt. When I was finally able to raise my head again, I saw Rojo-Cade sail by me like a bullet, at least four feet off the ground. He hit a tree and clung there like a spider, his fingers and feet sticking to the trunk. Then he sprung, his hands like claws, his teeth bared in an inhuman howl.

But he wasn't swooping down at me; he shot past me to pounce on another figure that stood in the clearing, legs braced, fists at the ready.

Danel.

They grappled. Rojo-Cade's mouth morphed into a shark-like maw; his fingers extended into razor claws. But Danel, with a simple maneuver, tossed him to one side and Rojo-Cade sped past me again, slamming into a tree with enough force to impale himself on one of the branches.

But it didn't. Instead, the branch shattered like glass into splinters and Cade, unharmed, dropped to the ground on all fours, ready to spring again.

At that moment, in my mind, it was Cade and Danel, fighting to the death, with powers that I couldn't begin to understand. As Cade flew at Danel, Danel turned and ripped up a pine tree; its trunk must have been two feet in diameter. He swung it at Cade like a baseball bat.

I still didn't have enough breath to scream; all I could do is rasp out a croaky squeal. In my panic-fogged brain, I couldn't separate the Cade I knew from the Rojo-infested Cade, and even though he had just tried to kill me, dismay rattled through me as the tree slammed into Cade, exploding in a cloud of dust and kindling.

Through the haze of the sawdust, I saw Cade fall.

But he wasn't dead. Incredibly, he pushed himself up onto his knees, shaking off the shock like it was so much water. But Danel wasn't about to give him the second he needed to recover and, as Cade staggered to his feet, he leapt, pouncing on him like a tiger.

With one brutal twist, he ripped Cade's arm off at the shoulder. Bile caught in my throat as Danel threw the arm into the air. It flew like a javelin above the trees and into the forest beyond. If I had to guess, I would think it wasn't going to come back down again for a couple of miles.

Cade screamed like an animal and dropped back to his knees but Danel wasn't finished and he immediately reached down and ripped off the other arm and sent it sailing in the other direction.

Cade fell flat on his face, not moving.

The forest went quiet. Unusually silent. I couldn't hear any of the night sounds. Not the crickets or the distant street traffic or even the hush of the wind through the leaves. It was dead quiet. I still lay on the carpet of leaves, shaking, unable to do more than use my arms to push my head up and watch.

And that's when things started to get really weird.

Cade still wasn't dead. Using his face for leverage, he pushed himself up to his knees and then stumbled to his feet. His arms were gone, his shirt was in shreds and he swayed drunkenly.

But there was no blood.

I tried to process what I was seeing. In the half light of twilight, I could see that there was no blood coming out of his wounds. Instead, I caught a glimpse of something gleaming between the scraps of tattered cloth, like mercury or silver gelatin, but there was no blood. And after a moment, when Cade looked like he had almost shaken off the effects of having both his arms ripped off, he stood and faced Danel, who smirked back at him.

"You're such a jerk." Cade hissed. "Sam is going to hear about this. Trust me."

And then, without a backward look toward me, he strode off, armless, into the woods, in the direction of where one of his limbs had been tossed.

My first thought was *I must be dreaming this.* The entire sequence was too bizarre to be real, and yet I knew I wasn't sleeping. And then I wondered if Mom and Doctor Phil might be right, and this was all some post-traumatic-stress symptom, but screw that. I was awake and relatively coherent and I knew what I'd seen.

Danel took a moment to brush the dust from his clothes. He looked down the path where Cade had disappeared and gave one last snort of amusement before turning his attention to me. The amusement died, and something flashed across his face. Regret? Resignation? He approached me gently, gingerly, like you would a wounded fawn. Unblinking, unable to move, I watched him advance.

His hands were gentle as he reached down to lift me up, setting me onto unsteady feet and holding my shoulders until I could support myself. At his touch, warmth flooded me and with it, I felt a buzzing in my blood. It was calming, but it couldn't offset the memory of what I'd just seen.

"What... are... you?" I managed to stutter out as I stared for answers in his eyes.

"Don't worry about it. It's just a bad dream." His voice was soft and even, mesmerizing.

"What?" Disbelief made me spit word out.

"In the morning, you won't remember any of this. It'll just be a bad dream."

I know when I'm dreaming and I know when I'm awake and this was definitely awake. I wanted to argue, but I didn't even know where to begin.

"You fell down in the woods," he continued gently. "You struck your neck on a branch and it left you with this bruise."

I was baffled as to why he was saying these things. "Is that the story you want me to tell my parents?"

Danel's hands began to move. They glided up my shoulders and his fingertips feather-touched the bruises on my neck. My skin tingled and my breath became jagged.

The sounds of the forest were returning. The wind in the leaves. The insects buzzing around my face. The pulse beating in my ears.

His fingers drifted up, pushed the hair off my forehead and gently caressed the bruise I'd got that morning.

"Poor little flower," he whispered. "You won't remember this in the morning either."

And then he did the last thing I expected, but maybe it was the one thing that I wanted.

He kissed me.

His lips were hot and soft, at first barely brushing mine, but then his hand cupped my neck and he pulled me into him and his mouth grew hard and demanding. Shock turned quickly into wildfire and I felt myself responding.

And then, even more abruptly than it had started, it was done.

I staggered back, suddenly free from his grasp. I thought Danel had leapt away, but I saw that he was flying backward in a high arc, having been thrown through the air by a new arrival to the glen.

Cade.

Chapter Nineteen

Cade was back, with both arms attached and a blazing fury in his face. He didn't wait for Danel to land, but dove at him, leaping high into the air.

Danel landed on his feet, spun around and leaped out of Cade's grasp, landing twenty feet away, his body tensed and poised to fend off another attack.

"Cade, wait!" Danel's voice was edged with panic as he tried to sound reasonable. "Let me expl---"

Cade was in no mood to talk. He landed on all fours and immediately sprung up again, twisting in mid-air, zeroing back in on Danel.

What followed was the strangest wrestling match I could ever imagine. Cade and Danel bounced off trees, maypoled around the barren trunks and ricocheted around the meadow like marbles in a pinball machine. Danel gave up trying to speak and focused on avoiding Cade's attack. At one point, Cade pulled up one of the dead tree trunks and began slamming it around, trying to bash Danel like he was a mole in an amusement park game.

I should have turned and run away, but I was too engrossed by the mayhem. I did edge away as far as I could, but it wasn't far enough. One of Cade's lashes sent splinters flying and a shard flew at me, grazing my leg like a bullet. I let out a squeal of pain and fell to my knees.

"Misty!" Cade's rage died like a spell broken. He dropped the tree trunk he had been swinging and, like a blur, rushed to me. Even before I finished falling, his arms were around me scooping me up like a baby.

The familiar electricity buzzed through my body and all the pain and bruises faded away, along with the terror that had haunted me. I looked up into Cade's eyes and saw... Cade. I started to cry.

"What is it? Are you badly hurt?" Cade sounded panicked.

"No. It's just that I'm so glad to see you. The real you." I tried to stop crying, but only succeeded in giving myself the hiccups.

Cade set me down gently on the leaves and his finger inspected the gash on my leg. He made a soft clucking sound with his tongue as he tore off a strip of his undershirt and used it to wipe away the blood before making a bandage from it. It wasn't that bad of a cut, and I was so busy staring at his face that I didn't even feel the pain.

"It is you. It is you," I whispered, repeating it over and over like a mantra.

Cade looked at me, concerned. "Of course it is. What happened to your forehead? And your neck?"

I didn't answer him. Instead, I cradled my head into the crook of his arm and took a deep breath. The sweet scent of the ocean was there. I closed my eyes and let go of all my qualms.

"Rojo's here in Wiccasset." Danel stood a dozen feet away, staring at us stonily.

"Rojo?" Cade said as he stood up quickly. As he moved away, I felt security slip away as well. "Where is he now?"

Danel jerked his head in the direction that the armless Cade had disappeared in. It wasn't until that moment that I realized that Rojo must have made himself look like Cade. It was no more surreal than anything else that had happened so far.

"Did you know he was coming?" Cade's anger was back. He moved right into Danel's face. "Is that why you sent me to see Sam? So that I would be out of the way when Rojo arrived?"

"Yeah, right." Danel didn't flinch. "And I just ripped off both of Rojo's arms for the fun of it. As if I like to get Rojo ticked off. He's going to be pissed at me for centuries."

Cade shot back a furtive look at me before grabbing Danel by the arm and dragging him to the other side of the meadow. They dropped their voices, so I crept closer until I could hear them.

"Hush!" Cade hissed. "She'll hear you. Did she see you dismember Rojo?"

"Yeah, but don't sweat it. I'll just wipe her memory."

Cade shoved Danel's chest with both hands but Danel barely moved.

"Is that why you stole a kiss? You assumed she wouldn't remember?"

"Why not?" Danel shrugged with a smirk.

"Unfortunately, we have a small problem with that plan." Cade stepped in to whisper to Danel. "She doesn't wipe."

"What?" At last, Danel seemed stunned. It amazed me that, with all the surreal things that had happened in the last half hour, Cade's comment, as enigmatic as it was, was the only thing that seemed to surprise him. Danel cast a blank look at me before whispering back to Cade. "Are you sure?"

"Have you tried? Have you not noticed? She brushes it off as if it were no more than an insect." Cade shot a look at me before pulling Danel further away. I edged closer. "Rojo tried to kill her this past summer by throwing her from a balcony. I tried for weeks to wipe that memory from her, but she will not wipe."

A flare of anger brought me to my feet. "What? I don't what?" I snapped as I stormed up to them, hobbling. "You've been trying to wipe my memory? You've got no right to mess with me like that!"

Danel found my fury amusing while Cade looked a little harassed.

"Now listen, Misty---" he started, but I was on a roll and all the crap from the last twenty-four hours was seething inside me. Besides, I had questions to ask and the big one came out first.

"What the hell are you guys?" I asked. "You and Rojo and this... this... Sam Jaza guy? What are you?"

They had both been taking my ranting rather calmly, but when I mentioned Sam Jaza, they both tensed. Cade strode back to me and caught me by the shoulders.

"What do you know of Sam Jaza?' Cade's whisper had an intensity that froze me. "Who told you of him?"

Before I could answer, Cade spoke again. It was weird, because I was staring at his face and his mouth hadn't moved, but it was definitely Cade's voice.

"It's enough that she knows about Sam," said Cade's voice. "And that she can't be wiped."

In sync, Cade and Danel spun to face a stand of trees that stood black in the darkness of the woods. Their shoulders met, not only shielding me from whatever was there, but also blocking my view. I tried to push way past them, but they were like a stone wall. I couldn't make them budge, so I stood on tiptoes so I could peer over their shoulders.

Another Cade stepped out of the shadows and into the dimly lit meadow. His shirt was in shreds, but his arms were attached. He looked identical to my Cade in almost every way, except for the clothes. And the smile.

"Rojo." I whispered.

"Observant little human, isn't she?" Rojo-Cade sneered. "And unwipe-able. Sam will need to be told. And you know what he's going to say."

Danel flicked one look at me before turning to Cade. "He's right you know. Might as well let him finish the job. No use putting off the inevitable."

"What?" Cade and I both exclaimed at the same time.

"Absolutely not!" Cade put his arm around my shoulder and turned me away, blocking me from Rojo-Cade. "We can find another way to handle this."

"Listen to reason, Cade," Danel stepped towards us, his voice soft and rational. "If we don't---"

Moving like lightning, Cade spun away from me and shoved Danel so hard, he flew backwards crashing into Rojo. As he landed, Danel's arm shot out, his hand tensed into a karate chop, and with a tearing sound like stone being split, he sliced off Rojo's head.

Rojo-Cade screamed. His head rolled across the grass.

And still he screamed.

His scream turned to curses, and then petered out to breathless mouthing as he ran out of air, no lungs to support voice. I stared, frozen, as his head rolled to a stop against a tree trunk, his mouth still snarling in silent fury.

Meanwhile, Cade and Danel both pounced on the beheaded body, tearing off the arms and legs and throwing them to the far corners of the clearing. Then, in a gruesome tug of war, they ripped the torso into two parts, kicking one away from the other.

Again, there was no blood, only that strange silver goo that quivered like it had its own life. And that's when I noticed that it wasn't just the goo that moved on its own, all the limbs were still twitching as well. And as they twitched, they edged their way back to the center of the meadow, as if trying to rejoin themselves, while Cade and Danel, playing some macabre game of soccer, kept kicking them away to the corners of the clearing.

Frozen in horror, I didn't notice Rojo-Cade's head until it was within feet of me. The blond locks of hair had grown and formed six leg-like appendages and the head scuttled toward me, spider-like. The face, still looking like Cade, was contorted with fury and its mouth snapped and chomped as if it wanted to bite me.

I screamed.

Danel was closer and with a movement too quick for my eye to follow, crossed the meadow and kicked the head away from me. With barely a look at me, he turned back to help Cade, who was still keeping the other body pieces at bay.

"Now where are we going to find seven sarcophagi?" Cade sounded more exasperated than puzzled as he kicked an arm back into the woods.

"There's a place in Nashua that makes lead lined valises for transporting nuclear isotopes." There was a twinge of glee in Danel's voice, as if he were enjoying this. "It'll take me less than an hour to get there and get back."

Why, with all the things that were happening that night, did that seem so unreasonable? Nashua was an hour and a half away in each direction. No way could he get there and back in an hour.

"First I must escort Misty home." Cade dropped the branch that he was using like a hockey stick to scatter the body parts and walked over to me.

Danel rolled his eyes. "She's a big girl. She can walk home by herself. She got here by herself."

As Cade placed an arm around my shoulder, he shot a look back at Danel as if to say "and look what happened."

Danel shrugged and went back to slapping apart the two pieces of the torso as it tried to seam itself back together. "Well, make it fast. I don't want to be doing this all night."

With that, Cade lifted me like a baby and, cradling me against his chest, whispered. "Close your eyes."

Of course I didn't. Cade leaped and flew down the path toward my house.

It wasn't actually flying, it was more like gliding. We were about six feet in the air, zipping down the path at what seemed like two hundred miles an hour. One of Cade's feet hit would the ground maybe once every hundred feet before launching back up. In seconds we were at the point in the woods that was just behind my house.

"I'll wait here until you get into the house," he said as he gently set me down. "And Misty, I know you're confused and frightened, but please, it would be better for everyone if you make no mention of this."

"Are you kidding? My parents want to send me to a shrink already. If I tell them anything about tonight, they'll think I've gone completely nuts and put me away." As it was, I wasn't sure if I wasn't losing it. Everything was too bizarre for me to even begin to rationalize.

"I'll see you tomorrow. I promise. But until then, not a word to anyone. Do you understand?"

I nodded mutely. He promised. He'd be there tomorrow and I believed him. That made everything okay.

"I'll watch from here until you are safe inside." When I didn't move, he gave me a gentle push. "Now go."

I stumbled out of the woods, looking back more than I was looking forward. When I got to the door, I could still see his silhouette, just barely lighter than the woods around him. He tipped his finger to his forehead in a little salute. I waved back weakly before I slipped into the house.

I closed the door and locked it, which is something I never do. I leaned against it and started to rehash all that had happened, but quickly put all that out of my mind. I didn't have time for that. I still had the parents to deal with.

"Misty? Is that you?" Mom called from the dining room. "Your dinner's getting cold."

I got to the foot of the stairs without being seen. "I'll be right down, Mom. I just got to change."

I ran up the stairs, I needed to get to a mirror before I let my mother see me.

"Change? Why are you changing?" I could hear her chair scraping as she stood to walk to the stairs, but I was in my bedroom before she made it to the hallway.

"I fell down in the woods, Mom," I said, elaborating on Danel's story. "A branch snapped back and hit me and ripped my jeans and shirt. I'll only be a minute."

"I called Chad." Mom called up the stairs. "He said that Captain Picard got home twenty minutes ago."

"That's nice." I looked in the mirror. My face had new scratches and my neck looked like I had a half a dozen hickeys. I rinsed my face, brushed my hair, and quickly changed out of my shirt and jeans and into a turtleneck and a pair of sweat pants. I ran my fingers over the bandage that was still on my leg. The cut wasn't that deep and I could probably take it off, but Cade had put it there and I was going to sleep with it tonight. I smiled at the thought.

My bruises ached as I bounded down the stairs. Tiff was in the middle of a monologue as she recreated the TV cartoon that she'd watched that afternoon. I was grateful for the babble; I could feel my parents watching me with wrinkled foreheads as I scooped out some vegetables and potatoes onto my plate. As I stabbed a breast of chicken, my mother reached over to drop some more vegetables onto my plate, like I was the three-year-old or something. I stifled a sigh, sat down and started to eat. After a moment, Dad cleared his throat and everyone froze. Even Tiff stopped babbling and looked up, puzzled.

"Misty." Dad looked towards me, but not at me, which was his way of letting me know that whatever he said was not open for discussion. "Your mother and I have discussed this and we agree that you should talk to Doctor Krajeski. You've had a very traumatic day and it can't hurt to speak to a professional. We've made our decision and I don't want to hear any arguments."

Normally, that wouldn't be enough to stop me, but I was not firing on all pistons at that moment so I just nodded and mumbled, "Okay."

I bent my head back to my plate and ignored the looks they shot each other. I knew what they were thinking: I had to be pretty traumatized to accept that order and not argue with them. I had no appetite for the chicken and the vegetables were cold. I put a half a teaspoon of potato in my mouth, pushed around the peas and then dropped my fork.

"I'm beat. Can I be excused?" I was already rising from my chair.

"But you haven't even touched your dinner!" Mom stood up and followed me into the kitchen where I was carrying my plate. She took it out of my hands. "I'll cover this up and put it in the fridge. When you get hungry later, you can heat it up."

I mumbled something about doing my homework and headed for the stairs.

"Goodnight sweetheart," I heard Dad call from the table. He sounded worried. If he only knew the truth.

I was glad to get to the privacy of my room. I winced as I put on the flannel sweatsuit that I used as pajamas when the nights started to get cold, pulling the soft cloth gently over my scrapes and bruises. I turned off the lights, but left the curtains open. The quarter moon didn't completely dim out the stars and I stared out the window, not really seeing them.

Cade was back. I'd see him tomorrow. He promised. My thoughts bounced all over my head but they always came back to that truth. I clung to it like a teddy bear as I tried to put everything I'd seen that night into some perspective.

But there was one truth that I kept avoiding and hours later, after the moon had long since disappeared, I finally admitted it to myself.

Danel's kiss had changed me in a way I couldn't begin to understand. All I knew was that, as much as I was in love with Cade, I wanted Danel to kiss me again.

Chapter Twenty

Doctor Krajeski was a bullet easily dodged. I overslept.

Mom started to try to wake me around six a.m. but since I'd only dropped off to sleep a couple of hours before, I didn't budge. Finally, around seven-thirty, I heard her calling the doctor's office to cancel. The conversation was longer than it needed to be. I couldn't make out her words too well, but I could tell that she was recounting everything that had happened yesterday. Everything that she knew about, anyway. Then she went into a half a dozen "uh-huhs" as she listened to the doctor's advice. I fell back asleep and didn't wake again until after ten a.m.

Crap. I was beyond late for school. I scampered to my feet and grabbed my shower stuff. "Mom! I'm late! Why did you let me sleep so late?"

Like it was her fault.

Once you're this late, you might as well just skip the whole day, but if Cade was back, I wanted to be in school. I'd already missed homeroom and Calculus, and Civics was half over, but if I rushed, I could get there by lunchtime. I could have lunch with Cade. I pushed the thought of Danel and Rojo out of my head. The night hadn't made anything clearer and all the questions would have to wait.

"Take your time, you're not going to school today," Mom called from downstairs. "When you're all showered and changed, come down. Your father and I want to talk to you."

I was in the bathroom by this point, but that dragged me back out. "Dad's here? He didn't go to work?"

"I took the day off." Dad stood at the foot of the stairs and spoke in his normal voice. I don't think I'd ever heard Dad yell up and down the stairs like Mom and I did. "There's something we need to discuss. Take your time and come down when you're ready."

I rushed. I still had every intention of going to school, but now, on top of my eagerness to see Cade, I added the curiosity of wondering what Mom and Dad were up to. I jumped into the shower. My body was a bruised purple nightmare with angry red scratches. Yesterday had been a rough day. I had to hope that today was going to be better.

My ripped clothes were missing. Mom must have scooped them when she was up trying to wake me. My clothes hamper was empty too. Mom must be doing my laundry. Cool. Getting beat up wasn't an even trade for having your mother suddenly wait on you hand and foot, but it was an unexpected bonus.

My second and fourth best jeans were missing. My third best jeans got ripped last night. That meant I had to wear my first best jeans, which, given the way the week was going, I really didn't want to risk them. I didn't have a second turtleneck sweater so I tried a scarf around my neck, but it made me look like an old lady, so I ended up in the same sweater I'd worn to dinner the night before. I hoped that my neck healed quickly; this sweater was going to get old, fast.

"Mom?" I started the question from my bedroom and ran down the stairs into the living room as I spoke. "Have you seen my second and fourth best jeans? They're not…"

I pulled up short. Mom and Dad weren't alone. They should have warned me. Bellowing down the stairs with un-blow-dried hair: kind of rude.

A strange woman sat in the living room with Mom and Dad. When I say "strange," I mean unknown, not weird. She was middle aged with a pleasant face, salt and pepper fluffy hair and dressed in khaki like she was ready to go on safari. They all stood up as I entered, the lady smiling warmly.

"Oops! Sorry," I said. "I didn't know we had company."

"Misty, this is Mrs. Phillipson from the Semester Aboard Program." Mom was bubbling with excitement. "She called this morning… Well, I'll let her tell you."

"We were very impressed with your application when we received it last year," Mrs. Phillipson began as she settled back down on the couch.

"Oh, thank you," I replied blankly. I'd applied for a scholarship for the Junior Year Aboard program, hoping to spend the fall semester on a ship cruising around the world. My parents couldn't afford the tuition and I'd received a rejection on my scholarship application almost immediately. I hadn't really thought about it much since. I wanted to ask, if they were impressed with my application, why did they reject me so quickly? but I didn't.

"Well, a last minute spot has opened up on the cruise. The young woman who had received the scholarship had an appendicitis attack last night and her doctor won't let her go. So there's a spot available."

I looked from Mom to Mrs. Phillipson to Dad, back to Mrs. Phillipson and then back to Mom. I didn't know what to say. To spend an entire semester on a cruise ship was a pie-in-the-sky dream-come-true. But now, when the chance of a lifetime was being handed to me, it was all I could do not to yell *No! Not now!* Last year I'd done nothing but daydream about how cool it would be to sail around the world, but that was before Cade. Now, if Cade was here in Wicassett, I wanted to be here in Wicassett.

Mom seemed distracted and unfocused. She spoke in a nervous rush. "The ship leaves this afternoon from Boston Harbor, so you have to leave now. I packed your suitcases while you were sleeping and Mrs. Phillipson will drive you to the ship. So give your father and I a hug and a kiss and call us when you can."

"WHAT?" Life had to stop moving so fast. I couldn't even sleep in one morning without everything careening out of control.

Mom seemed clumsy as she pulled me to my feet and herded me to the front door. Dad picked up two suitcases that were in the hallway. I hadn't noticed them when I'd run down the stairs. The door was wide open, which might explain all the flies I heard buzzing in the living room.

"I've packed everything you need and we've changed your cellphone service so that you can use it in other countries, but don't use it except for emergencies, it's very expensive."

"But---" I was being propelled down the front steps to the driveway where a blue station wagon was parked.

"Mrs. Phillipson says you'll have internet available to you, so you can send us emails. And pictures! I've packed your camera and rechargeable batteries. Be sure to take lots of pictures."

"But Mom," The door to the station wagon was open and I braced myself against the frame, fighting against be shoved into the abyss. "I don't know if I want---"

"Of course you do! It's all you talked about last winter! And now you're going to get to go! Now I know that it's sudden, but you don't have time to dawdle. Give your father a kiss goodbye and get into the car."

Dad stepped forward, his arm extended like he was going to shake hands. This was so weird, it took me a minute to realize that he was pressing something into my hand. "Here's a little cash and a credit card. Only use it in emergencies. Do exactly what you're told and follow all the rules and you'll be fine." He gave me an awkward hug and stepped back.

"I'M... NOT... GOING!" I was trying for assertiveness, but my voice quavered.

Mom and Dad shot each other a look before Dad spoke.

"Listen Misty." Dad's normal sang-froid held an edge of anxiety. "Sergeant Huebner was by yesterday and he's concerned about some of the new boys at the school. And the attention that they've been directing to you. Considering what happened yesterday, we believe it would be better to take you out of that situation for a while. When Mrs. Phillipson called this morning, we decided that this is the perfect opportunity. You're not going back to the high school this semester, so it's either a semester on a cruise ship, or Saint Ignatius. You decide."

It was dead quiet on the driveway for a long minute. No one spoke and there was no sound except for one of those ever-present black flies buzzing around my face. As I brushed it away, I caught a stray scent of leather and cinnamon. I turned my head quickly as I stared at Mrs. Phillipson intently for the first time.

"Come along, Melissa," Mrs. Phillipson said, a tiny half smile twitched on one of her cheeks. "We'll miss the boat."

The buzzing. I looked back at my parents, noticing the slight vacantness in their eyes and the placid smiles on their faces. My temper flared and I glared back at "Mrs. Phillipson" or whatever he was calling himself. What was he up to? He might be able to sway my parents into letting me go with him, but what would happen after we pulled away and the "buzzing" wore off?

I wavered and Mom, taking advantage of my hesitation, pushed me into the car. She hit the button to roll down the window before she slammed the door shut.

"Your father and I love you very much! Have fun! Be careful!"

And then the car started down the driveway, onto Camden Place, and on to God-knew-where.

But at least I had a fairly strong idea of who was taking me.

Chapter Twenty One

I waved weakly as the car pulled out of the driveway and kept it up until we'd turned the corner. Then I turned my attention to the driver.

"Where's Cade?" I asked.

"Who, dear?" Mrs. Phillipson asked innocently, but I could see her brow wrinkle slightly. I took a deep whiff, just to confirm my hunch. There it was. The scent of cinnamon and leather and something faintly woodsie, like pine. I crossed my arms and glared at "her."

"Don't give me that. Even if I was so gullible as to believe that I'd won a last minute scholarship on a round-the-world cruise, I can still smell a rat when it kidnaps me."

Mrs. Phillipson barked out a very un-Mrs. Phillipson laugh.

"Kidnap? Is that what you'd call this? I think of it as more like rescuing you from a semester of boredom and frustration."

"Where are we going?" I pressed myself as far away from "Mrs. Phillipson" as I could manage. Even in his current incarnation, the memory of last night's kiss was a distraction.

"On the trip of a lifetime, my dear." Mrs. Phillipson said sweetly. "I explained it to you earlier. You're going on a fabulous adventure."

For a fraction of a second, I wondered if my psycho imagination was running away with me again. I watched Mrs. Phillipson closely. I had to be right. That one-cheek smile was completely Danel. I don't how he did it, but now that I knew he could shape shift, I was almost a hundred percent certain this was Danel.

"Knock it off." I said with a scowl. "Where's Cade?"

Mrs. Danel-Phillipson shot me a probing look and I felt the familiar wave of heat flush over me.

"When you do that heat wave thing," I asked. "Is it because you're angry? Or is there another reason?"

The wave of heat stopped as abruptly as it started and Mrs. Danel-Phillipson's expression changed from intense to wary.

"What heat wave thing?"

"I thought, at first, it was because you were mad at me, but it's not that, is it? You're not angry now. What were you trying to do to me?"

Mrs. Danel-Phillipson stared at me, unblinking, while as we took the entrance ramp on to Route 93 perhaps a little faster than it was designed for.

"Do you ever look at the road when you're driving?" I asked, trying for nonchalant while I braced myself against the dashboard.

Mrs. Danel-Phillipson turned back to face the road, but I don't think he was looking at it any more closely than when he had been staring at me.

"What are you?" he muttered softly.

"Funny," My eyes flicked from the traffic to the driver, unsure as to which one was the more immediate threat. "That's exactly the next question I was going to ask *you*. What are you? And what is Cade? And Rojo? Are you aliens from another planet?"

"Trust me. It would be better for you not to know. Safer."

"Right. Like that's going to fly." I snapped back. "I'll ask Cade. He'll tell me."

"No he won't."

"Yes he will," I muttered with a certainty that I didn't feel. I settled back into my seat with a huff, my arms crossed across my chest. One way or another, I was going to find out.

It was quiet as we headed down Route 93 toward Boston. I stared at Mrs. Phillipson, a little freaked out by how perfect Danel looked as a middle-aged white lady. Despite the voice, when I didn't look at him, I knew he was Danel, but as soon as I turned to see him, I would get jarred again.

Danel-Phillipson broke the silence.

"How do you know that I'm not Cade?" Danel's words came out of Mrs. Phillipson's mouth.

I pffted at that. "I can tell."

"How?"

The question was casual, but I could tell that Danel was more than a little curious. It was easier to talk to him if I didn't look at him, so I stared out the window.

"I don't know," I shrugged. "You smell different."

Danel didn't answer but I felt the heat of his stare and after a minute, I made myself turn and look. Again, the weirdness with him looking like a middle-aged lady, but I met his eyes and waited.

"I smell different?" he asked at last.

"Yeah, you smell like a Christmas potpourri."

I was aiming to annoy him, but he only seemed fascinated.

"Could you glance at the road, just occasionally, just to please me?" I said when his stare didn't waver. "It's too weird, you driving and not looking."

He faced front again, but I don't think it was to please me. He glanced for a microsecond in the rear view mirror, and then started driving like a regular person.

"What?" I turned to look behind us. "What did you see?"

"Don't turn around again, but I believe Sergeant Huebner is escorting us out of the state." Danel was talking and acting like Mrs. Phillipson again. "We'll be at the Massachusetts border in about twenty minutes. It'll be interesting to find out if he follows us over the border."

I didn't look back, even though I really wanted to. I made myself stare ahead. "So, am I really going on a cruise ship? Are you and Cade coming too?"

"No and no." Danel said, the Mrs. Phillipson voice slipping a little. "We need to run a little errand and I'm not going to do it by myself. Cade won't do it alone either and we both agreed that it would be best not to leave you behind in Wicassett, so you're coming with us."

I had to admit, I was a little disappointed. The world cruise sounded awesome, and if Cade and Danel had been going, it could have been a blast. I sighed.

"What kind of errand? And what am I going to tell my parents when I show up back at home tomorrow? That I missed the boat? That it was all a mistake?"

"You won't be home tomorrow. This errand will take us at least a couple of weeks. Possibly longer."

An alarm bell sounded in my head. "Then where are we going? And where's Cade?"

"At the moment, Cade is following us in my car. I would have preferred to have ditched this car and this body long before this, but I'd rather wait until we lose Sergeant Huebner. If he gives up at the border, then we'll pull over somewhere in Massachusetts and meet up."

I started to twist around to look behind, but stopped when Danel snapped "Don't look!"

"I wasn't looking for Sergeant Huebner!" I huffed. "I was looking for Cade. Is he driving that cone-egg car?"

Again, the eyes and the heat. "How did you know I drive a Koenigsegg CCX?"

"You followed me up from North Carolina in it. And then you drove pass the bus yesterday. Everyone saw it."

"But how did you know I was driving?"

"I could tell it was you."

"From the way I smell?"

I pffted again. "No, of course not! You were in your car! I couldn't smell you from the bus."

"Then how?"

"The heat thing. Like you're doing right now. When you stare at me like you're trying to push into my head."

Again, the heat wave stopped abruptly and Danel turned back to face the road.

"Interesting," Danel was trying for blasé, but I could tell that my being able to feel that heat wave was unsettling to him. "Rojo was right. You are unusually observant."

The mention of Rojo brought last night back to me like a slap. The image of him getting ripped into pieces, with no blood flowing wasn't as weird as his head running after me and his limbs flailing around the clearing. I shook my head to try to clear the memory.

"Rojo isn't dead, is he." I said. It wasn't a question. I was almost certain.

Danel didn't answer for a long moment. "No," he said at last. "He can't be killed."

I didn't expect that. I shivered as the implications chilled me. "Then you and Cade… you can't die either?" I whispered.

"I think it would be best if you stopped asking questions."

A brittle silence settled on the car. I stared out the window, not seeing the traffic and trees and buildings pass by.

Aliens from another planet? Androids? Some new kind of synthetic robots? Every explanation seemed ridiculous, but not as bizarre as the facts that I kept trying to puzzle together.

We were slowing down. I hadn't even been aware that we'd crossed over into Massachusetts. The station wagon was pulling onto an exit ramp and into the parking lot of a highway hotel. I turned to look at Danel, getting the same jolt of disorientation from seeing him as Mrs. Phillipson. A flicker of movement outside the car drew my eye and the Koenigsegg CCX slid into the parking lot, pulling up besides the station wagon. I got out quickly.

Cade was still extracting himself from the driver's seat when I slammed into him. He stood and wrapped me in his arms and I plastered myself into his chest, my eyes closing as I let go of the tension that I'd been holding inside.

"Time is of the essence," he said quickly, more to Danel then to me. "Officer Huebner is still in pursuit."

"I'll lose him and meet you at the airport." Danel said, reaching over to close my door. There was a scream of rubber as the station wagon tore out of the parking lot, horns blaring as it jumped back onto the highway.

The pressure from Cade's arm herded me toward the passenger door, but I pulled free, crossing my arms and giving him what I hoped was a determined glare.

There is no time now, Misty," Cade said, looking harassed. "Please get in the car. I'll explain on the way."

I let Cade guide me to the car and in a moment, I was seated in a black leather cocoon staring at a dashboard that looked more like a movie prop from a science fiction series than a real car. The strange wing door swung shut almost silently and the feeling of being in a cocoon grew even stronger. A millisecond later and the driver's door opened and Cade slid in. The car's purr intensified to a hum and as we pulled out slowly onto the street, I fumbled with the seatbelt. We didn't go back up onto Route 93, but cruised along the side streets, stopping at lights every two minutes, but heading roughly south, alongside the highway.

Cade looked uncomfortable so I took the opportunity to go on the attack.

"How old are you?" I shot the question at him like a bullet.

"What is age anyway? It's no more than a number."

"You don't know how old you are?"

His brow furrowed as he shot me a quick look before turning his attention back to the road, but he didn't answer.

"Danel told me that you can't die. So how old are you?"

We were stopped at a light, so he turned to face me, shocked. "Danel?"

I sighed. "Danel? You know, a.k.a. Mrs. Phillipson? He told me that he and Rojo and you can't die. So, how old are you?"

A blare of a horn and the car swerved. As I grabbed the dashboard, a more burning question came to mind. "You do have your license, don't you? Your driver's license?"

"Of course." Cade's knuckles were white from gripping the wheel.

I wasn't reassured. "Let me rephrase that. Do you know how to drive?"

"Theoretically."

"Theoretically?" Lack of confidence was morphing into panic. "What do you mean, theoretically?"

"I've read several pamphlets on the subject. I understand the basic principles." He flashed me a nervous smile. "And I played 'Grand Theft Auto' for sixteen hours."

I closed my eyes. If I was going to die, let it be in a million dollar car with a Greek god beside me. Another blare of a horn, and I changed my mind. I wasn't ready to die. I opened my eyes.

"I'm tired of this. I need to get some straight answers. I need to know what's going on and I need to know now."

Cade bit his lip. He was weakening. I was wearing him down, I could tell. It was only a matter of time before I got my way. I was just settling down to some serious wheedling when something thumped me from under my seat. Hard.

"What the heck is that?" I tried to crane my body down to see under the seat, but the seatbelt decided to lock and I couldn't lean forward. I stretched my arms down. My fingers touched the cold metal of a box wedged beneath my seat. "Something just thumped me."

"Pay no attention to it."

"Pay no attention to what? There's something alive in that box!" It took me another millisecond to figure it out. "Rojo? Is that Rojo under my seat?"

A second angry thud answered me more than Cade's silence.

"You brought Rojo with you?" I hugged my calves as I pulled my feet up off the floor as if at any moment Rojo would lunge out and grab my ankles.

"Only his head."

"Uh… uh…" Words stuttered in my throat. I was being driven to who-knew-where by a who-knew-what with a dismembered un-dead head beneath my seat. I was still trying to make words happen when I felt another thump from behind me.

Something else, not-dead was rattling around in the trunk. I turned, glassy-eyed, to Cade.

"Oh, and perhaps one of his legs."

Words were still not happening for me.

Cade spoke quickly, shooting me a wary glance as if wondering if I was going to melt down completely. "The rest of him is at the airport, but we didn't think it would be wise to leave all his parts in one place, unguarded."

"Of course not," I managed to answer.

"I planned to bring more of him along, but this is a ridiculous car. The trunk is absurdly small."

"Ridiculous." I agreed.

152

"Misty?"

"Hmm?" was the best response I could manage.

"Are you okay?" Cade turned to look at me, but a blare of a horn and a screech of tires pulled his attention back to the road.

I grabbed for the only straw that seemed rational at the moment. "Airport? What airport?"

"Hanscom." Cade seemed relieved to be able this simple question. "It's a small private airport outside of Boston."

"Why? Are we flying somewhere?"

"Yes, we have a series of tasks that need to be done and we will need to fly to execute them."

"Where are we going?"

"That is something that we haven't yet decided upon."

I held my tongue. We were pulling back onto Route 93 and I thought that it was probably better for my health if I didn't distract him while he was driving. I lowered my feet back down but kept them as far away from the box under my seat as I could. It rattled now and again and, as I tried to ignore it, I wondered what I was getting myself into.

Chapter Twenty Two

We drove right onto the tarmac at Hanscom Field, pulling up next to a small sleek jet parked there. The doors unfurled and Cade was out of the car and around to my side before I could even get the seatbelt undone. He pulled a small chrome suitcase out from under my seat and then popped the trunk to reveal a second one. He was holding both suitcases by the time an airport attendant ran out from the terminal building to help. I felt a huge wave of relief from Cade as he tossed the keys to the attendant.

The guy's eyes lit up like it was Christmas.

"We'll be sending someone to pick up the car shortly." An icy voice spoke from a little distance away and I looked around, trying to find the source. It was Danel, standing at the foot of the stairs, looking cool, stern and very male. He had a black turtleneck sweater, black slacks and a black leather bombers jacket. He looked older, and like a real pilot. There was nothing Mrs. Phillipson about him. The memory of last night's kiss trembled through me.

Despite the suitcases he carried, I leaned into Cade as if that could push the memory away.

"Yes sir, Mr. Stark," the attendant replied, his enthusiasm untouched by Danel's coldness. He tenderly closed each door before sliding into the driver's seat and pulling away.

"How did you like it?" Danel asked with his one-cheek smirk.

"Ridiculous vehicle," muttered Cade as he pushed past Danel and headed up the stairs into the plane. Not knowing what else to do, I followed Cade. Danel kept the half smile on his face as I passed him.

"Find out much?" Danel whispered.

"Loads," I lied and felt a small satisfaction as Danel's grin dimmed slightly. I could hear him follow me up the steps.

I stood a little stunned as I stepped into the plane. It was like walking into some rich guy's living room. Cream colored leather recliners, chrome coffee tables and wood paneled walls were not what I had been expecting. The few times I'd flown (that one time to North Carolina and twice to Disneyworld) I'd only been on commercial jets and only in coach.

The leather couch would have been have been a lot more inviting if there weren't two brushed chrome suitcases already on it, each one strapped down with its own seat belt, and each shuddering occasionally. Cade belted his two cases into two of the reclining chairs. I counted four valises, but I thought they said there were supposed to be seven. Warily, I looked around for the last three. They weren't in sight.

The thrill of actually being in a private jet was seriously squelched by the quivering suitcases and my not knowing what was going on. I stepped past Cade to the rear of the plane so I could face both of them.

"Okay, someone had better start telling me what's going on here or I'm leaving."

Cade took a deep breath before shooting a look at Danel. Danel barely caught his eye before reaching into an overhead compartment, pulling out a rolled up map.

"We will tell you what you need to know," Cade started, "but only what you need to know. It will be safer for you, Misty. Trust us."

There was no way I was going to be satisfied with that, but at least it was something. I folded my arms as I took a seat in one of the chairs unoccupied by pieces of Rojo.

"As you've managed to cajole from Danel…" Cade pointedly ignored Danel's dagger glance. "…Rojo cannot be killed. Since he has decided he wants to kill you, we need to immobilize him for the rest of your natural life. We will do this by taking his dismembered body parts and burying them far from each other. It will take him decades just to kick and claw his way out of these cases and then at least a couple of more decades for the parts to find each other. So we envisage six to ten decades before he'll be able to threaten you. Given the typical human lifespan, you should be safe from him for the rest of your life."

You get to the point where you stop feeling shock and you just go with the flow. I nodded as I absorbed all this. It kind of made sense, in a fantastic, irrational sort of way. "What about Sam Jaza?"

Both Cade and Danel stiffened.

"It would be so much safer for you if you forgot you ever heard that name." Danel's voice was cold and harsh.

There were no insects in the cabin, yet the buzzing was there. This time though, I recognized it for what it was.

"Stop pushing at me," I snapped at Danel. Shock flickered across his face and the buzzing stopped.

Cade gently took my shoulders, mindful of the half-healed bruises beneath my sweater. His eyes caught mine and held them as he spoke softly. "Perhaps forgetting is not possible, Misty, but I'm asking you not to mention that name again. For all our sakes."

His eyes were so clear and blue and deep, I found myself falling into them. I wondered if this was what skydivers felt as they plummeted to earth, tumbling and dropping, but never seeming to land. I nodded mutely.

Danel broke the spell with an abrupt movement. He unrolled a map of the world onto the coffee table and waited for Cade and me to join him. As we moved to the map, I twitched when one of the boxes thumped angrily as I passed. I skittered past it to stand between Cade and Danel.

Danel tapped a spot a couple of inches below the Hawaiian Islands.

"We'll dump his head here, refuel here," he tapped the island of Maui on the map, "and then decide what to do with the rest of the parts from there." Danel turned and gave me a half-smile. "You can spend the time studying the map and thinking about where we should put the rest of him. But don't say anything out loud. He can still hear you. That's why we'll dump the head first. This way, he won't know where the rest of his body is and it'll be harder for him to call his parts together."

Danel and Cade moved to the front of the plane while I split my attention between studying the map and glancing at the Rojo head valise that was strapped to one of the recliners. I was almost feeling sorry for Rojo, creep though he was. As Danel and Cade disappeared into the cabin,

"You're enjoying this, aren't you?" I called after them. "You think this is fun."

Danel, settling himself into the pilot's chair, turned and grinned. "It keeps me off the streets."

As I followed them into the cockpit, a new realization hit me. "You guys aren't going to really fly this thing, are you? Don't you need licenses and certifications and stuff like that?"

"Don't worry, little bloodhound," Danel answered, his hands flicking switches and writing down gibberish on a pad of paper. "We've got it covered."

"Cade? How 'bout you? Can you fly this thing?"

Cade turned and winked at me. "Theoretically."

My stomach sank. "I hope you can theoretically fly a plane better than you can theoretically drive a car."

Cade's smile faded as Danel burst out laughing. I'd never heard Danel laugh like that before. His eyes were tearing.

"Perhaps you'd like to go into the cabin and strap in while we're taking off." Cade said to me as he shot a less-than-amused look at Danel.

I half turned to go back into the cabin, but then I realized that it would just be me and bits of Rojo. "I'm not sitting back there by myself."

"You can pull out the jump seat and sit up here." Danel said, nodding to a small seat folded up against the wall.

"You'll be more comfortable in the main cabin," said Cade.

"No, I won't," I said as I pulled down the jump seat and settled in. "You know, that's a really stupidly small window for such a big plane. I've seen go-carts with bigger windshields."

"We manage," answered Danel. "Now strap in."

As I clicked my seatbelt, I listened to them call in the flight plan to the tower and prepare the plane for take-off. A couple of days ago, they were just two really cute high school boys. Yesterday, they were superhuman fighting machines. And now today, when they weren't being little old ladies, they were totally mature, seemingly competent jet pilots.

I really should have been scared out of my mind, but I wasn't. I trusted them. Both of them, not just Cade. I thought about that as we taxied to the runway; looked deep into myself and realized that the jitters I was feeling wasn't fear, but excitement. I was flying to Hawaii, and then to anywhere in the world I wanted to go with two heartstoppingly gorgeous guys. I wasn't just excited. I was psyched half out of my mind. By the time we were airborne, I was already antsy.

"Can I get up now?" Unbuckling my seatbelt even as I asked. "I want to take a look at that map."

"Certainly." Cade's eyes laughed at me.

"You may want to email your parents," Danel added. "Just a quick note telling them that you made it on the ship and everything is okay. Don't go into much detail. Tell them you'll write more later."

I was halfway out of the cockpit, but that brought me back in.

"We get internet up here?"

"This is a G550. Of course it has wi-fi," Danel answered coolly.

"Sweet." I wasn't about to be put off by Danel copping an attitude. "Where's my stuff?"

"In the storage compartment in the rear," Cade replied. "Will you be alright by yourself? It may take a few more minutes before one of us can leave the controls."

"I'm good." I said as I headed into the main cabin. I bravely ran the gauntlet between Rojo parts and found the rear compartment exactly where it was supposed to be, in the rear. Go figure.

"Yuck! You're using my luggage to separate Rojo bits? Eeew!"

My two suitcases were strapped down between two chome Rojo valises. They twitched angrily as I opened up the suitcase that held my laptop.

There were only two recliners that weren't taken up by Rojo. I took the one that faced the cockpit. The coffee table and the map were behind me, a tempting distraction that I promised myself I'd indulge later. We were going to be flying for hours, there'd be time enough later to figure out where we could go after Hawaii.

"How long are we going to stay---" I yelled, catching myself before I said *Maui* "---you know, there?" I yelled to the cockpit.

Cade didn't yell back. Instead, he used the intercom system. I started as his voice answered in stereo-surround like a deejay. "That would be your choice. How long would you like to stay?"

I didn't answer. I just gurgled happily to myself as my laptop booted up.

This was going to be an awesome semester.

Chapter Twenty Three

Writing the e-mail to my parents was harder than I expected. It didn't seem right to lie to them, but they'd completely freak to the point of meltdown if they knew everything, so not telling them the complete truth was for their own good, right?

In the end, I settled on a quick, ambiguous note that wasn't the entire truth, but wasn't an outright lie either. I said that we'd made it on time and I was on board in my cabin and that I was excited beyond words. All of which was true. I said I'd write them again when I could, but I didn't know when I'd have a chance to write so don't be worried if they didn't hear from me regularly. Also true. Then I said I loved them both very much and thanked them for this opportunity and I expected to have an absolute blast. See? All true. No need to feel guilty.

Except I did. I pushed the send button and did my best to shake off the funk.

Rojo #4 thumped angrily as I moved over to look at the world map. I rapped sharply on the top of the case. "Knock it off in there." I said quietly.

There was a moment of shocked silence, and then all the Rojo bits started to thrash violently. I decided to abandon the map and was heading for the cockpit when a thought hit me. Ignoring the percussion tantrum around me, I settled back into my recliner and re-opened my laptop.

Google Search: "Sam Jaza."

I could have searched for this earlier, but I didn't bother to kick myself now. There were a couple of hundred entries for

"Sam Jaza," but there were very few in English. Some were in Arabic, some in other languages. It's risky to click on foreign sites and I wondered if I was seriously infecting my computer. The third one I clicked on looked halfway between drugged out weirdness and soft porn. I quickly moved to close it but then something caught my eye.

Samjaza – Name of the leader of the rebel angels that were cast from heaven.

Whacked, right? Almost as whacked as all the weird things that had been happening to me in the last few days. I tried a search for Samjaza as one word.

Did you mean Semjaza?

I don't know. Did I mean *Semjaza*? I clicked on *Semjaza*.

Why, when I asked for Semjaza, did it give me the Wikipedia entry for Samyaza? I didn't waste much energy pursuing that mystery, but dove into the article.

Fragments of sentences flared at me.

…fallen angel…

…another name for Satan…

…most powerful angel…

…cast out by God…

…demon…

I closed the laptop and stared ahead blindly.

"Is everything all right back there?" This time Cade didn't use the sound system, but called from the cockpit.

"Fine. All good." I said quickly.

I opened the laptop again and re-read the page. I clicked on the links and tried to absorb all the different entries. Half of them contradicted the others, but they all seemed to share one reference in common. The Book of Enoch. I searched and found an online rendition of it and, curling my legs beneath me, read what had to be the oldest written reference to Sam Jaza, or Semyaza or whatever his name might be.

162

The Book of Enoch is the kind of stuff that makes you yearn for good old incoherent Elizabethan English Lit. It's written like it's part of the Old Testament with lots of smiting and quaking and judgments on the wicked and ungodly. Not exactly a curl-up-on-the-sofa happy-read. But once you got past the perishing and sunder renting, there really was something very weird happening in this book. Supposedly angels, sent by God to watch humans, had crossed the line and started having sex with them.

Seriously! That's what the book says! And then they taught humans a lot of stuff, some good and some bad, like weapons and makeup and astrology, and then people started killing each other and then God got pissed and the good angels cast one of the bad angels into a pit and condemned the rest of them to live forever. Oh, and then there was this bit about giants. The whole thing was really out there, and normally, I'd just write it off as ancient mythology, but let's face it. I was dealing with something that was so obviously outside-the-box, I needed to be ready to accept the unacceptable.

Angels? Fallen Angels? Demons? I stared through the open cockpit door, my eyes glazing as I wrestled with the concept. As if they could feel my stare, both Cade and Danel turned and looked back. Danel's dark eyes narrowed and I felt the wave of heat that I began to recognize as his attempts to probe into my head. Cade's clear blue eyes were wide, but they both were asking the same silent question. I closed my laptop and walked back into the cockpit. They watched me approach.

"The Book of Enoch." I said it like I was answering a question.

As one, they both turned to look out the tiny windshield. Cade fiddled with switches while Danel's fingers tapped furiously on the plane's yoke.

"You and this Sam Jaza guy go way back, then. WAY back."

Still no response from the pilot seats.

"You want to start talking or are you going to make me keep stabbing around in the dark?"

Cade broke the silence first. "What do you want to know?"

Danel gave a twitch but didn't say anything.

"For starters, what exactly are you? Fallen Angels?" I had to force myself to go on, but the word needed to be said. "Demons?"

It was Cade who flinched this time like I'd slapped him across the face. "We prefer to call ourselves 'Watchers,'" he said.

"And what does God call you?"

It was silent for a long moment, and then it was Danel who spoke.

"Not at all." His words were barely a whisper.

The cockpit was so charged, I expected the electricity in the air to short out the control panel, but it was Danel who shorted out. He flicked two or three switches with suppressed fury, then stood up from his seat and strode past me into the main cabin. He didn't touch me, but his anger was like a shove as he passed. He picked up one of the Rojo cases, the one with the head in it, and carried it to the back of the plane. Pulling out some gearboxes, he wedged the head-case into a compartment and then piled the gearboxes in front of it. His wrath gave him a supernatural speed as he strode back to the cabin. He stopped abruptly, his face inches from mine.

"You have no idea the peril you are tempting. All humans die, but the when and the how are not all equal. The choices you are making, the questions you are asking, are leading you to an end that may not only be horrific, but may threaten your very soul. When we say it is better for you not to know, it is neither our souls nor our lives we seek to protect, but yours." He throbbed like a flame for a moment before sliding himself back into his seat, muttering to himself as he clicked the switches to turn off the autopilot. "We have neither souls nor lives to save."

The words were alarming, and yet in that moment, with his face so close to mine, all I could remember was the kiss from what seemed like a lifetime ago. I stepped back, not out of fear, but frightened that I might forget myself. I turned back to Cade, who watched all this with a veiled expression.

Maybe it wasn't wise to push this any farther, but I couldn't see us continuing on without my having at least some clue about what I was dealing with.

"So, how old are you?"

The veil over Cade's eyes dropped away, leaving only resignation.

"Define *age*," he said quietly.

"Oh, c'mon! Are you running for President? It's a simple question. How many years have you been alive?"

"Define *alive*."

I flipped down the jumpseat with a snap and sat on it. I folded my arms across my chest and glared. This game was getting old.

Cade gave it up with a sigh. "Since our definition of time is not the same as yours, we don't define 'life' in the same way either."

I couldn't even begin to come up with a valid response to that one, so I just waited.

"We have existed since before time. And outside of time."

"What do you mean, *outside of time*?" I was way over my head. "What is *outside of time*?"

Cade pulled his fingers through his hair with a long loud sigh. "It's similar to reading a book. And then you read it a second time. You know what will happen next, you remember. But while you're re-reading it, it's immediate. So even though you know how it will turn out, you feel as if you're living it for the first time. Again."

I nodded slowly, almost understanding.

"That's what it's like for an angel. They know everything that ever happened and that will happen, the same way you know a character is going to break a glass and cut her hand, but even though you knew it was going to happen, you couldn't stop it and you couldn't change it."

Danel was ashen. His fingers gripped the yoke. He stared out the windshield, unblinking. It didn't even look like he was breathing.

"So you guys know the future? Everything that will ever happen?" My eyes unfocused as I thought about the ramifications. Heck, never mind knowing the questions on a college entrance exam. My mind reeled with the possibilities of lottery tickets and stock market speculation.

"Not anymore." Cade seemed unaware of where my mind had headed. "When we were sent here to watch, our existence became locked into your time standard. We have knowledge of Creation and memory of the past, but our vision of the future is gone. God blinded us to the future when He placed us here. Through us, He wanted to experience the phenomena of time the same way humans do. Living minute by minute, second by second."

"Bit of a head trip, that was." Danel whispered with a small ugly laugh.

Cade smiled crookedly. "Yes. It took us centuries to adjust. Being surprised. Not knowing what would happen next until it happened. Not even knowing what the other Watchers were thinking or what they were going to do or say until they did it. We were as twitchy as rabbits surrounded by wolves. Even though nothing could permanently harm our bodies, we actually experienced fear. It was… unnerving."

166

I sat listening, not moving, not even blinking. Cade was unfurling before me. It was if in revealing his history, he was purging some black venom from his depths. He wanted to tell me. He wanted me to know. And I wanted to know too. Every detail.

"And joy," he continued. "And boredom. Angels are never bored. Every tiny detail of your life is fascinating to them. When you throw a pebble into the water, they follow it to where it lands and study it. Your strategy when you play solitaire. Everything. Angels are infinitely interested in everything every human does. But when we actually came down to earth and got bound by time, we started to prioritize. Humans getting angry and fighting was more interesting than humans sleeping. Humans building and creating was more intriguing than when they lay on their backs with their bellies full and watched clouds pass by. And the most interesting of all was love. Human love."

"And sex." Danel added.

"Not just the intercourse." Cade flicked a scowl at Danel. "Well, yes, the entire concept of sex was fascinating to us. But… human love. And how humans create a family with love. Before we descended, we watched it and thought we understood it, but we saw it as an extension of the animal function of reproduction. But when we actually walked on earth, living moment to moment, it added a sense of urgency to the entire process. Success or failure not only has a physical factor, but mental and emotional and even spiritual." Cade, his eyes deeper and brighter than I'd ever seen before, raised his hand and touched my face, his fingers barely gliding over my cheek. "Love, human love, is perhaps one of the most thrilling dynamics in all of Creation."

I shivered, my eyes unblinking as I stared into Cade's.

"And therein lay our downfall." Danel broke in curtly.

Danel's words were ice cold and shattered the spell of Cade's eyes.

"Why?" Feeling a little light-headed, I broke away from Cade and turned to Danel. "What happened?"

"Jannah." Danel spat the word like it was a swear.

"It's not right to place the blame on Jannah. It's not as if she were at fault," Cade snapped at Danel before turning back to me. "Jannah was a very pretty, very happy human girl who lived about eight thousand years ago. We, the Watchers, hadn't taken on full human bodies yet. While we could take on any form, we tended to stay in spirit form, floating like a mist as we observed humanity. And it was while he was in his mist form that Azazel became obsessed with Jannah."

Cade stopped, looking over at Danel as if expecting him to pick up the story. But Danel stared silently at the horizon, ignoring us as if we were the nebulous mists. So with a barely a shrug, Cade continued, picking his words with careful hesitation.

"Jannah had a joyous soul. She smiled and sang while she worked. As Azazel studied her, he would devise all types of adversity to challenge her, but still she smiled and perservered. So he decided to make himself visible to her, taking on the shape of a man. But on this occasion, he did not take on the human form the same way we had done in the past. Before the fall, when we occasionally took human form, it was just the outer shape that would be human-like, but it was just a façade. Our bodies would be a glowing colorless white, going from opaque to transparent as needed. Since it was never supposed to be part of the plan to be seen by humans, just to pass among them and watch, we rarely used human form. But that day, when Azazel decided to appear as a man to Jannah, he went too far. He took on the full physiology of a human man and he wasn't prepared for the full impact of the testosterone flooding his body." Cade paused, unwilling to continue.

Danel broke the silence.

"He raped her to death and buried the body." Danel spoke this so tonelessly, at first I thought the words meant nothing to him. My horror quickly flared to anger, but then I saw that his vacant look hid something deeper: remorse, disgust, pain, and maybe guilt. I was still staring at him when Cade continued.

"The rest of us had no idea. We couldn't read each other's thoughts and the idea that one of us could actually commit such an act didn't seem possible." Cade had turned back to face out the windshield of the cockpit, watching the cloud cover pass beneath us, not meeting my eyes. "Decades passed. A long time by your reckoning, but only days or weeks by our measure. Since Watchers are limited by time and space, we lack the ability to be everywhere at all times. We cover a lot of territory, but we tend to spread out, crossing each others' paths only occasionally. I believe I was the first to notice the sporadic disappearance of women, scattered among different tribes over a large area that is now central Africa. I canvassed the jungles and probed the minds of all the peoples within miles of the women's disappearances, but I found nothing of note. Those that knew of the missing women felt only fear or sadness or concern, but no one felt any guilt. If they'd been killed by an animal, I should have found remains. I was puzzled and I reported back to Danel who reported back to Sam Jaza."

"And Sam reported back to Gabriel, chief of all angels," Danel added. "And since the rest of the angels aren't limited by time and space, they knew all that Azazel had done."

Cade nodded for Danel to carry on, but Danel, instead of taking up the story, gave a quick glance to the back of the plane where Rojo's head was stored, and pressed his lips together, returning to focus on the horizon.

Cade shrugged and continued. "So when Sam Jaza summoned us to gather, we thought it was to confront Azazel with his crimes. And I believe that was what he first intended, but nothing happened the way we expected. Not then. And not since then." Cade's jaw clenched and he's eyes hardened. He was still looking in my direction, but I could tell he didn't see me. He was lost in events of a dozen millennia ago.

"We attended in spirit form, which was how we almost always existed back then. If you were to see us, it would look to you like a room full of swirling fog, but Azazel appeared before the tribunal in full human form, looking more beautiful and glorious than any human we'd ever seen. He wore white robes, like the kind you might see centuries later in Greece. He stood there, proud and arrogant." His eyes came back to me. "We were unused to having bodies; normally we just misted. In the past, when we would assume bodies, we never covered them. And yet, suddenly, even in mist form, I remember feeling naked… and vulnerable. It had only been a dozen or so centuries since we'd descended and we were still skittish about our limited state. And there was Azazel, standing there awesome and proud, every inch of him screaming *This is what I am meant to be. What you are meant to be.*

"And that is basically what he said. That the taking on of human form and living among humans, this was our true vocation. How could God expect us to fully understand humanity unless we walked as one of them? And then he started talking about sex, and how it was such an amazing experience and how could we hope to understand mankind unless we experienced every human aspect."

Cade spoke more quickly now, as if some dam had broken. I felt relief flowing from him. This was something the thing that he had been holding back from me all these months and now, that he'd decided to share it, it was cathartic.

"We'd been given free will when we'd descended, but none of us had ever thought about actually using it. We just followed our instructions. We reported back to our archangel, who reported back to Sam Jaza who reported back to Gabriel. To actually make a decision, to consciously do an act that we had not been specifically directed to do, was so foreign, we didn't know how to respond. We all turned to Sam Jaza for direction, but at first, he did nothing."

Cade's back was to me as he stared out the clouds passing beneath us. I couldn't see his face, but I could feel his emotions. Confusion. Pain. Isolation. And a deep and throbbing guilt. I wanted to touch him, to connect and comfort, but he wasn't ready. He wasn't done with his telling.

"Perhaps Sam too was stunned for he said that he would 'take this under consultation.' We thought he meant he was going to communicate with Gabriel who would then tell him what to do. Since, in our earth-bound state, we could no longer hear God directly, we relied on the chain of command.

"But Sam Jaza didn't speak with Gabriel about this. He spoke with Azazel privately instead. And Azazel convinced him to take on human form, to try it, just for an hour, and then make his decision.

"And Sam Jaza assumed human form and became corrupted. Decades past before he gathered us again and by then, he had completely fallen to vice.

"It was the strangest conclave. We drew together in mist form to the place where Sam had called us. It was a huge hall with towering pillars. It was like nothing that had ever been seen before on earth. Sam had not only shown himself to humans, but he'd convinced them he was some kind of god himself, ordering them to build him a temple to worship him. They stood before us, Sam and Azazel, in glorious human form, larger than most men, with white robes and gold bands around their necks, arms and heads.

"We were horrified. This was so obviously wrong, so completely against everything we'd been told to do, but here was our archangel, the commander appointed by God to lead us, telling us to that we should dismiss everything that we knew was right and to follow him instead.

"He kept using the words 'choose' and 'choice' and it baffled us. Humans were given choice. Angels follow direction. Now we were being told to make a decision about our own destinies. It was heady. But frightening as well. We swirled around like sharks in a feeding frenzy, not knowing what to bite.

"In the end, it was curiosity that did us in." Cade's bitterness made each syllable bite. "We wanted to know what it was like to be human. We were already living minute to minute and to experience the rest of the physical elements of humanity was too tempting.

"Est dropped from the mist first, choosing a female body. We watched as she experienced for the first time a nearly human body. Her face lit up with ecstasy and she laughed." Cade was torn between amazement and grief. "Laughter! Like a human! We couldn't resist. One by one, we fell into human-like bodies, reveling in the sensation of being so connected to ourselves… and yet so disconnected from the rest of creation." Cade stared at his own hand as if seeing it for the first time. "So completely alone, but not really lonely. We felt, for the first time, the independence and isolation that all humans feel. We were beyond stunned. We felt… god-like."

He stopped talking then, caught up in reliving that moment. I looked over at Danel who had sat stony during Cade's long tale, his eyes now fixed on me, unblinking.

"And then Sam Jaza asked for the promise," Cade continued. "The pledge that would bind us to him for the rest of time. The promise that doomed us all. Reveling in our new bodies, ecstatic with a million new sensations, we agreed. One by one, we all said yes, pledging to stand with Sam Jaza and take this step together.

"And one by one, we damned ourselves for eternity."

I reached out now, resting my hand on Cade's shoulder. The need to touch him was overpowering and, as before, the energy was there, leaping between us like it always had. But this time there was something else. A wall had fallen and I felt a peace from him that hadn't been there before. And trust as well.

But a glance over at Danel told me something that I'd already felt. There was more to this story. There was something that Cade hadn't told me and I could see from Danel's expression that it was going to be bad.

But it would have to wait until Cade was ready to tell me. And I knew that, whatever it was, it would not change the love I had for him. I could be patient. For Cade.

The silence hung heavily until it was broken by a ping from the plane's controls. Almost grateful for the interruption, they turned to the panel, tapping screens and responding to air traffic control with the mindless relief of routine.

I fidgeted in the jump seat, allowing the trivial annoyance of discomfort to distract me as a wordless tension resettled on the cockpit.

"Can't you change your mind?" I asked at last. "You know. Ask for forgiveness?"

"Forgiveness is a grace given only to humans." Danel finally spoke, his voice dead of all emotion. "There is no clemency for our kind."

"Well, that's not fair."

"It may not be fair," Danel said quietly, "but it is just."

That sounded lame. "Just what? Just stupid?"

Cade smiled at my sulkiness, but it was a bittersweet smile. "Why don't you go back in the cabin and try to take a nap. We're picking up nine hours on this flight, so it'll be the middle of the day by the time we get to Hawaii. Why don't you try to get some sleep."

I actually stood up and started toward the cabin before I balked. "Are you kidding?" I turned back to face the pair of them. "There's filet of demon on every seat! Where do you expect me to sleep?"

Cade stood with a chuckle and slipped past me while Danel glanced at us, his face expressionless except for one raised eyebrow.

"I'm glad you find her amusing." Danel muttered with a sigh before turning back to the control panel.

I stuck out my tongue to the back of his head.

Meanwhile, Cade was unstrapping Rojo cases from the seats and moving them back into the rear storage area. He pulled out the head-case and moved it up to the cabin. "The rest of him will settle down once we dump the head," he said with a nonchalance that was eerie, considering what he was saying. "The closer his head is to the rest of the body parts, the more he can call to them and the more they thrash. We'll jettison his head before we land."

"Okay," was the best I could come up with.

Cade paused as he passed, the last two Rojo cases under one arm. With his free hand, he glided his fingers across my cheek. The electricity pulsed and I felt the surge pull all the way through me. I froze when his fingertips rested on my lips.

"Thank you," he said with a whisper, "for listening. For not judging. For being you."

He carried the last two cases with him through the galley. I stood there staring at him as he disappeared into the cockpit.

Yeah. Right. Like I was going to get any sleep at all after that.

Chapter Twenty Four

"Don't think about it!" Cade's voice cracked. "Just do it!"

He was doing a lousy job of hiding his laughter as he straddled his board in the shallows, having ridden the last wave in as if his board was stationary and it was just the rest of the world that was flashing past him. "All you need do is paddle until you get enough speed and then stand up like we practiced on the beach. It's easy!"

"Says the guy who learned surfing from a pamphlet he picked up in the hotel lobby," I muttered. My arms were aching as I lay on my belly and let another wave surge beneath me. I was a soggy mess after having wiped out a dozen or more times. We were paddling on an isolated beach on the western side of Kauai. It had taken Cade and Danel a half hour to swim here, pulling the surfboards with me riding on top of one. They swam so fast, I'd actually managed to stand up on the board on the way here, but now that it was just me and the wave, I was hopeless.

Danel had been gone for a few minutes, disappearing under the surface. He had beached his board, preferring diving to surfing, leaving the ever-patient Cade to try to teach me the fine art of surfing. He paddled back out to me as I pushed myself up to kneel on the board.

"And, no. I didn't learn surfing from that booklet." Cade said as he drew closer. "I learned it from Chief Lohi Kelo centuries ago. I just wanted to brush up on the latest technology. Lohi would have loved these boards."

Both Cade and Danel had very good hearing. Maybe all the Watchers did. That's what I thought of them as: *Watchers*.

It was a nicer word than *Demons* and a lot easier to swallow than *Fallen Angels.*

"Go on now," Cade urged. "Give it another try. The third wave behind us. That one should crest just right. Paddle until you pick up speed, then kneel up into a crouch. You can do it!"

We'd been hopping between Maui and Kauai since we'd jettisoned Rojo's head out the hatchway into the middle of the Pacific about a week ago. As promised, the other suitcases had immediately settled down as soon as the head-case dropped. Since Danel and Cade hadn't seemed in any rush to get rid of the rest of Rojo, I hadn't given him much thought and focused on more important things. Like surfing. And suntans. And Cade.

And Danel.

Now don't get me wrong, I was completely and entirely in love with Cade. It's just that, at night, when I was laying down in my bedroom in the oceanfront condo that they had rented and listening to the beat of the surf, there was something about Danel's kiss that kept me awake. It bothered me, like maybe he had got into my head and was pushing me somehow. I no longer wanted Cade to kiss me. I NEEDED Cade to kiss me. I just didn't know how to force the issue. Every time I started to approach him about it either something would come up, or he'd retreat. I was getting to the boiling point and as I knelt on that surfboard, a million miles from the rest of the world, I knew it had to be broached and I was going to broach it now.

"Cade," I started and I could see the veil drop over his face. He could tell from the tone of my voice where I was going with this but he couldn't very well run away and leave me in the middle of the Pacific Ocean.

"We can talk later." Panic gave his words a little more speed than usual. "Your wave is almost here. Start paddling."

"Nevermind the wave. We need to t---"

Before I could finish that sentence, my board caught the wave perfectly and I found myself cruising along. Everything else washed from my head as I rose to a crouch.

I was still moving! I hadn't wiped! It was the most amazing feeling. Imagine flying, then imagine something ten times cooler. It was like the entire ocean was a huge hand that was sweeping me along. All I had to do was stay on the board. I centered my balance and straightened up even more.

I rode that wave all the way in. I actually crouched down at the end and glided into the shallows, still on my board. The whole event left me speechless. I turned to look at Cade, who was still out beyond the breakers, straddling his board and shaking his head at me, ruefully.

"What?" I yelled out to him, annoyed at his expression. "I did it! I surfed all the way in! It was amazing!"

Just then Danel burst out of the water, breaching like a dolphin before standing on a sandbar, looking smug. Realization dawned.

"You pushed me!" I slapped the water and a spray hit him in the face. "You jerk! Here I was, thinking I'd actually surfed all by myself, and you were under my board, pushing me all the time!"

Danel was trying not to laugh. "No, you were surfing! I just gave you a little push to get you started."

"And then?" I scowled at him, trying for intimidation.

"Okay," he admitted with a shrug. "I may have guided your board a little, but it really isn't reasonable for Cade to expect you to handle waves this big this soon. You should practice in the lagoon near the condo."

I held my scowl, but I was beginning to agree with him. I was taking a beating from all the wipeouts and I was getting tired.

Cade paddled over, his eyes narrow as he looked at me. "Nice ride." His voice was exceptionally neutral. "Would you like to try again?"

I looked up at the sun. "We've been out for at least four hours, it's got to be lunchtime. I'm getting hungry."

"After that breakfast you had?" The laugh was back in Cade's eyes. "That should have lasted you until tomorrow morning!"

Danel had grabbed the leads on both boards and was swimming south, back towards the beach near our condo. Which just left Cade and me, straddling the boards and cruising in style.

We talked about nothing on the way back. I wanted to get to the question of the kiss, but it was too weird with Danel being so close.

I would have to bide my time.

Chapter Twenty Five

People walk by all the time and you never notice them.

Or at least you don't think you notice them.

They walk by you, toward you, away from you, around you, and you never see them.

Or at least you don't think you see them.

But even if you're sitting at a window seat overlooking the ocean in a fancy restaurant with two beautiful men and you are completely focused on them, there's still a small sliver of your brain that's aware of the people in the background.

Which is how I noticed the woman walking towards us long before she reached our table. The back of your brain processes all the familiar movement: waiters hurrying, guests meandering to and from their seats, bus boys puttering about, and ignores it. But when someone moves in a non-familiar way, your brain goes into some instinctive mode and a warning flares. Maybe that's why, even though I was sitting with two Watchers, I was the first one to notice the woman striding directly toward us, her eyes fixed on me like a leopard on an impala. I stiffened and Cade broke off mid-syllable from his story about surfing monster waves in an earlier century. Both Cade and Danel turned to face the woman.

Shelly, looking tall and fabulous, strode toward us, a smile like a cobra on her face. Instinctively, I edged closer to Cade.

"Cade! Darling!" She purred as she stepped around me like I was a puddle that a dog had made on the floor. Her fingers glided over his shoulder and played with a golden curl above his ear. I bristled and I felt as if my fingers were morphing into dagger long claws. "Whatever happened to you? We thought you were going to Monaco for the Viscountess' birthday party! I looked and looked for you there, but couldn't find you. You naughty boy! Did you blow off the Viscountess? She'll probably forgive you, but I may not."

Cade reached up and clasped her wrist in an apparently light grip, but Shelly gave a little gasp and tensed. Beneath her flawless tan, she paled, but her smile glittered on the same. "Private party, Shelly," Cade said softly with no hint in his voice of the threat that I knew was there. "You're not invited."

"Silly man." Shelly wasn't even slightly slowed by the cool reception. "I'm always invited." A nod to a waiter and a fourth chair appeared. She went to sit down. "Aren't you going to introduce me to your friend?"

Friend. Singular. And I was pretty certain she wasn't talking about me, even if we had met ever so briefly last summer. She was looking at Danel, completely ignoring me. The invisible treatment made me feel like a stupid little kid, all dressed up and sitting at the grown-up table. But when I glanced over at Danel, he had only a bored smirk for Shelly, as if she were an awkward brat and her silly games just barely amused him.

Cade rose and stood behind my chair, as if to pull it out. "Are you finished, Misty?" he asked.

I looked down at my plate. I had only eaten half of my pasta pomodoro and it was really good. As I stood up, I shoveled two more forkfuls into my mouth and washed it down with a mouthful of ginger ale. "But I'm still starving! Can we stop for ice cream?"

The stricken look on Shelly's face was hard to describe. Pain? Jealousy? Hunger? And then I realized that she was staring at my dinner plate. I bet that to keep her shape she'd probably spent the last twenty years dieting religiously. My cat claws popped out.

"I'm always hungry!" I widened my eyes innocently at her. "You know what it's like when you're sixteen. It seems you can eat and eat and never get full."

Danel bit his lip as he gestured for the bill.

"Tell you what, Misty," said Cade from behind me. "We'll stop and get you a sundae. Whipped cream and a cherry, too, if you like."

"Okay," the smile I directed to Shelly was all sweetness and light, "but I don't need a cherry. I still have mine."

The mask slipped from Shelly's face and for a split second, I could see that my barb had been perfectly aimed. She might be rich and glamorous and beautiful, but she'd never be sixteen again and she'd have to switch from martinis to Shirley Temples before she could ever offer someone a cherry.

This was as cattish as I'd ever been in my life and I was amazed by my own nerve. I leaned on Cade as I felt my knees shake. But I wasn't frightened. It felt like adrenalin, like I was in the middle of a battle and I was winning. Me versus the fabulous Shelly and I was winning. Cade, maybe sensing how tenuous my victory was, guided me to the elevator while Danel paid the bill. I held my cool façade together until Shelly's fuming face was lost to the closing elevator doors.

Cade collapsed. His legs went out from under him and he slid to the floor, his infectious laugh sputtering almost silent as tears slid down his face. "That was brilliant!"

A flicker of remorse stifled my laughter. "Yeah, but it was kind of mean."

That sobered him quickly. "Misty, don't mistake her. She was well aware that Rojo meant no good when he lured you into the Shack." He rose to his feet in a smooth motion as the elevator doors opened. His hand was on the small of my back as he guided me into an alcove in the hotel lobby and onto a plush sofa.

"Is she, um, human?" I asked quietly, a quick glance around to make sure no one was close enough to hear me.

"Shelly?" Cade seemed distracted as he sat down. "Oh, yes. She's one of those humans that seek us out and cling to us. They have no idea what we are, but they lust after power and wealth and will do anything they're told for no more than the opportunity to walk in our shadows."

Was that me? Did the feelings that I had for Cade, and Danel too, make me like Shelly? Some kind of demon groupie?

Cade must have read my face because he took my chin in his fingers and turned my face to his. At his touch, my mind sputtered to a stop and I stared unblinking into his eyes. "Not you, Misty," he said with that smile. "You treasure family and friends and all the free joys of life. The shallow and mundane trappings of wealth have no appeal to you compared to the delight of a sunny afternoon or the moments spent with people you love. I'd forgotten how beautiful humans could be until I met you."

I didn't want to burst Cade's bubble or destroy this image he had of me, but to be honest, I kind of like the things that money buys, like private jets and beachfront condos. Yet, at that moment, with Cade's fingers on my chin and his face so close, I could only think of one thing. I leaned closer to him and paused.

"Now would be a good time." I whispered.

Confusion flickered in his eyes for a half a moment but then I could see him understand what I was thinking about. His face paled and his chin trembled slightly as he clenched his jaw as if the very act of standing still was a herculean effort. But he didn't pull away and I drew my face to within an inch of his. I reached up to stroke his cheek.

"Shelly's been looking for Rojo." Danel's voice startled us both and we parted with a guilty jerk. Fuming with frustration, I turned to find Danel standing in front of us, his expression stony. "I'm not familiar with her. Is she one of Rojo's sycophants?"

Cade pulled himself together with an effort, his cheeks flushing, redder than a day spent in the sun could account for. "She's his principal liason here in the New World. She arranges his debaucheries and cleans up his dregs. He pays for her amusements and her surgeries. She's a nothing."

I shook off my temper enough to notice that something was seriously bothering Danel.

"Who else does she know?" Danel's question had an intensity that caused Cade to tighten beside me. I looked from one to the other, trying to grasp the real meaning behind the question.

"She's mentioned Sobro and Min. I don't think she really knows them, but she may have met them at some point while she was with Rojo."

"Sobro's not that hard to find. He keeps a high profile." Danel's brow grew darker. "I think we've lingered here too long. We need to finish scattering Rojo before Shelly can track down Sobro or Min."

Danel reached down and grabbed my arm, pulling me to my feet. Off-balance, I almost slammed into him, my hands pressing against his chest to steady myself. A surge of warmth ran through me and I pulled away in confusion.

Danel didn't seem to notice. Still not even looking at me, he released my arm and I found my feet. "You two go back to the condo, pack up and check out. Meet me at the airport. I'll prep the plane."

He turned and strode to the door, leaving Cade and me staring after him. I looked at Cade, too many questions in my head to even start.

"Danel's right." Cade said softly. "If Rojo's attempts to kill you were ordered from a higher stratum, then eventually there will be someone following up for confirmation. We need to dispose of all of Rojo, and do it well, so they won't be able to reconstruct him too quickly. All we need is fifty or sixty years, but if Shelly draws their attention now, they'll be looking for him too soon."

"You say 'fifty or sixty years' like it was 'fifty or sixty minutes.'"

"That's a pretty good analogy," Cade said with a crooked smile. "I doubt I'm very close to the top of Sam's issue list, so I probably won't cross his mind again for a couple of decades, so long as no one mentions me."

The Hawaiian heat hit us like a blanket as we walked out of the hotel and onto the sidewalk. Cade's arm around my shoulder guided me toward the condo, a couple of blocks away.

"Why did Rojo try to kill me?" I tried to keep the question cool and casual, but it's not easy to keep a little resentment out of a question like that. "Is it because Sam wants me dead? And if he does, then why?"

Cade slowed his steps, his brow furrowed as he weighed how to answer. "It's not you, personally, that he wants dead."

"Oh, good. I can't tell you what a relief it is that it's not personal."

Cade's arm tightened around my shoulders as he huffed a breath of a laugh. "It's only…" he paused and I let the silence sit there, which was probably a good thing, since after a moment, he continued. "There's a war going on. Right now. All around you. Humans are the warriors, the weapons and the collateral damage, and they don't even know that it's happening. Humanity has been contaminated by the Fallen and the battle rages as the Others try to purge us from earth. Over the ages, both sides have been ruthless and Sam demands all the resources he can husband. This not only includes the power that corruptible humans give him, but also the strength that he draws from us, those who fell with him all those ages ago. He doesn't really care what we do, as long as we're available for him to draw on. One thing he doesn't allow, however, is for us to become too committed since he says that loving someone weakens his hold on us. I really wasn't aware how deeply I'd fallen in love with you until Rojo tried to kill you."

My breath came out in short, frantic huffs. I should have been terrified, the king of all demons wanted me dead, but all I could focus on was Cade's words *I'd fallen in love with you* and they left me gasping for air.

Cade, mistaking my jagged breathing, curled me into him and I pressed myself into his chest. "Don't be frightened, Misty," he whispered softly, his hand cradling my neck, pressing my cheek into his shoulder. "I will always be here to protect you."

Boy, when Cade was wrong, he was way wrong. I raised my face to his and slid my hands behind his shoulders. Staring into his eyes, I whispered "Now would be a good time."

A hundred thoughts flickered through his eyes before he slid me away, holding me at arms length. "Misty, Misty, Misty." His throaty laugh made me shiver. "No. Now would certainly not be a good time for that."

A frustrated sigh escaped me as he guided me through the gate of the condo complex and onto the path that wound its way through the buildings. We walked up the stairs to our unit in silence and in moments, I stood in the cool, airconditioned living room, sulking as he disappeared into his room.

"Misty, you may pout as you pack." Cade called from his room. "Come now, we'll need to move quickly."

I spun around and stomped into my room. "I am not pouting. I'm sulking. There's a difference." I slammed the door shut and wasted four seconds glaring at my beautiful room with its private balcony overlooking the Pacific Ocean.

Then I got over it and packed my stuff.

Chapter Twenty Six

The plane was on the tarmac waiting when we pulled up. Among the many cool things about a private jet is that you can drive your car right up to the plane and just walk up the steps. Danel stood at the foot of the stairs, once again looking like a movie actor playing a pilot with only a resemblance to the seventeen-year-old boy that he'd been playing an hour ago. It made me remember that the image of them as teenagers was as unreal as their older personas. The truth of their nature was far more alien than I could fully grasp.

And yet I trusted them. Both of them. The logical part of my mind needed pages to catalogue all the reasons why I shouldn't, but as I stood there in the cabin, clutching my pack and suitcase and watching them strap down the Rojo cases, I shredded that mental list and flushed it down the cerebral toilet.

The hair on my arms fuzzed as Danel slid by without touching me, locking the hatchway and striding into the cockpit. Cade passed more slowly, his hand pressing into the small of my back, steering me to one of the main cabin seats.

"Strap in, Misty. Danel already checked out the plane and we're taking off immediately." Cade followed Danel, sitting quickly into the co-pilot's chair.

I stood for a moment, looking at the two of them, then to the huge plush swivel chair, and then back to the cockpit.

A moment later, I was strapping myself into the hard little fold down jumpseat.

"You'll be more comfortable---" Cade started.

"Don't waste your breath," Danel cut him off with a mutter.

I smiled smugly.

"So," I asked as I fastened my seatbelt. "Where are we headed next?"

"North." Danel was terse as he flicked switches and adjusted his headset.

"To Alaska?" Cade asked.

Danel gave a small nod.

And the rush was on.

Fairbanks Alaska in October is not nearly as cold as one might expect. At least, not as cold as I expected. The sky was clear, the sun was bright and a brisk wind made it feel perhaps only a little colder than a late autumn morning in New England. I stood at the top of the gangway steps, encased in four layers of clothes that included my winter hat, a scarf, boots and thermal underwear. I was sweating bullets. On the tarmac, Danel chatted with a ground crew guy, both looking quite comfortable in jackets and sweaters. Danel cocked his head as he looked up at me, his single raised eyebrow mocking me. I gave him a dirty look before I spun quickly around, slamming into Cade who had moved to stand silently behind me.

"I'm going to change." I mumbled as I edged around him, heading back into the plane, to the rear of the main cabin where my suitcase was. I caught a weird look on Cade's face as he looked after me, and then he turned to stare down at Danel, his eyes narrowing.

"What?" I asked as I pulled off my jacket. Despite the privacy curtain that I yanked shut, I camped dressed as I pulled off one shirt and my thermal underwear. I tossed the extra clothes along with my scarf into my suitcase, but shoved the gloves and hat into my jacket pocket. It wasn't that cold out, but I didn't know where we'd be going. I pulled open the curtain and found Cade staring at me with narrowed eyes.

"What?" I asked again. "What's the matter?"

"Nothing," he mumbled. He stepped back to let me get past him to the gangway, but I stood staring at him.

"No, something's bugging you." I crossed my arms in front of my chest and waited. He wouldn't meet my eyes, which was unusual. "What is it?"

He took a deep breath, then hissed it out through his nose. "It's of no matter," he said quietly as he headed out the hatchway and pounded down the stairs. I followed slowly.

Cade opened the back door of a waiting Humvee and climbed in. I was barely aware of Danel as he passed me up the stairs and disappeared back into the jet; my eyes were on Cade. I walked around to the other side, pulling myself up and into the backseat.

The bench seats in a Humvee are huge, bigger than most sofas   and Cade had positioned himself as far away from me as he could manage. I wanted to close the gap, but he had put out an invisible "do not disturb" sign and I didn't know how to get past it. I pulled my legs up so I could hug my knees and stared at him silently and waited.

A practically ageless angel is a heck of lot better at waiting than I am. It felt like weeks had passed before the rattle of the rear hatch startled me. Danel was grim as he looked from Cade to me before swinging a canvas bag into the rear compartment. I peeked over the back of the seat. There was a lump in the bag roughly the size of a Rojo case. I hugged myself tighter and went back to staring at Cade as Danel walked around to climb into the driver's seat.

"Am I the chauffeur now?" Danel spoke lightly but with an edge. "You know, there's enough space in the front for all three of us."

I didn't say anything but kept staring at Cade.

"Go ahead," Cade said at last. "You know you want to."

"What?" I asked loudly as Danel, at the same time spat out "Shove it, Cade."

I could see Cade simmering, seconds from exploding, but suddenly, so was I.

"What are you talking about?" I uncurled and pounced liked a tiger, crawling across the seat until my face was inches from Cade's. "What would I want to do? Go in the front seat? What's bugging you?"

"Forget it," Cade muttered as he wrenched open the door. In a millisecond, he was out of the car and around to the passenger's side door. He opened both the front and back doors and stood waiting. "Come on."

There was no other way to describe it: Cade was sulking. Slowly, I climbed out of the back seat, my brow furrowed as I passed him before sliding into the front seat. I twitched when the back door slammed angrily but I was ready for the second door slam after Cade had landed on the seat beside me.

No one spoke as we drove out of the airport. The awesomeness of being in Alaska was being completely eclipsed by Cade's bad mood. I needed to talk to Cade alone. Something was bugging him about Danel. And me. Which was stupid. For five minutes, I matched Cade sulk for sulk until the landscape finally distracted me.

"Where are we headed?" I asked.

"Denali National Park," Danel answered.

"Cool," I replied brightly as a new tactic occurred to me. I wasn't going to waste my first (and possibly only) chance of seeing in Alaska by letting Cade wreck it for me. At some point, we were going to get some alone time and then I would get to the bottom of all this. For now, I was going to enjoy the moment.

You would think, having lived in New Hampshire all my life, I'd have seen enough foliage to make me pretty jaded, but I have to say, Alaska in the fall is amazing. I mean, this late in the season, the trees were half bare, and while the gold leaves were beautiful, they didn't have the deeper reds that New England has, but nonetheless, the landscape was stunning. It's just that it's so much vaster. The forests roll on for miles right up into the foothills. And then you have purple mountains with white caps and brilliantly blue skies. I took about a million pictures, but they couldn't begin to capture what I saw. I'm not saying that I forgot about Cade's sulking, but I will say that I enjoyed the scenery more than Cade's attitude.

We drove for another hour inside the park before Danel turned off the paved road and onto a gravelly path that was more like a pair of overgrown ruts than an actual road. For some reason, I was the only one who had to hang on to avoid being bounced off the dashboard. The two guys rode it out like they had shock absorbers in their jeans. Cade's temper seemed to have slightly mellowed from sullen to pensive, but when an unusually fierce bump sent me flying clear out of my seat and I landed, sprawled across his lap, he tensed and made no attempt to steady me.

Stretched face down across the seat, my face in Cade's lap, my feet kicking Danel, I squirmed clumsily but only managed to lose even more coordination and dignity. I couldn't seem to find a safe place to put my hands to push myself back up to a sitting position and the more I squirmed, the worse it got. Beneath me, I could feel Cade stiffen.

Then the tension got to me and I started to laugh. I gave up trying to right myself and collapsed into a heap. I was laughing so hard, I started to roll off Cade's lap. I was starting to fall into the footwell when he finally reached out and grabbed my shoulders. With one gentle but powerful motion, he lifted me up and righted me onto his lap. I couldn't see him clearly, my eyes were wet with laughter, but I could tell he was struggling with something.

And then he laughed. That brilliantly beautiful Cade-laugh that could make the Alaska tundra as warm as a beach in Hawaii. He held me there for a moment, laughing into my face until he slid me off his lap and tucked me against his chest, his arm cradling my shoulders.

And all was once more right with the world. I still didn't know what had been bothering him, but I wasn't going to bring it up now. I'd felt like an empty seashell when Cade put up those walls and I wasn't going to risk going there again.

The jostling of the Hummer was a lot easier to handle with Cade's arm around my shoulder and I actually felt a twinge of disappointment when Danel slowed the vehicle to a stop and killed the engine.

We were parked under a tree near a rough hewn wood shingled barn. I went to slide off the seat, but Cade grabbed me by my waist and lifted me out. We stood there, his hands on my hips, until Danel strode around from the driver's side. Cade's hands slid slowly away, making me shiver, and I wheedled myself under his arm, needing his warmth not nearly as much wanting his touch.

We'd been steadily climbing uphill, but I hadn't been aware as to how much higher we were. It was noticeably cooler up here and I zipped up my jacket and pulled out my gloves. It wasn't bitterly cold, but it was a lot chillier than down at the airport. I shouldn't have left my scarf on the plane.

A man lumbered out from behind the building and stood sizing us up. He looked as weathered as the shingles on the side of the barn, both his skin and his clothes. Every inch of him, from his boots to his hat, looked faded and thrashed, like they'd been left out on the prairie for years. Except his eyes, which gleamed bright brown at us.

"You be the ones that called?" His accent sounded like an old Western movie.

"Yep," Danel answered. I looked over at him, surprised. His voice had changed and suddenly, the high-school-student a/k/a jet pilot was now a seasoned cowboy. Weird.

The scruffy guy gave Danel and Cade a quick glance and then a longer one at me before moseying around the corner of the building. If you could see the way he walked, you'd know why I say "moseying." His stance was wide, like he was straddling an invisible horse, and his pace was rhythmic. Danel followed him, matching him step by step and Cade and I fell in behind.

"Danel's kind of like a chameleon, isn't he?" I walked close to Cade so I could whisper.

Cade went stiff again. "What do you mean?"

"I mean the way he changes all the time. I wonder who the real Danel is. Or what."

"You know what he is. What we both are." Cade's voice was cool.

"Yeah, but even when you're a pilot or a lifeguard or a high school student, you're still the same you. But with Danel, he seems like a completely different person from one role to the next." I looked up into Cade's face, worried about the biting set of his jaw. "It's no big deal, I was just noticing."

"You seem to 'notice' Danel a lot lately." Cade muttered this so softly that I could have pretended that I didn't hear it.

But I had. It took me a minute before all the pieces fell together and then I grabbed his arm and jerked him to face me.

"Are you *jealous*?" It was such a ridiculous notion that my voice squeaked. "Of *Danel*?"

"It's of no matter." Cade shrugged off my grip, but I grabbed him again. I made him face me as the full realization hit me. I could feel the heat surge to my face as I sputtered to respond.

"You're jealous!" My voice rose high enough so that the cowboy walking in front with Danel turned to glance, but Danel kept walking as if deaf.

Cade grunted and pulled his arm free. He continued to walk ahead but I stood where I was, stunned.

Danel and the cowboy disappeared into the barn but Cade waited by the entrance, his back to me.

Finally, I pulled myself back together enough to be able to speak.

"That," I whispered, "is the sweetest thing you've ever said to me."

That made him turn around and I saw the flicker of confusion in his eyes quickly surrendering to a smile. He bit on his lip to stifle a laugh.

"No, really! That you could actually think that Danel could like me like that is so... flattering!" I skipped toward him and didn't stop until I slid my arms around his waist. He didn't stiffen or pull back and I felt as if all the gravity which had been beating down on me all morning suddenly dissipated. If I hadn't been hanging on to his chest, I'd have floated away.

Slowly, his arms curled around me and I melted into him, breathing deep the scent of sunshine that clung to him even here on a grey day at the top of the world. We stood there, not moving for an eon or two until he finally started to loosen his grasp. I gave him one last squeeze before letting my arms drop, but I didn't step back. Instead, I kept leaning into him like I was a magnet and he was a refrigerator.

"He does, you know," Cade's whisper was nearly soundless, "like you like that."

I chuckled as I looked up. "That is so cute!"

Cade laughed then too, like his old carefree laugh, and he draped his arm over my shoulder and guided me into the stable. I figured that this was the end of it. Together, we had slain the dragon of jealously. The idea that Danel even *liked* me was ridiculous.

Right?

Chapter Twenty Seven

My horse was named Rambo. He was golden brown with a dark brown mane and tail. He eyed me blearily, at once recognizing me as a complete non-horse person, beneath contempt. He snorted and proceeded to ignore me.

Fine with me.

Cade threw me up onto Rambo's back and the horse didn't so much as twitch. I patted his neck and jiggled the reins but as far as I could tell, Rambo didn't even know that I existed. Cade and Danel mounted their horses with smooth practiced movements. A fourth horse carried the canvas bag with the box inside.

I was the only one that waved to the cowboy as we left the ranch and headed into the mountains.

Try as they might, Danel and Cade couldn't make Rambo walk three abreast. The path was wide enough, but Rambo had a follower mentality. Cade urged me to kick him, but the look of dismay on my face was enough to set Danel chuckling.

"You won't hurt him." Cade was exasperated.

"I'll hurt his feelings." I reached forward to pat Rambo's neck. He rewarded me with a contemptuous snicker.

Finally, Rambo compromised by allowing Cade to ride next to us, with Danel and the pack horse ahead.

The sun was bright and although the day was cold, it was almost warm when we were in the sunlight. We left the towering trees behind and trotted across tall grassy fields, brown from the frost, and chilly burbling streams that looked like they should have frozen the hooves off the horses, but Rambo ignored the frigid water the same way he ignored everything else. Maybe I could have kicked him. I doubt he would have noticed.

We trotted for an hour or more and we were all happy to ride quietly with our own thoughts. And my thoughts, on their own volition, wandered back to what Cade had said about Danel.

Cade wasn't wrong often, but boy, was he wrong about that one. While I was relieved that Danel seemed to have gotten over his initial nearly homicidal rage about me, and I had got to the point where I did trust him some, there's a big gap between no longer wanting to kill me and love. I wondered when I started to trust him and thought that maybe it was the day he'd saved me from Gary Kasanjian and the Jackets. But the more I thought I about it, I think it started before that.

It was ridiculous, but my mind kept meandering back to that stolen kiss and I found myself staring at Danel's back. I shook my head to break that train of thought and turned to see Cade watching me with narrowed eyes.

"Why won't you kiss me?" The words slipped like a dog out an open door. But I didn't regret saying them.

Cade pulled his horse to a stop and Rambo followed suit. The Alpo reject would follow direction, so long as it wasn't mine. Danel, still playing deaf, kept moving forward. Cade sat stone still on top of his horse, his eyes on me, until Danel was out of earshot.

"Well?" I dropped my reins and folded my arms over my chest. Why bother with reins when you're on a horse that ignores you. "Why won't you kiss me?"

"I want to," he whispered at last, his eyes skimming away from mine. "There is nothing more on earth or in heaven that I want more."

My knees nudged Rambo, trying to steer him closer to Cade's horse but, surprise, surprise, it ignored me and I was stuck having to ask the million dollar question from six feet away.

"Then why don't you?" You could see my question, a white mist in the cold air. We were on an open prairie, Danel was way ahead and I was probably the only human being for a dozen miles. And yet my voice dropped to a hush. "Now is good."

Cade gave me half of a smile but wouldn't meet my eyes. "I don't know if I could stop."

His words vibrated through me like a swarm of tiny butterflies, leaving me stuttering. Even on the chilly tundra, I could feel my cheeks flush hot.

"Maybe I wouldn't want you to." I managed to whisper.

His head snapped as he met my eyes at last. "You don't know what you're talking about."

He gave a click of his tongue and his horse trotted forward. Rambo followed without warning and I flailed to hold on.

"Wait!" I cried as my fingers slipped off the saddle horn. I reached down to grab the reins but that just brought my weight forward and I toppled headfirst to the frost-hard earth with a thump.

My ankle twisted in the stirrup before my foot slipped free. I let out half of a squeak before I hit the ground, the air knocked from my chest. For a second, I laid there, looking up at the piercing blue sky and then Cade was there. Before I could even take an inventory of my bruises, I was being lifted up.

He tried to set me on my feet, but I let out a cry as my ankle protested. I balanced on one foot and leaned into his chest. Actually, this was fine with me and I stayed, leaning, his arms warm around me.

"Are you hurt?"

198

With my head pressed against his chest, I could hear his words rasp beneath his jacket. His fingers glided over my head, neck and back, which made me tingle and burn. Ignoring my twisted ankle and bruises, I turned my face up to his.

"Now would be a good a time."

Relief made his laugh louder than normal. "Misty! You scared me half to death." He glided his fingers across my cheek, as light as a rose petal. "Humans break so easily."

Suddenly, the Alaskan tundra was hotter than Kauai.

"Um, how about now?"

"Misty…" Cade's voice held both amusement and reproach.

Frustration made me hop back on one leg and push him away. I tried to put my hands on my hips, but lost my balance and ended up having to grab his arm to steady myself, which completely undermined the attitude I was aiming for.

"Why can't you? I don't get it. It can't be an angel thing 'cause Danel had no problem kissing me."

"And you liked that?" Cade went cool and accusatory.

"Yes I did." I was too pissed to lie to him. "I liked it a lot, but I'd much rather that you kiss me. Why won't you?"

"I told you." Cade stepped back and I hobbled on one foot. "I don't know if I can control myself."

"You had the same issue this summer, on the beach, just touching me, and you were able to handle that!"

"Yeah, but you couldn't. You nearly passed out."

"But I got over it. We worked it out. And we can work this out too." I switched to my wheedling voice. "C'mon, Cade."

I could see cracks in the walls of Cade's resolution. I knew it was going to take some serious battering to get through those barriers, but I was up for it.

"Tonight then," he said, derailing my offense. "We'll discuss this tonight."

"Discuss it?" I hissed with disgust. "This is getting ridiculous. You'd think we were talking about going all the way, not just a kiss."

That brought him up short. He stopped in his tracks and eyed me carefully. "And if it led to something more? If it led to 'going all the way,' are you ready for that?"

I couldn't lie to him. I had thought about it. A lot. Just because I was still a virgin, didn't mean I didn't think about. Most times, I thought I would want to go all the way, someday. But I just wasn't always sure when.

He read the indecision on my face and gently stepped forward. "I don't think you're ready for that yet, Misty. And I don't want to wreck it for you by rushing you into something that you're not sure about. You have no idea the effect you have on me and how much I want you, not just a kiss but every inch of you, inside and out."

His draped his arms around my waist, resting them on my hips. I raised my hands to his shoulders, ready for anything. Except for when he lifted me up onto Rambo's back. I squeaked as he released me, and I grabbed at the saddle horn to hang on. He handed me the reins.

Wordlessly he remounted, a small regretful smile on his face as he urged his horse forward. Rambo followed and we trotted for a stretch until Danel drew back into sight. Then we dropped back into a silent walk.

Cade's last words had unleashed a thousand questions and a million emotions and I couldn't even begin to sort them out.

But I was going to try.

"When was the last time you kissed a girl?"

A stranger might have thought that Cade hadn't heard me, but I wasn't fooled. I waited.

"Gregorian Calendar or Julian?" he responded at last.

I let out a disgusted snort. "I don't care! Mayan! Whatever! Just answer the question! How long has it been since you've kissed a girl?"

"One thousand six hundred forty seven years." He said baldly. "And a couple of months."

I was speechless for a few moments.

"That's ... quite the dry spell." I said at last. "Do you always go this long between relationships?"

"Depends how you define relationships."

"You know, if the watcher-thing starts to get old, you could always go into politics." I left those words to settle for a second before I continued. "How often have you wanted to kiss a girl like you want to kiss me?"

Cade's response was swift and unexpected. He grabbed Rambo's bridle right below the bit and pulled him until our horses were side by side and our thighs were touching. His eyes burned into mine with a light I'd never seen before.

"Never. I have never, since time began, wanted a woman in the way that I want you. All of creation is real again. And new. And meaningful. And it's only because of you." He released the bridle and turned his horse back to the trail. "It terrifies me."

I was speechless.

His next words were so faint with ache, I barely caught them. "And I can't bear to think of the time that you will not be with me."

I stared blindly at the trail ahead, crushed. My own mortality would defeat us both. I might have another half a dozen decades, maybe a little more, but the day would come that I would be gone and Cade would have to deal with a future that I would never have to face. A life alone.

I wanted to hold him. To leap from my horse and wrap my arms around him and comfort him and tell him that it would be all right. That I would never leave him. But it was a lie. I would leave him one day, not by my own choice, but I'd leave him nonetheless. And he would be left to carry on. Alone.

There was nothing I could say. Nothing I could do. Nothing I could change. We rode on silently, our thoughts dealing with two different views of the same grim reality.

Danel had stopped in a clearing on a bluff, surrounded on three sides by towering pine trees. The fourth side overlooked the stillest lake I'd ever seen. Golden mountains with white peaks reflected like a mirror giving the entire vista an Alice-Through-The-Looking-Glass feel. He had tied up his horse and was loosening the girth when we entered the clearing. Cade quickly slid off his horse, grabbed Rambo's reins and helped me dismount.

I gave a tiny gasp as I landed and Cade immediately scooped me up and carried me to a nearby boulder. I steadied myself with my hands on his shoulders as he sat me down.

"What's the matter?" Danel appeared at my side faster than I expected and I flinched in surprise.

"I don't think it's sprained, just twisted." I slipped off my sneaker and rolled down my sock. The ankle was black and blue and a little swollen. "I fell off the horse and my foot got caught in the stirrup."

Danel stared at my foot like it had twelve toes. His face was cold and blank and he had never seemed more alien. It unnerved me.

"What? It's no big deal. I've had worse. It'll heal."

Danel turned and walked away without saying a word. He stopped at the edge of the bluff with his back to us, looking out over the lake.

I shot Cade a "what-was-that-about?" look but Cade just shrugged and turned away.

With my fingers, I gently prodded my ankle. I could move it, but it was painful. I was about to try to pull my sock back over it when Danel suddenly did one of his lightning moves. One second he was at the bluff, then he was at his horse. He fiddled with the saddle bag for a half a moment and then, moving like light, he was beside us again. In his hand was an ace bandage which he handed to Cade.

With a smileless nod, Cade took the bandage and knelt down before me. His fingers were warm and gentle as he removed my sock so that he could wrap the bandage around my ankle and under the arch of my foot. I was so intent on watching Cade that it took me a minute to realize that Danel was still there, focusing on my foot with more intensity than a twisted ankle deserved.

I gave an involuntary hum of pleasure when Cade rubbed warmth back into my toes before gently rolling my sock back up. I felt like a hillbilly Cinderella as he slipped my sneaker back on. I held Cade's arm as I slid off the rock, gingerly testing the weight on my foot. It wasn't bad and when I looked up to give him an encouraging smile, I noticed that Danel was gone again. I knew he could move that fast, but usually he paced himself around me. Now, for some reason, he was flashing around the clearing. One second he was at his horse, the next, he was brushing clear an area under a patch of sunlight. Then he'd be at his horse again, and then over to the bluff. But it wasn't until he flashed over to the spare horse that carried the canvas bag that I tensed. I must have made a sound because Danel looked up and caught my eye as he pulled free the ropes that secured the bag to the saddle horn. It was then that he finally smiled and I felt something inside me relax. I was far from understanding Danel's moods and I'd been worried that he was about to go into one of his suppressed homicidal rages. But whatever it was, it seemed to have passed and his smile looked almost mischievous, which seemed weird, considering what he was holding.

He walked over and placed the bag down into the patch of sunlight. I hung back with Cade, not really wanting to be close when he did whatever he intended to do with the bag.

Reaching into the bag, Danel pulled out a large plaid blanket which he promptly spread on the ground with a dramatic flourish. Then, after casting one enigmatic look over to me, he reached in and pulled out… a large straw picnic basket.

"What!" I exclaimed as he tossed the bag away. It sailed across the clearing and I jumped when it landed in a heap near my feet. Empty. "Where's Rojo?"

I prodded the bag with my bad foot, ready to jump if Rojo's arm should decide to make a grab for me, but the bag was empty. I looked from Cade to Danel, confused.

Cade took my arm and helped me over to the blanket where Danel was unpacking a gourmet picnic lunch complete with three crystal wine glasses.

"It's a red herring," Danel said as he handed me a tiny pastry tart topped with tiny wet black beads. I pulled back from the fishy smell.

"Yuck. No thanks." I pushed the appetizer away and made myself comfortable on the blanket. "What are we doing here?"

"Not the canapé," Danel placed the tart into my reluctant hands. "*Why* we're here. It's a red herring."

"Ah." I said, like I understood, which I didn't.

"Danel's concerned about the others coming too soon to look for Rojo." Cade said, pouring what looked like champagne into one of the glasses.

"They might be able to find his head quickly." Danel took the glass that Cade offered and savored a sip as he spoke. "Even if it takes them a couple of years before they start looking, they'll be able to track the plane's flight path and it shouldn't take them that long to canvas that area. A two hour drive into Denali and then an hour on horseback should make this leg pretty untraceable. They'll have to search over two thousand square miles before they'll give up. This side trip alone should slow them down at least for a decade."

I stared at the canapé in my hand, not seeing it. I'd been suppressing the entire purpose for this anti-scavenger hunt, but the lurking uneasiness that I'd been feeling since this adventure started began to morph into a serious dread.

"It's caviar," said Cade, misinterpreting my expression.

"I'm in serious danger, aren't I?" I said, not really hearing him.

"Not from the caviar." Cade held out one of the two filled glasses.

With my mind a million miles away from the moment, I popped the little appetizer into my mouth.

Mistake.

It tasted bitter and salty. I gagged and then spat it out into the bushes, but still the residue coated my mouth. I rubbed the back of my hand across my tongue trying to purge the dregs as I grabbed the wine glass and took a gulp.

Mistake #2.

In the past, the few times that I've tasted wine, it's always been something pretty lightweight and I hadn't really liked them, but they were chocolate milkshakes compared to champagne.

The champagne followed the caviar into the bushes. Hopefully, whatever bugs lived under in the shrubs had a taste for caviar and champagne. Heaven knows, I didn't.

The picnic basket wasn't a complete disaster. Cade pulled out a tuna sandwich and a grape soda which I grabbed gratefully.

Danel was watching with that almost a half a smile on his face, but it disappeared at my next comment.

"Yuck! We won't have to worry about Sam Jaza's hoods if you poison me first!"

Those words left Danel and Cade suddenly chilled and silent.

"If you can't forget that name," Danel's voice throbbed with tension, "could you at least refrain from using it?"

"You're kidding, right? We're in the middle of the Denali National Park, twenty miles from the nearest person, human or otherwise. And the name Sam has got to be one of the most common names in the Western Hemisphere. What's your problem?"

"Words are powerful." Danel spoke with an inhuman lack of emotion which made his words all the creepier. "Modern humans have lost the understanding that they can influence the universe with their words. Elements, especially angels, can be beckoned with a word. And even though fallen angels aren't as receptive as the others, they can still be influenced."

I chewed my sandwich slowly as I thought about that. "You mean just using the name too much can help him find me? What if I called him 'Bob' or something?"

Danel relaxed visibly. "That would help."

This sounded remarkably lame to me, but I was game to go with the flow. "*Bob* it is. From now on, I'll call him *Bob Cratchit.*"

Cade chuckled and handed me a strawberry.

This should have been one of the most golden moments of my life. Alone with Cade and Danel with a picnic basket and an epic landscape, but anxiety rumbled uneasily in my stomach and I kept glancing back at the shadows, wondering if Bob Cratchit and the ghosts of Christmases-Never-To-Be might be closing in.

Chapter Twenty Eight

From Alaska we flew to Australia.

I had them detour so that we could fly over the Hawaiian Islands. I wanted to see them one more time. I didn't know if I'd ever get there again.

In Australia, we spent four days hiking deep into the Outback, then we hiked back out, still carrying all the cases. We stopped to refuel at a small airport in the Northern Territory and Danel left us for a few hours to drop one of Rojo's legs in a sinkhole in the Kakadu Wetlands.

After that, we flew north. Destination: To Be Determined.

I started the flight in the main cabin, getting caught up on emails. This was tough since I couldn't very well describe to people where I'd actually been and what I'd been doing and I wasn't very good at making up stuff, so I settled for ambiguous and vague. Kat had long since got over being pissed at me for taking off without saying goodbye. Her emails kept me up to date on all the gossip from school. There had been a major buzz when the kids found out that I was off on a Semester Aboard and an even bigger buzz when Cade and Danel disappeared at the same time. I played ignorant about Danel, but I told Kat that I was still in touch with Cade and that he'd had family issues he had to go take care of. Mom and Dad were harder to put off, but I managed to write them enough to keep them from worrying. I closed my laptop with a sigh of relief. It was late and I needed to sleep. Who knew what we'd be up to tomorrow, or where. But like a cat to a fishbowl, I was drawn to the cockpit.

The door to the cockpit was open. I stopped and stared. They looked so cute. I know they'd probably hate to hear me say that they looked cute, but they did. They had on their pilot uniforms as they lounged in their seats and Cade's hair was all jumbled, the flickering control lights made his curls glitter gold and wild. Danel's black locks were tight and neat. I felt the urge to rush in and neaten Cade's hair and, at the same time, muss up Danel's.

I decided to just enjoy the moment. One or the other of them always seemed to be watching me, so now with both of their attention on the controls, I took advantage of the opportunity. The cabin's foremost seat was faced away from the cockpit so I knelt on it, rested my chin on my arms on the seatback and settled in.

Oh yeah, they were good to look at.

"I'm still liking the Gobi Desert," Cade was saying.

Danel gave a sniff of disdain. "When were you last in Mongolia?"

Cade shrugged. "I don't know, five, six hundred years ago. Are you telling me it's changed?"

"Hardly," Danel conceded, "but with the shifting sands, it'll be too easy for him to wiggle free."

"We'll be dumping the upper torso next, right?" Cade made it sound like they were dropping off laundry. "The torso's the least mobile. It'll have to flop around out there until the legs catch up. I say we dump it in the Gobi."

"No, there's a dam in South China that they're just finishing. We can bury it along the shoreline and within a year it'll be under two hundred feet of water."

It was Cade's turn to shrug. "Okay. We'll dump it China, but we can buzz the Gobi. Another red herring."

Danel agreed with a silent nod and started to fiddle with the controls.

A silence descended on them as they retreated into their own thoughts. Finally Danel spoke.

"Is it bad? Not the pain, but being dismembered?"

"What? Are you feeling bad for Rojo?" Cade turned, the laugh in his voice almost bitter.

"No. I was just curious."

"You've never been dismembered?"

Danel shook his head.

"Well, you can't go by me. At the time, I didn't care." Cade turned back to the controls.

Cade had been dismembered once? I felt sick. I slid down in my seat so only my eyes peeked over the top. It was silent again. I wanted them to go on. At last, it was Cade who spoke.

"Did you pity me when you ripped me to pieces?" Cade's tone was too distant to even be called cold and yet I shivered.

"No." Danel was just as remote. "We didn't know what else to do."

"Because I was a little depressed?" Cade asked.

"A little?" Danel gave a small snort. "You sat on that glacier for over a century without moving. We had to chip you out to find you."

"It just seemed pointless." Cade shrugged. "Life. Earth. Creation. There's no redemption for us. Why bother."

"You were dismembered and scattered for over a century." Danel sounded like he was the injured party. "When we finally came to dig you out, you hadn't even twitched."

Again Cade shrugged.

"But now?" Danel asked softly.

Life started to return to Cade's voice. "I suppose I should thank Rojo. He had Shelly set up that beach house and fill it with every kind of decadent vice he could think of, trying to get me interested. And I have to tell you, when it comes to debauchery, Rojo has an unparalleled imagination. He dragged me there, but it only disgusted me. I walked out and tried to find a place far away from Rojo and the Shack and all of humanity. I didn't even have the energy to despise them. I still felt as detached from everything as when I was dismembered. So I found an abandoned lifeguard tower and sat there. It suited me. I felt like I was once more doing what I'd been sent for, to watch. I didn't care. I didn't interfere. I just watched.

"And then, one morning, this girl comes to the beach. She was taking care of a pair of toddlers and I could tell from the way she looked at the other teenagers as they walked by that she wanted to be with them and not taking care of someone else's babies. I watched her. Every morning she came to the beach and every morning she'd stare at the other teenagers, but she never neglected those kids. I waited for the inevitability of human nature to set in. For that moment when she turned her disappointment on the smaller ones and lashed out in frustration. But she never did.

"A couple of times, I tried to push her into snapping, but I couldn't sway her. It was like I was a fly that she'd brush away. For a week I watched her. And listened to her as she chatted at those kids. She was clever and smart and funny and the more she spoke, the more I wanted to hear. I cursed at the sun whenever it started to set because I knew she'd be heading back inside for the evening. And I'd stay on the lifeguard tower all night, just waiting for her to return."

He paused, and when he continued, his voice was low and tight. "I was obsessed, and my own feelings terrified me. I wasn't sure if I should run away or just dive in deeper. In the end, I couldn't leave and when I finally broke the ice and spoke to her, it was if I had entered an entirely new universe."

I slid down into the chair, hugging myself as if to hold Cade's words inside me. I couldn't understand how he could feel for me the way he did, but the fact that he did, sent a warmth spinning deep within me. I could have sat there for a year, but then Danel spoke.

"She will die someday." Danel made it sound like nothing. "You do understand that. If we can manage it, she should last at least another half century, maybe even a full century, but the day will come when she'll go on."

"I have hated time for eons," Cade said softly, "but I can't hate it now. While I have her, I will cherish each second like sips of fine wine. Maybe, when it is over, I will hate time again. Or maybe the memory will be enough. I don't know. But for now, I'm going to live like a human, thinking only of the moment and ignoring the future as if it could be wished away."

They fell silent then. I slipped to the rear of the cabin, curled on the sofa and pulled the blankets up over my head.

I wept. I don't know if my tears were from joy or grief, but they slid down my face and dripped into my ears. Finally, I slept.

Chapter Twenty Nine

"Ka-ching."

"*Chong-ching*," Cade corrected me.

"*Chun-king?*" I've never been good at languages.

"*Chong. Ching*," Cade was patient.

"*Chong Ching*." I repeated obediently.

Chinese is hard because, when written with western letters, the same word can get spelled a lot of different ways. *Chongqing* was the most common spelling, but it was still too ultra-foreign for a girl from New England.

As was much of China. Some things were familiar, like skyscrapers and Kentucky Fried Chicken, but for me, coming from Nowhere, New Hampshire, it was exotic and exciting and a little frightening. I stared out the window of our hotel room, eighteen floors up, and listened with half an ear to the conversation between Danel and Cade.

"It will only take one of us." Cade was saying.

"You're not familiar with human's current level of technology." Danel kept his voice low. I noticed that he always whispered whenever he spoke about humans like they were aliens. I wondered if he did that for me, or because he was concerned about being overheard. "One of us needs to monitor the surveillance control room. I can't get all the way to the dam without triggering their alarms. I'll block their perception while you get down to the waterline and bury the case."

"Why does Cade have to go down to the water?" I jumped into the discussion, stepping between them. "Is it more dangerous? Is that why you're asking him to do it?"

Danel turned away, exasperated, but Cade just grinned.

"I won't be in danger." Cade smiled as he turned me to face him. "There won't be any risk."

"Not to us." Danel was the voice of doom and Cade's smile faded quickly.

"I'll make the run to the river." Cade was speaking to Danel, but I could tell he was saying this for my ears. "You're right that I'm not up to speed with current technology. You'll be better at getting them to ignore and misinterpret their equipment."

"What do you want me to do?" I asked.

"You'll have to stay here, Misty." Cade's forehead made interesting Vs when he furrowed his brow and I tried to stroke them away with my fingertip. "We're going to be in disguise and you won't be."

I started to argue, but Cade's smile stopped me. With a faint squishy sound, his hair grew darker, his skin changed tone and he shrank about four inches. Within seconds, Cade's smile was on a non-descript Asian man.

"If you're wondering," I fumbled for words, disconcerted, "that really freaks me out when you do that."

Cade quickly morphed back into his normal self, but I was still unsettled.

"What do you guys really look like?" I asked. "You know, *really* look like?"

"What we look like, *really*, is nothing at all." Cade seemed wistful. "But when we walk as humans, most of us keep the same bodies that we first materialized into. Or pretty close to it. The longer we stay with a body, the more powerful it becomes. Rojo changes shape so often, he's a lightweight wimp."

I remember Rojo in the woods, nearly taking off my head with a backhand. Even a wimp demon is nothing to piff at.

Danel had turned away and was staring out the window. He was worried about something.

I walked over to stand beside him and we both stared down into the streets below. Cars slogged along slowly, like a swarm of drunken bumble bees, bicycles like gnats weaving between them. Even from this height, the muffled sounds of the traffic filtered through the glass.

"What is it?" I looked down into the street, trying to figure out what he saw that was freaking him out. He turned from the window and moved quickly to grab one of the Rojo cases, not meeting my eyes.

"We've dawdled too long. They're closing in. We need to finish dumping Rojo and work on getting you off the radar. Stay here. We'll be back in two hours."

Cade, echoing Danel's urgency, grabbed a small duffle bag from beside the bed before turning back to me.

"You can watch TV and order room service." I trembled as his fingers skimmed my cheek. "We'll be right back." he whispered.

And then, before he walked out the door, he placed a light kiss on my forehead. He disappeared into the hallway and the door closed quietly behind him.

I leapt forward, pulling open the door and yelling down the hallway.

"That doesn't count!" I hollered. "Don't think it!"

He'd already disappeared around the bend in the hallway, but I heard his chuckle drift back to me.

Chapter Thirty

The scents of Cade and Danel mixed in my dreams. It was strange, but I was kissing Cade, but it felt like Danel's kiss. With a faint squishy sound, the two of them mingled together and changed from one to another.

The pounding of my heart woke me. I was lying on the bed, hot and disoriented. Clinging to the fading shards of my dream, I took a deep breath to pull myself back together and that's when I realized I wasn't alone.

Cade and Danel were back. I savored their fragrances while I stretched. When I opened my eyes, I found Cade staring at me, a worried smile on his face.

"Wake up, Morning Mist," he said, giving my bare feet a nudge. "You can catch up on your beauty sleep later. We're moving."

"I'm not tired," I yawned. "I was napping out of boredom."

I rolled to my feet, rubbing my eyes. We'd never unpacked so it didn't surprise me to see Danel standing by the door, carrying the three remaining Rojo cases as well as his own valise.

"Why so fast?" I asked. "We just got here. Can't we get dinner first?"

Cade grabbed my bags and his with one arm and with the other, herded me into the hallway. "No time. We need to move now."

Danel had disappeared down the hall and around the corner. By the time Cade and I got to the elevator, Danel was already inside, holding the door open.

I was getting a little tired of being shuffled around like an eighth Rojo case, but there was something in their energy that kept me from complaining. They looked as calm as usual, but there was an intensity to their action that worried me. I bit my tongue and said nothing.

We sailed through the lobby unnoticed, which was strange. I could feel a faint buzzing and I realized that either Danel or Cade were influencing everyone. Even those few people that were looking roughly in our direction didn't seem to notice us. I felt invisible.

Even the car valet didn't notice Danel when he stepped into his office and lifted a set of car keys from the tack board. In moments we were in the car and backing out of the garage.

"Okay, so tell me now. What's going on?"

Cade, beside me in the back seat, didn't seem to know where to begin.

I was surprised when Danel answered me from the front.

"We ran into two Watchers today." He glanced into the rear view mirror to catch my eye. "And it wasn't a coincidence."

I felt chill. Cade wrapped an arm around me and I huddled into his warmth, but it didn't seem to help. "What happened?"

"We 'bumped' into them when we were heading back to the car at the dam." Danel didn't need to look at the road that much to drive, but his eyes were all over the place, checking his mirrors and glancing to the side. "They didn't even try to act surprised. They weren't looking for Rojo. They were looking for us."

"Why?" The word came out of me like a breathy squeak.

"It's been over seven thousand years since the Fall, but it's been about ten thousand years since we first descended." Danel rattled off those mindboggling dates like they were nothing. "Enoch foretold that the Fallen would be brought to judgment after ten thousand years and ever since that prophecy, Sam has been building his defenses, readying all of mankind to be his weapons when he defies God on the Day of Judgment. But we've always assumed that it was going to be ten thousand years after the fall and that we still had another three thousand years."

I shivered to hear Danel talking about Judgment Day and going to war with God in such an offhand way.

"You talk as if that's changed." I stared at the rear view mirror, trying to read Danel's eyes. "What happened?"

Cade answered, his arm tightening around me almost painfully. "Enoch didn't give us much of a guideline, but he did give a name to the Time of Judgment."

I waited. I could tell that they were building toward something and that it wasn't going to be good.

Cade took my chin in his hand and turned my face to his. His eyes were warm with concern. "He called that time, *the Year of Mystery*."

That was so not what I was expecting. I tried hard not to laugh in his face. And failed.

"Are you serious? That's what you're worried about?" I forced myself to laugh, trying to diffuse the tension, but it wasn't working. "Because my flaky mother named me 'Mystery'? Do you want to know why she named me Mystery? Because there's a park in southern New Hampshire with a stone circle and one night, on Spring Equinox, my mother snuck in there with my father and they did the dirty in the middle of the stone circle. And nine months later, I was born. Do you want to know the name of that place? Mystery Hill! My father's last name is Hill and Mom thought it would be funny to name me after the place where I was conceived. That's the whole story. It has nothing to do with the Book of Enoch or Judgment Day or anything like that!"

I really thought Cade would laugh at that story. Or at least smile. But if anything, he seemed more worried. "You were conceived in a stone circle on the night of a Spring Equinox?"

"Oh, c'mon!" I pulled away from Cade. "You act like that's a big deal!"

Cade looked more somber than I'd ever seen him.

"It doesn't matter what we think," said Danel from the front seat. "It's what Sam thinks that counts. If he suspects that you're a catalyst for the Endtimes, then he'll be looking to eliminate you. And not because of Cade's interest in you."

"Catalyst? Endtimes? Seriously?"

"You've been pushed to the top of his to-do list." Cade curled me back into his chest.

"To-do?"

"To kill."

Chapter Thirty One

My stomach was in knots. Nothing I said seemed to make a difference. If anything, they both looked more troubled. I finally shut up and stared out the window.

"Where are we going?" I asked, seeing the cityscape quickly change to fields. "It wasn't this far to the airport last time."

"We can't use the jet," Danel explained. "That's probably how they tracked us here. We're going to have to travel with a lower profile until we lose them."

"Lose them?" Somehow, I doubted that Sam Jaza would give up just because he lost track of me. "For how long?"

It had started to drizzle and the wiper blades slid dully against the windshield. Other than that, it was silent in the car. Beside me, Cade wouldn't look at me and in the rear view mirror, Danel didn't meet my eyes.

"We may have to kill you," Danel said at last.

My heart stopped.

"Not for real," Cade was quick to assure, "but we may have to fake your death, and do it well, if we're to throw Sam off your scent for a century or so."

"But, he must know that I live in New Hampshire. What happens when we go back?"

"You can't go back, Misty." Danel was ice hard. "Ever."

Can't go back? Ever? My chest was tight and my throat was closing up. Cade wrapped both arms around me as I started to shake. I was never going to see my family again? Or my friends? My parents would be devastated. Tiff wouldn't have a big sister anymore. Kat would flunk math. I would never see anyone or anything that I'd known before.

I felt like I was dead already.

"But I didn't do anything wrong!" I hiccupped as the words caught in my chest. "It's not fair. I didn't do anything wrong!"

Both of them were silent as my hiccups faded.

"I don't know, Danel," Cade said softly. "I think, maybe, she should go home. Get one last chance to see everyone before she 'dies.' If she disappears while she's supposed to be on a world cruise, it'll raise too many questions."

Danel was silent in the front seat. The rain was falling harder and the windshield wipers beat angrily.

"Okay," Danel said at last. "We'll head back to New Hampshire. However we decide to kill you, if it's believable enough for Sam, it'll be more than enough for human forensics."

It was a small concession. I really didn't want to die, either way. For real or for show.

"There's no other choice, is there?" I asked, pretty much already knowing the answer. "Couldn't we explain to Sam that I'm just an ordinary boring human and nothing for him to be interested in?"

"Sam wouldn't care." Danel glanced in his mirrors as he slowed the car to pull over. "He doesn't value human life. He'd rather be safe than sorry. He doesn't see the value in letting someone who might be a threat to him live one second longer than it takes for him to kill. You all die eventually."

I bristled at the tone of his voice. "You sound jealous," I snapped.

With the car parked alongside the highway, Danel turned to face me. "*'Tis a consummation devoutly to be wished.*"

"Shakespeare?" I asked, suddenly wistful for Mr. Gallagher's English Lit class.

"We should have left you in New Hampshire." Danel muttered curtly as he opened the car door. He was out in a second and I could see him, in the pouring rain, opening the trunk. I turned to Cade, puzzled about the stop.

"No use in scattering Rojo over twenty time zones." Cade answered my unasked question. "We'll toss the last three cases here in China. It'll still take him years to break free and pull himself together. We'll have your situation resolved long before then."

Resolved. He spoke with a forced cheerfulness but I could feel the tension beneath his words. I buried my own fear as well. It wasn't going to help anything if I melted down. The trunk slammed shut. I turned to look out the back in time to catch a glimpse of Danel, disappearing like a flash into the mist.

"So," I was trying for chipper, but my voice sounded wispy to me, "where to next?"

"We're heading to Cheng-du." Cade seemed relieved to be able to talk about something relatively normal. "From there, we'll pick up a commuter flight to Shanghai and then fly back to the United States."

Part of my head kept thinking that when I got back to the United States, to New Hampshire, I'd be safe. That Mom and Dad and Sergeant Huebner and Principal DeVeau would be more than enough to handle Sam Jaza and his minions. But the more rational part of my brain knew otherwise.

"How am I going to die?" It's a weird question to ask, especially when it's not rhetorical.

Cade thought for a moment. "Airplane crash?"

"By myself?"

"Well, maybe that's not a good idea then," he shrugged. I got the feeling he was giving up the idea, not because of the death toll, but because I was horrified.

"Were you really considering killing a whole plane full of people just to mask my death?"

Gently, Cade reached out to cradle my face with his hands, his fingers pushing the strands of hair from face. "Misty, all humans die. Some sooner than others. At this very moment, there are tens of thousands of humans in the process of taking their last breaths, while at the same time there are even more being born. If we have to sacrifice a couple of hundred to protect you, then that's what we'll do."

I pulled back, appalled.

"Cade! That's wrong! How can you---" I couldn't continue.

"You're right." Cade's voice was soothing as his hands drew me back. "I know you'd never agree to that. We'll figure something out."

I wasn't going to let him glaze this over. "But you'd have no problem with that? With killing innocent people?"

"They're going to die anyway, Misty." He hunched his shoulders defensively. "It's not as if they're immortal."

"Like you." This was a side of Cade I'd never seen and I didn't like it. I pulled away and crammed myself into the farthest corner of the car. "And Danel, and Rojo and Sa--- Bob Cratchit and all the other Watchers. You're the important ones. The rest of us are just a pile of dying leaves."

Cade pulled his fingers through his hair. "Just the opposite," he said quietly.

I waited for him to explain that comment.

"You nailed it, earlier, when you accused Danel of being jealous. He is. We all are. You might call us immortals because we don't die, but humans are the true immortals. The Fallen will only exist for as long as time and then we shall perish. But humans continue on, rejoining God after their time here is done."

"So you're saying death is good a thing?" I wasn't buying this.

"What I'm saying, Misty, is that fearing death is just a programmed response, but if you think about it, it's like being afraid of the setting sun. You know it will set and there's nothing you can do about it."

"Yeah, but the sun rises again in the morning."

"Exactly. The sun always rises. Maybe that why I call you *Morning Mist*," he added with a feeble laugh.

"Then if I shouldn't fear death, why bother with all these strategies?" I sounded pettish, but this conversation was disturbing me. "Why don't we just let Bob Cratchit finish me off now rather than later?"

"Because I'm selfish, Misty." There was an edge in Cade's voice that scared me, but at the same time, made me want to cradle him like a child. "Because, while I don't want you to fear your death, it is my single greatest fear. Every moment I spend with you only makes me dread your passing all the more. I fear the night, Misty, because on the day when that sun sets, for me, it will not rise again."

Chapter Thirty Two

Danel returned two hours later, soaking wet but lighter by two Rojo cases. Cade and I had made an uneasy peace and, from one glance in the rear view mirror, I could tell that Danel picked up on it.

I counted six cases gone. There must still be one more in the trunk. "Are we taking the last Rojo case with us?"

"Yes," Danel answered as he pulled the car back into traffic. "We'll keep it with us for the time being. It's the lower torso. He won't be able to function without it. You need at least the head and both torso parts to be able to speak."

At some point, conversations like this will stop freaking me out, but I wasn't there yet. Gamely, I pushed on. "That'll make interesting checked luggage."

"We'll carry it on," Danel said.

"Are you serious?" I looked from Danel to Cade and then back again. "You'll never get that through airport security. They won't be able to scan it, and then they'll open it. That'll be messy, to say the least."

Cade and Danel just smiled.

The name on my ticket wasn't even close to my real name. Of course, I couldn't read the Mandarin characters, but they reprinted everything with western letters, so I was able to figure it out. Even assuming a bad translation, Mystery Elizabeth Hill is not spelled "Tsai Lu." Cade hushed me when I started to argue.

"We don't want 'certain people' to track us," he whispered in my ear. "We'll need to travel under false names until we get to the United States."

How we were going to get past airport security was the next question I wanted to ask, but I bit my tongue and waited. Sure enough, when we approached the security checkpoint, I felt the familiar buzzing. The guard looked at my U.S. Passport and my Tsai Lu ticket, nodded and let me pass. Cade and Danel were waved through as well.

The same treatment at the luggage scan. I watched the attendant as he stared at the image of the Rojo case. The lead lined case resisted the x-rays, but the attendant, with a glazed look in his eyes, just nodded and let it pass. I wondered what he thought he saw. The buzzing didn't fade until we cleared security.

The flight to Shanghai was four hours and I didn't miss the private jet. The seats in coach were cramped but I was seated between Cade and Danel. I didn't mind at all. It was actually more comfortable than the jump seat in the cockpit, so I sipped on a strange orange soda and enjoyed the moment. I flipped up the armrests and cuddled up with Cade. I felt so safe, I dozed until we started to land.

Shanghai Airport was as modern and frantic as any U.S. airport. The obvious differences were that the signs and announcements and almost all the people were Chinese. It felt weird, being different. I'd never been a minority before. It's not that anyone looked at me funny; it was just that I looked at me funny. I wedged myself between Cade and Danel as we headed for the luggage claim.

The babble of travelers in the terminal seemed loud and jarring to me, so I didn't pick up on it right away when the pitch of their voices rose, but Cade and Danel did. I suddenly found myself sandwiched between them.

"Hey!" I started to complain, but anything else I might have added died on my lips as a strangely muffled ratatat sound punctuated a rising crescendo of screams.

Cade's arm covered my head and I was pushed to the ground and smothered by his body. Danel crouched, straddling the two of us as a wave of bullets shattered the civilized chaos of Shanghai Airport, turning it into a deathtrap. I could feel the impact of the bullets as they pummeled Danel and Cade, but pinned to the ground I could only see a sliver of the carnage around us. Bodies were falling, bleeding and shattered, and beyond the dropping corpses I saw figures running, some fleeing in terror, but others, dressed in black, their heads hidden in hoods, trotted slowly, emptying their weapons in sprays of hell.

Instinct made me want to flee. I pushed up against Cade, but it was useless; he wanted me flat against the ground and I wasn't moving. My line of vision was limited and a rising pile of bodies reduced it even more, but I saw one guerilla speaking to another, gesturing toward Danel who was one of the few figures still standing. Bullets arched toward him as Danel leapt toward the gunmen. A blur of movement, and the guerillas fell.

I couldn't see any more action, but the screams of terror were fading and the gunshots grew sporadic, making unearthly echoes in the vaulted terminal. I caught a glimpse of Danel, flashing back and forth like an arcade pinball as he neutralized the gunmen. Occasionally, a terrified sob could be faintly heard, but as the guerillas fell, one by one, the silence became so absolute, my pounding heart became the loudest sound I could hear.

I bit my lip, choking back hysteria that threatened to rise into my chest. Adrenalin made me hyper-aware. I breathed deep and shuddered. The stench of blood and fear and death nearly overpowered Cade's familiar scent.

The gunshots stopped and I sensed Danel's return. Cade made a move as if to rise, but stopped at Danel's whispered command.

"Stay down." Danel's hand came into my line of sight as it touched Cade's shoulder. "That was too easy."

"Too easy?" The words squeaked out of me.

Cade's voice was calm and steady in my ear. "Mindless violence is not a natural condition of men. It's unlikely that this terrorist attack is a coincidence."

Sam Jaza.

I froze, spellbound by the thought that the demon overlord could be the catalyst of not only this attack, but in other terrorist assassinations around the world. I moved my head and found the unblinking death stare of a young man who didn't look much older than me. I couldn't even begin to calculate the body count around me. That I might be the motivation for all this carnage made my stomach clench in dry heaves.

A wave of blue garbed soldiers, marching shoulder to shoulder, clutching clear acrylic shields, flowed into the terminal. Spreading out in formation, they stepped over the dead and dying. I watched, bleary, as a second flank of support personnel followed them, pulling out the casualties from behind their line and retreating with the bodies. The soldiers slowed at the downed guerillas, kicked away their weapons and muttered with puzzlement to each other, unable to figure out why some of the gunmen were unconscious or dead.

As I watched, one of the soldiers flipped over one of the assassins and began to rummage under his jacket. I felt Cade stiffen and Danel yelled something in Chinese that sounded like "May-Yu!" Danel's body dropped to cover my head only milliseconds before a blast mushroomed through the hall.

I couldn't breathe. Between Danel and Cade's bodies, nearly every inch of my body was covered, but in those hair thin gaps, I was seared by flame. Percussion followed percussion and I realized that all the guerillas must have been wired with suicide bombs. I fought for breath, but Danel wouldn't move. I sucked in hard to steal what air I could get. The sweet winter scent of Danel couldn't mask the stench of melted plastic, frying hair and burning flesh. Desperate for oxygen, I wavered on the edge of consciousness until another blast, stronger and closer, sent us rolling and scattering across the floor.

I was being carried. We were moving quickly, much faster than a human could run. Screams and chaos grew stronger, but the reek of hell was fading. I gulped the air greedily, vaguely aware of a new scent. Sweet and cloying, like baby powder. Buzzing circled my head as I dropped into blackness.

The world was trembling. It was the first thing that I became aware of. I was lying down, shaking, a vague sense of panic gripping me, but for a long moment, I couldn't remember what was terrifying me. The sofa that I was lying on rumbled faintly. Something buzzed around my head. My hand rose to brush it away, but it didn't help. I took a deep breath and opened my eyes.

I was in the jet. My first thought was relief. It was familiar. There was a hazy black dread lurking in the back of my half-waking mind: I knew something bad had happened, but if I was on the jet, I was with Cade and Danel and they could handle whatever it was. I took another deep breath.

Memory flooded back. The unblinking eyes of the corpses, the smell of death and the mind-numbing fear were all there. I screamed.

"It's all right, Misty." I heard Danel's voice over the speaker system. "Sit tight. We'll be in the air in a few minutes."

All right? The buzzing around my head was annoying. I scrubbed my fingers through against my scalp, trying to rub away both the hum outside my head and the images inside. Why were they wasting their time buzzing me? They knew it had no effect. My eyes filled with tears and I wished I could let their mind-wiping work on me. Having that memory flushed or even dimmed would be a relief. I stumbled to the door of the cockpit.

"Oh, God!" I was sobbing. "What happened?"

The buzzing intensified. "Nothing to worry about." Danel flashed a smile at me. "There's a little delay in letting us take off. They had a problem in one of the terminals. Doesn't concern us. Just take your seat and strap in."

I stared at Danel. He was acting so un-Danel. His smile was all wrong. And Cade hadn't even turned to look at me. I sniffed. My sinuses were blocked from crying, but I could still pull a shallow breath through my nose.

The scent was wrong. Sweet and cloying. Was it my stuffy nose? Was that why I couldn't smell Danel's cinnamon-pine scent or Cade's sea-breeze tang? I started to shake. The buzzing grew stronger.

"Go sit down, Misty." Cade's voice ordered baldly. "We'll be taking off shortly."

I was frozen, unable to speak. I stumbled back a few steps and my head nodded blindly.

They didn't seem to notice my weirdness. I thought back to the Jacket guys in the boys' room and their confused glazed looks. Maybe that's what they expected from the mind buzzing.

Too many things were happening all at once, but one fact was absolutely clear.

That wasn't Cade and Danel in the cockpit.

I stood in the middle of the cabin, staring at nothing. The buzzing faded a little but was still present.

I had only one card up my sleeve.

They were faster than me and stronger than me. They outnumbered me and were indestructible. My only ace: for some weird reason, I was the only human that could withstand their mind buzz. They were trying to cloud my memory, wipe my mind and make me think that everything was alright. But I still held my own thoughts, my own will. They told me to sit, so I stood.

My backpack was tossed into a corner. Who knows how many people had died that day, but my pack had made it intact. Singed, stained and stinking of dirty flame, it had survived. I pushed that thought away as I grabbed it.

The jet was still on the tarmac, but it was starting to roll.

I glanced at the closed door to the cockpit. I didn't need to advertise my defiance, so I sat on the couch as I fished through my pack. My cell phone was still there.

I flipped it open to call Cade, but stopped. Cade and Danel had phenomenal hearing; the two imposters in the cockpit probably had the same. I couldn't risk even a whispered conversation. My fingers trembled as I punched out a text message.

I'm on the jet w 2 watchers that look like u and Danel. RU ok?

My phone had a signal, but I didn't know if it could send text messages in China. I also didn't know where Cade's phone had been during the blasts and if it had survived. The shaking in my hands spread to my whole body as I waited for a response.

What jet? The response came back at last.

The knot in my chest passed like a giant kidney stone. They were alive. I hadn't wanted to think about it, but until that moment, I wasn't sure if even they could have survived those blasts. I took a deep breath as I texted back.

Our jet. We're on the tarmac. I don't know where we're going. They don't know that I know they're not u.

Don't let them know you can't be wiped. Play stupid. It's what they'll expect.

Something about that comment rankled. I typed back:

This is Danel, isn't it?

A pause, and then the message came back.

Can you smell me from through the phone?

I could read the smirk in his message and I actually smiled back, but then a bigger worry set in.

Where's Cade? Is he ok?

Right here. He's not good at texting.

That would be right. Even though my Cade could fly a plane and drive a race car, technology made him uncomfortable. I slid my fingers across the line of text as if by touching it, I was touching him.

We've found the flight plan. They're taking you to Egypt. Sam will want to see you. We are following. Play safe and stupid. We will catch up. They won't hurt you if they think you're under control.

"All set back there?" Dopple-Danel's voice came over the speaker. The accent and pitch were the same, but it wasn't Danel. It made my stomach ill, but part of me knew that my survival depended on my knowing the difference. I pressed the speaker button to call up to the cockpit.

"Just playing on my computer." My voice was brittle as I aimed for chipper. "How long before we get home?"

Hey, Danel had asked for stupid.

"It'll be a long flight. Twelve hours. Make yourself comfortable."

Comfortable. Right.

Shanghai Airport is shut down. We're heading to Beijing to pick up a flight there. Text if you need to reach us. We'll be about six hours behind you. If you can stall them safely, do it.

K

Part of me wanted to keep that message chain on my phone as an anchor during this trip, but I didn't dare. I purged the messages and closed the phone.

The jet rolled along the tarmac, picking up speed as it approached the runway. I hugged myself as it paused and then, with a roar of engines, we accelerated.

We were in the air and I was on my own.

Chapter Thirty Three

I sat in the lap of luxury, heading for a rendezvous with the lord of all demons and certain death.

My fingers ached from gripping the cell phone. I stared at it as the signal bars disappeared one by one. The lifeline was severed, but still I clutched it.

I aged twenty years in the next twelve hours.

For twelve hours I sat there, waiting for the impersonators to come out of the cockpit, worrying about what they would say. What I would say. What they would expect.

I shouldn't have worried. Apparently, the last thing the Dopple Demons wanted was to chat with me. The buzzing was persistent, so whatever they were trying to get me to think, it satisfied them so they didn't need to bother actually looking in on me. That reprieve should have helped, but instead I was a nervous wreck. By the time we landed, I was actually relieved. It gets to the point when facing the enemy for real is less terrifying than facing them in your imagination.

I don't know if I would have seen the pyramids as we landed. I was too busy watching for the reception bars on my cell phone to reappear. As soon as I got a signal, I pushed the send button on the message that I'd spent the last twelve hours composing.

Landing. U are probably still in the air. I wish I could talk to u now. They're buzzing me but did not talk to me the whole flight. Don't know if u should text me back. I'll text u when I can.

I watched for what seemed like forever as the little timer icon on the screen spun, taking its time sending it out. Finally the message sent. I read the message through one more time before I deleted it from the phone's memory. Then I went back to staring at the screen, hoping against hope for a response.

In vain. I waited until the plane was on the runway and we were taxiing to the gate before slipping the phone into my jacket pocket. I hoisted my backpack onto my shoulders and sat waiting. The buzzing intensified as the plane rolled to a stop. I pasted a vacant smile on my face as the door to the cockpit opened.

"Sleep well?" asked the far-too-perky Dopple-Danel. Dopple-Cade still wouldn't look at me.

I was exhausted but wired. I blinked and smiled. "Oh yes. Like a rock." I didn't know how far to go with the role of a brainwashed-ditz, but I figured a couple of obvious questions might be expected. "Are we back in the U.S. yet?"

The buzzing intensified and Dopple-Danel's brow wrinkled. "No, we've stopped in Egypt to refuel."

Evidently even obvious questions weren't expected. Good. It would be easier to just nod and smile like a bobble-head doll then to try to talk to them.

"Okay." I stood up and blankly faced them. This must be what they expected since the buzzing eased off a little.

"Would you like to go look at the pyramids while we're refueling?"

"Okay." How can I delay them when all I could do was keep saying "okay" and act like some drugged out zombie?

They didn't seem to care that I kept my backpack with me as we headed down the ramp and onto the tarmac. They walked beside me, hemming me in.

I used to enjoy walking down the rolling stairs and not having to mess with the crowding that regular plane passengers dealt with, but today I looked over at the distant people getting shuffled through their covered ramps and longed for the safety of numbers. If I was going to get away or even delay them, I needed a diversion.

The Dopple-Cade made no attempt to hide his disgust for me and it took a real effort for me not to react to that. Something about me really pushed his buttons and since I felt like I needed to do something, I decided to use it.

I grabbed his hand and draped his arm around my shoulder. The temperature of his body wasn't cold, but there was a chill that seeped into me like an ice shard. I suppressed a shudder as I pressed his hand against my cheek.

Dopple-Cade stopped in his tracks. The look on his face was of such revulsion, he barely looked like Cade any more. Dopple-Danel snickered as Dopple-Cade tried to pull away, but I held on as I looked up at him with goo-goo eyes.

"Caydee Waydee?" I was going way over the top on this one, but since they had no idea how Cade and I really spoke to each other, I figured I was safe. "I have to go wee wee."

"No you don't." Dopple-Cade said as he disengaged his arm. The buzzing increased as I moved to cling to his chest. I was hoping that the idea that I was immune their mind buzzing was so out there for them that they'd figure bodily functions couldn't be completely suppressed.

You could almost see Dopple-Cade's skin crawling. "Why didn't you go on the plane?"

"I don't know." I was playing the vapid moron about ten times bigger than I should have, but I wasn't used to faking stuff. "I didn't need to go then."

Dopple-Danel had an ugly grin on his face. "You can go in the terminal. Come on."

There was a separate reception terminal for the private jets. It was elegant, quiet and nearly empty. Dark haired men in crisp suits stepped forward to offer us fruit juice in tulip glasses and warm towels to wipe our hands and face. One tried to take my backpack for me, but I shrugged him off and made a bee-line for the ladies room. The Dopple-Demons made no objection, stopping right outside the door as they gave quiet orders to one of the concierges.

The ladies room was huge, opulent, empty, and windowless. I checked each stall. The ceiling vents were only about nine inches wide. I looked under the sinks for service doors or any other exit, but it was as secure a prison cell. I pulled my fingers through my hair as I fell back onto a sofa.

If I couldn't get away, I need to stall for six hours so that the real Cade and Danel could show up. I pulled out my phone and sent them a text: *In Cairo at airport. Dopple Demons taking me to the pyramids. Don't know how long I can stall.*

As I pushed the send button, I thought about all the other things I could have added, but as much as I needed to kill time, I couldn't waste any of it on soppy texts. I shoved the phone back into my jeans and gazed up at the ceiling. I couldn't think of any way that the light fixture could help me, but I was climbing up on the back of the couch to check out its wiring when the door opened.

A miasma of black fabric swarmed into the room. The door closed gently with a whisper behind them and they all stopped to stare up at me.

There were eight human figures, draped head to toe in black silk broken only by a strip of netting through which their eyes glinting faintly, unblinking.

I froze. I could see my reflection in the mirror and I looked both guilty and ridiculous at the same time. For a long tense minute, we just stared at each other and then, as if on some signal, the black figures twitched into action.

They pulled off their veils and robes, giggling and chattering in a foreign language as they filled the sitting area. What, a moment before, had appeared to be a coven of black hooded demons, now looked like a bevy of jean-clad, bling/grunge teenage girls with a sad predilection for *Hello Kitty.*

236

There were two older women there as well, one of whom raced past me into the adjoining room that had the stalls while the other pulled out a cosmetic case and began to inspect the makeup on her face with a clinical urgency.

Having nothing else to do, I decided to brave it out and continue to fiddle with the light fixture. One of the girls with a strong partiality to the color pink approached me.

She asked me a question. Probably *what are you doing?* I couldn't understand a word of it, but I answered anyway.

"Um, nothing."

This seemed to more than satisfy her. She turned to the others and nodded knowingly, "Ahhh! American!"

Like a switch, it appeared that was all the explanation they needed. The woman at the mirror flicked a glance at me for a microsecond before returning to the crisis of smeared mascara. The others relaxed and went back to chatting, but now they did it in English. It amazed me how many people around the world spoke fluent English.

The pink girl, now only mildly curious, looked up at the light fixture. "What are you doing?" she asked, this time in English.

What the hell. "Trying to escape."

I had their full attention again. Even the woman at the mirror paused in mid-eyeliner to focus on my reflection. The others gathered closer, staring up at the ceiling in curiosity.

"Through a light fixture?"

"I'm desperate."

They seemed to understand. They nodded in sympathy.

"Where are you from?" the Pink Girl asked, still watching my hands as they unscrewed the shade.

"The United States."

"Hollywood, California?"

"No. Wicassett, New Hampshire."

This seemed to baffle them more than escaping through a light fixture. There was a puzzled silence until the mascara woman said cryptically, "On Golden Pond."

This didn't seem to clarify things any further. As one, they turned to look at a small dark plump girl who pursed her lips in concentration.

"Jumanji!"she announced at last with a flash of triumph.

They all nodded, satisfied by this obscure announcement before turning back to watching me remove the light fixture.

"I didn't think American girls had to escape their family-men," The pink girl said, conversationally.

"Well, not normally," I said, twisting screws, "but this isn't a normal situation."

My fingers slipped and I grunted impatiently. I had bent back a fingernail, painfully. I sucked on it for a second before getting back to work. The girls seemed torn between sympathy for my predicament and horrified by the broken nail. Finally, the light fixture came free with a cascade of dust.

Not surprising, it was a dead end. I don't know what I'd been hoping for. Maybe a ventilation shaft that I could wiggle my way through. Or maybe a drop ceiling that led to another room that the Dopple Demons wouldn't be watching. But it was a no-go. The ceiling was a solid sheet of plaster with bare inches to the concrete floor above. I dropped to the couch, frustrated. The girls shrieked as they snatched their robes away from the cloud of dust settling around me. I sulked for a moment, staring at the girls as they shook the dirt off their robes.

And veils.

The pink girl met my eye as we both had the same thought.

Five minutes later, shrouded head to toe, I bustled out of the lady's room, hidden in a wave of black silk. I had to waddle low because the burqa we had "borrowed" was made for a woman about a foot shorter than me. The other girls had thought that this was a great joke to play on their aunt who was still on the toilet and was not very well-liked.

The buzzing was vague but insistent as we re-entered the airport terminal. The Dopples were lounging impatiently near a bar. They barely spared a glance at the four well-dressed men who stood up to escort us out of the terminal.

The girls stopped giggling, stifled by the buzzing, but as soon as we cleared the terminal, the buzzing faded and their humor returned. I paused as we were guided toward a line of black stretch limos lined up at the curb. Pinky hustled me toward the second to last one, pushing me into it. I climbed in quickly, not wanting to say a word that would betray me, but not sure if I wasn't stepping out of the frying pan and into the fire.

None of the men followed us into the car and dark curtains protected us from the eyes of the driver. There were two other girls beside Pinky and me, and as soon as the door closed, they peeled back their cowls and pulled off their veils. Their giggles quickly escalated into squeals. They found this entire adventure too funny for English and they babbled in Arabic as they straightened each other's hair.

I wished I could consider this all a big joke as well, but I turned in my seat to look out the back window. I bit the inside of my cheek to prevent myself from screaming with impatience. The rest of the party was taking forever to load up into the cars. Pinky turned to stare out the back window as well, curious as to what was making me so tense.

"Do not worry," she whispered, her head close to mine. "Even if your family men suspect that you are here, our guards would never permit them to enter this vehicle."

I forced a smile, but I wasn't comforted. It would take more than a heavily armed band of Arabian security to stop the Dopple Demons, but I couldn't tell Pinky that.

Barely two minutes later, but it seemed like two hours, the Dopples stormed out of the terminal, their eyes raking in all direction. A wave of buzzing, more intense than I'd felt before, washed through the limo, silencing the girls like a mute button. I froze. Despite the deeply tinted windows, I ducked my head down, only my eyes peeking over the back of the seat. The men packing the luggage into the trunks slowed their movements as if they were pushing through syrup.

In my panic, I thought that Dopple-Cade's eyes had locked on to mine, seeing me through the blackened glass, but after a millisecond, his gaze passed on. Then, with no visible acknowledgement to each other, the Dopples split up, blurring to streaks as they raced in opposite directions. The buzzing faded and the people on the sidewalk resumed normal movement. Inside the limo, the girls picked up in mid-syllable, unaware of the time warp they'd just endured.

Pinky too, continued chatting to me, oblivious, even though we'd both been looking directly at the doors when the buzzing had started. I forced myself to exhale, but I couldn't relax.

Finally, the cars began to pull forward, moving at what seemed like the pace of a baby crawling. Stopped at a light near the airport exit, I saw Dopple-Danel glaring in all directions, both livid and panicked at the same time. Then with a blur the Dopple-Cade stood beside Dopple-Danel as if appearing from nowhere. How could no one see that? They conferred for a brief furious moment before they both disappeared in a streak. I looked at the pedestrians around them, but if anyone had noticed anything, they didn't show it.

"We are we going?" I asked Pinky as I pulled out my cell phone and started to text Cade.

"Oh, I don't know." Pinky was not impressed with my phone. She sniffed as she pulled out her phone. It was the same kind, but hers was two generations better and covered with enough pink rhinestones to double its weight. "Just some ancient historic stuff. It's supposed to be educational."

The small dark plump girl, who had been watching us gravely the whole time, gave an annoyed groan. "It is the Valley of the Kings! Some of the oldest man-made monuments in the world! The Pyramids! The Sphinx!"

"Whatever." Pinky said, sounding more like a L.A. brat than a Saudi Princess. "They will drag us all over the place and it will be boring."

"Not so boring now!" cried a girl with Cleopatra eyeliner. "We left Suma at the airport! There will be no one to lecture us!"

Cheers filled the car. Even the small dark plump girl smiled. I found myself grinning as well as I punched in a message into my phone. I supposed there must be worse ways to kill six hours.

Ditched the Dopple Demons. Heading for the Sphinx with a posse of Persian Princesses. Will try to keep a low profile until you get here.

Chapter Thirty Four

Blame it on bad jeans.

I tried to crouch down as I got out of the limo, but my stupid long legs stuck out from under the burqas and one of the princesses' brothers noticed it. It wasn't that the other girls weren't wearing jeans, it was just that their jeans weren't ripped, charred and bloodstained from the Shanghai Airport Massacre.

What followed was a scene about forty times more melodramatic than any reality show could manufacture. I have to hand it to Pinky. If being shrouded head to toe hindered her even one decibel, unshrouded, she could be a military-grade assault weapon.

And yet, despite Pinky's fury, the end result was the same. I was left standing burqa-less on the sidewalk in front of the Sphinx while Pinky and the Princesses were hustled back into the limo and back to the airport to pick up their stranded aunt. The last I saw of Pinky was a bangled, rosy-nailed hand waving out a crack in the window.

I waved back weakly as I watched them pull away. I felt a whole lot more forlorn than I should have, considering I'd only known them for less than an hour. I took a deep breath and looked around me.

There were so many western tourists here at the Sphinx, I didn't look as much out of place as I would have elsewhere in Cairo, but my clothes were still tattered and stained. I had tried to clean up as best as I could on the plane, but my luggage was somewhere amidst the ruins of Shanghai Airport and there's only so much you can do with linen hand towels.

The sun was just setting and the sky was going pink and purple with dusk. The night air was cooling quickly, but the desert sands were still hot and the heat pounded against the chill, pressing odd breezes and eddies through the crowd.

Despite the looming darkness, the crowds seem to be growing larger, shoving and pushing as they hurried toward the huge statue, crouching in the sand.

Really? I thought irritably, as I was bumped for the fourth time. It's been lying there for tens of centuries, are they worried it's finally going to stand up and walk away now?

I stopped at the thought. With all the recent weirdness, I shouldn't joke, even to myself, about that kind of stuff.

The sweet smell of something pizza-scented flew past my nose and I closed my eyes and inhaled deeply, my stomach rumbling in response. Yes. Whatever it was, it smelled just like pizza and I had to admit, I was famished. I tried to remember when the last time I ate. Other than some stale cheetos that I'd found on the plane, it had been more than a day since I'd really eaten.

I was about to start following my nose to the pizza-smell, when I sensed something else. A familiar ominous buzzing, distant but building.

The Fallen were nearby and getting closer.

My appetite disappeared as dread clenched my my stomach. Tensing, I looked around but couldn't see anything familiar. Then I realized, if the Dopples weren't looking like Danel and Cade, I had no idea what to look for. They could be among any of the thousands of tourists and peddlers that pushed and ebbed around me. A boy, no more than eight or nine, caught my eye. He was staring at more intently then a stranger should. My mouth went dry as a sly smile cracked his face and he approached.

"Hey pretty lady! You buy statue?" A crudely hewn figurine of a sitting cat, carved from green stone was shoved near my face. "Real jade! Bargain! For you, only twenty dollars U.S.! Because you pretty lady! What you say? Real jade! Such a bargain!"

I forced myself to breathe, backing away from the urchin. "No thank you. I don't need a statue."

The boy was persistent, and as I turned and headed down the street, he followed, spewing out a convoluted speech about how his father would beat him or selling such a precious relic for such a sum, but that I was so pretty that he wanted me to have it. My saving grace was that I could move much faster than he and as I pulled away, the price fell dramatically. The last I heard, I could have had the precious relic for "five dollars, U.S., final offer!"

I headed up a street that ran parallel to the Sphinx. In the distance, I could see the Pyramids, lit with colored lights. The street swarmed with people who clamored up the banks, sitting themselves on blankets and folding chairs, positioning themselves to look at the Sphinx. I pushed through the crowd, no time for curiousity, but as the boy fell back, I forced myself to drop to a walk and tried to blend in with the turmoil.

A tour bus pushed its way slowly through the crowd before rolling to a stop almost next to me. A group of Americans poured out and a woman, dressed in a tailored orange business suit and carrying a frilly violet umbrella, promptly began shepherding them together. She led them back down the street, bellowing out cheerful commands as she held the parasol high above her head like a beacon.

The buzzing started again. I jerked my head back and forth, trying to pinpoint the source in the crowd, but I couldn't seem to get a bead on it. On impulse, I joined the flock of tourists as they passed.

Most of the sightseers looked like they were retirees, but I noticed at least one girl about my age so I hoped I didn't look as out of place as I felt. A couple of the tourists noticed me and gave disapproving sniffs, but their escort was too focused on guiding them through the mob for them to tattle on me, so I worked my way to the center of the pack, hunching down as I scoped out the crowds.

The buzzing was vague but insistent. I was so intent on my surveillance, I didn't notice that the young girl from the tour group was walking beside me until she spoke.

"Hi!" She smiled up at me, breathless from trying to match my stride. "Are you from the U.S.?"

She was a short, bone thin girl that looked to be around fourteen or fifteen. She had cropped blond hair and huge blue eyes, too big for her face. Her goofy smile reminded me of Kat, only prettier.

"Uh-huh." I nodded, maybe a little too brusquely. I tried to soften my expression, but I think it came out as a distracted grimace. She didn't seem to notice.

"Me too!" she bubbled. "I'm from California. Where are you from?"

"New Hampshire."

"Are you travelling with your parents?" She asked, but then didn't wait for an answer. "My mother is doing this world tour thing and she's been dragging me to all the most stupid places. I am so bored that I could eat meat."

"Eat meat?"

"Yeah, I'm vegan. Are you vegan?" I shook my head, no and she kept talking. "You really should, you know. Eating animals is so disgusting. So, are you here with your family?"

"Um, no." I didn't know how much to say. "I'm travelling with friends."

"Really? I thought you were my age. Are you on a school trip?"

"No, just with friends." I felt the need to get control of the conversation. "How old are you?"

"I'm sixteen." She rolled her eyes. "I know, I know. Everyone thinks I'm younger, but that just because I'm so short. I'm Estelle."

"I'm Misty."

"How old are you?" she asked with friendly intensity of a puppy dog.

"Seventeen," I meant to lie, as if it didn't sound as weird for a seventeen year old American girl to be wandering on her own around Cairo. But then I realized that it might not be a lie. It had been more than three months since I'd left Wicasset and my seventeenth birthday must be soon. I didn't even know what day it was. I pulled out my cell phone and, for the first time, noticed that it was December 20th.

My birthday was tomorrow. I was lost in Egypt, being hunted by homicidal demons and I was going to be seventeen years old tomorrow.

Assuming I was still alive.

"Have you graduated?" Estelle rambled on, oblivious to my mood. "My mother tells everyone she's home-schooling me, but then she just hires a tutor to come along. Sometimes he's a hottie, but this trip, I got stuck with some old lady. You want to go out for a hamburger? I found a BK only two blocks away and their stuff is almost as good as back home."

"I thought you were vegan?"

"This is a special occasion."

I didn't understand that at all.

My stomach rumbled loudly, undermining my first impulse, which was to stay with the group, hiding in plain sight, but then I figured that a Burger King in Cairo might be just as good, or just as stupid a place to wait as anywhere else.

The tour guide was directing her group to climb up a set of bleachers where they could get a clear view of the Sphinx and the Pyramids. Dusk was deepening to a gloomy darkness, but the ancient monuments were glowing with fluorescent

246

colors. From dozens of speakers hidden around the plaza, a tinny soundtrack resonated with a turgid majesty.

No one seemed to notice Estelle as she slipped away from her group. She grinned at me gaily, beckoning me to follow her. We made our way upstream, against the flow of tourists rushing to see the light show.

Steps away from the Sphinx, a small strip mall faced the plaza. We passed a Kentucky Fried Chicken and a Pizza Hut, packed with people hoping to experience the penultimate Egyptian cultural event: eating American fast food while watching modern technology desecrate one of the Seven Wonders of the Ancient World.

I wanted to stay and watch, but Estelle led me around the corner.

We stepped into another world. I could still faintly hear the soundtrack to the lightshow, but ten paces back, it had been all buses and tourists. Here it was honking cars and locals walking quickly, many dressed in traditional robes, some even with turbans. The streets were three lanes in each direction, but the drivers ignored the lines and straddled the lanes. Sedans and small trucks formed a quagmire of vehicles, weaving in and out like worms, all lightly beeping their horns with a near constant pulse. I stopped for a moment to stare, but Estelle grabbed my arm and pulled me along.

Up ahead, I could see the familiar Burger King logo jutting out from a building, the scrolling Arabic lettering beneath the familiar western alphabet. My stomach dragged me forward more than Estelle did and within moments, we were inside.

"I'll have two triple whoppers and a mega size Dr. Pepper." She turned to me. "What do you want?"

I slapped my pockets on my jeans, knowing even as I did it that I had no money in them. I swung my backpack around and burrowed through it, fishing out a couple of bills and some change from the bottom, all that was left of the money that my father had given me, months ago. Dismayed, I look down at the money and then up at the menu board, which was in Egyptian Pounds.

Estelle laughed. "Don't sweat it! I've got this one."

I smiled gratefully. "Thanks, Estelle. You rock." Turning back to the clerk, I ordered two chicken sandwiches, fries and a root beer.

As we stepped aside to wait for our order, I scanned the crowd carefully to see if anyone was watching us. A group of dark haired boys, about our age and crammed together in a booth, were trying to catch our attention. They made kissy faces at us and giggled like baboons. Estelle rolled her eyes in disgust and turned her back on them. She looked at me thoughtfully and, thinking that she was about to start asking questions that I wasn't sure how I could answer, I beat her to the punch .

"So, what do your parents do that has them travelling so much?" I asked, scoping the crowd while ignoring the boys, who were getting louder.

"Mom was a porn actress," Estelle said cheerfully. "She married 'the rich old goat,' as she called him, and made him very happy for about a year and a half before he popped off. Now she's stupid rich. Cool huh?"

I didn't know what to say to this so I was glad that our order came up. We grabbed our food and then took a table as far from the ogling boys as we could. Before I started eating, I took the moment to pull out my phone and texted Cade.

Got ditched by the princesses. Met a girl from the US. Hanging with her til you get here. Call me.

"Who you texting?" Estelle asked between bites.

"Friends." I answered vaguely. I felt bad. Estelle was so open with me, and here I was, hedging. "I'm, um, hoping they can help me get a plane ticket home."

"Well, if they choke on you, maybe I can help."

"Really?" My sandwich hung in front of my face, waiting. I still had my passport. If I could get back to the airport and get an airline ticket... "I'd pay you back as soon as I got home."

"Whatever," Estelle chirped merrily, brushing this off. "So where are your friends that you're traveling with? Any cuties? Or at least, any guys under thirty? I am SO tired of the geriatric lechers on that tour bus."

I looked at Estelle, her cute little head cocked to one side, waiting for my answer. I needed to tell her something, not the truth, at least, not all of it. But maybe enough of it to get her to help me.

"I'm in trouble, Estelle." I leaned toward her, whispering. "Big trouble. I've been separated from my friends and I'm being followed by some… creeps."

Estelle's eyes got even bigger. "Cops?" she asked hopefully.

"No," I answered. "Worse than cops. Really bad dudes. I need a place to hide for tonight, or at least five or so more hours, until my friends can catch up with me."

A look of glee lit up her face, making her freakishly large eyes look even bigger. "I know the most perfect place to hide! No one knows about it. It is uber-uber-awesome!"

We'd only finished one of our sandwiches, so she grabbed her drink and the rest of our meal and stood up.

"C'mon! I'll show you!" she said, heading for the exit. "You'll freak! It's brilliant!"

Dusk had darkened into night when we stepped out onto the street. We headed back toward the Plaza of the Sphinx and I stopped for a moment, mesmerized by the change. The music throbbed from all sides and the Sphinx was bathed with a fuchsia blush while the pyramids in the distance behind glowed blue. As I stood watching, the lights changed, pulsing with the music.

"I know, garish isn't it?" Estelle was far too young to be so jaded.

She pulled me through the crowds of late arrivals who jockeyed for a spot to watch. We pushed our way against the flow of the mob as Estelle led me to a road that ran alongside the Sphinx.

Tourists filled the road too. They climbed up the embankments, scrambling for a viewing spot. With the Sphinx on our left, we kept to the right side of the road, but even with the obstruction of a hundred heads, I could still see it. I didn't want to seem like some lame gawker, but I really hoped that, from wherever Estelle's hideout was, we'd be able to see the lightshow.

As we headed up the street, I saw small niches that had been cut out of the embankment. From the hieroglyphics carved into the lintels, I figured they were really old. Maybe they were small tombs for second-best royalty or nobility, but with the Sphinx and the pyramids, no one seemed to pay these little nooks any attention. They had the feeblest little gates blocking the public's access so I wasn't surprised when, with a sharp poke, Estelle was able to push one of them open. It creaked wide, but not one of the hundreds of people on the street noticed. We stepped into the shadows and Estelle closed the gate behind us.

There was a painted steel door in the back of the grotto. Estelle grabbed the handle and rattled it back and forth. The door opened with an angry squeal. I looked around anxiously, but even though, a dozen yards away, people were walking by us on the street, no one looked our way.

My guess that it was an ancient burial chamber was probably correct. The room was about six feet wide and eight feet deep. The ceiling was not much more than five feet high; I had to stoop, but little Estelle waltzed right in. There wasn't a sarcophagus or anything like that; it had probably been taken long ago by grave robbers or archeologists. Carved hieroglyphs on the wall were disfigured and heaps of trash, beer cans and cigarette butts littered the floor and created dunes in the corners. The place stank of urine and stale tobacco.

Given the choice between spending the night in a five star hotel or in a trashed crypt by a busy street, you can probably guess which one I would have chosen, but beggars can't be choosy. I gave a little sigh of disgust and kicked at the trash, trying to clear away a place to sit.

"How do you know about this place, anyway?" I asked, trying to keep the disappointment out of my voice.

"Fajid. He's the son of the chief archeologist. Last time we visited Cairo, he brought me here."

"Last time?" I asked. "You've been to Egypt before?"

"Yeah, this my third trip." Estelle rolled her eyes. "My mom's psychic told her that she's channeling Cleopatra's spirit, so she keeps coming back and dragging me along." Then Estelle broke out into a mischievous smile, "but this is not what I wanted to show you."

"Oh, you mean it gets better than this?" Insert sarcasm here.

Estelle just giggled. She stood at the back of the crypt, her hands running over a vertical crack that ran from the floor to the ceiling. It looked like a solid stone wall, but when she stuck her fingers into the crack and tugged, the back wall moved. I was so surprised, I just stood there for a moment and watched her grunt and pull, but when I finally came over to help her, I was amazed at how easily the wall moved. It looked like solid stone, but it must have been counterweighted because it moved with only a little resistance.

We shifted the wall only about a foot and a half, but that was more than enough for Estelle and me to slip through.

It was black as death in the inner room, only the faintest glow from the street bled through. I fished through my pockets and pulled out my cell phone, flicking it on. The faint light from the screen did little to light up the room. I couldn't make out the walls, but I could see Estelle, feeling around on the ground off to my right. I crouched down next to her, shining the feeble light on whatever it was she was doing.

With a flare of a lighter, a kerosene lantern flickered to life. Estelle handed it to me and then turned to close the sliding panel. I was so amazed at what the light revealed, I completely forgot to help Estelle with the door. I raised the lantern high.

The room was a cube, twenty feet wide by twenty feet deep with the ceiling about twenty feet high. The walls were carved with murals and hieroglyphics, colored brightly, looking freshly painted and gleaming with gold leaf. In the center was an ornate marble sarcophagus on a large stone dais. Estelle set the Burger King bags on the slab and then nimbly vaulted up beside them. She sat like a smug elf, quite proud of herself, as if she had personally created all of this splendor.

"Estelle!" I was breathless. "This is… amazing!"

"Yeah, I know! The archeologists only found this about a year or so ago. They haven't announced it to the public yet, they're still cataloguing everything first. After we done eating, I'll show you the rest of it."

She was already devouring her sandwich, her legs crossed beneath her. It felt sacrilegious to be eating on the dais, but I supposed just being there was some kind of descration, so I pulled myself up beside her.

"Rest of what?" I asked.

Her mouth full, she gestured to a corner where the lantern's light didn't reach. I realized that it was because it was the opening to a passage. A faint breeze flowed from it.

"Cool!" I slid down from the dais. "Let's check it out!"

"Eat first," she said between mouthfuls. "Tell me about your friends."

I hopped back up onto the slab, absently picking up my sandwich. As I took a bite, I felt my mouth soften into a foolish smile. I stared at the flickering shadows on the wall and thought about Cade and Danel.

"There are two of them." I started softly. "Cade... Cade has the most wonderful smile. He laughs so easy and when he does, it seems like the entire world has to turn and find and out what so funny. He is the sweetest, most gentle person I've ever met. When I'm with him, it feels like the entire universe is in balance." I hugged the memory into myself, but then shifted my weight as my thoughts changed direction. "Now Danel is a completely different story. They're both very strong, and really good looking, but Danel is a lot more decisive. He's always got 'The Plan.' I don't always agree with 'The Plan,' but he's always got one. And while he hardly ever laughs, I always feel like he's laughing at me. Not in a mean way, but sometimes he makes me feel like I'm a dumb little kid." Memory of that stolen kiss came back and hijacked my brain. I shook it off. "But not like a kid sister. No, definitely not like a kid sister."

I turned to look at Estelle, who was staring at me, so intrigued that she had actually stopped eating. "Can I meet them when they get here? It sounds like you've got dibs on Cade. Can I call dibs on Danel?"

I smiled, thinking how Danel would handle being pursued by the indomitable Estelle. He'd hate it.

"Deal." I said not bothering to hide a grin. I pulled out my cell phone. I doubted that Danel and Cade were in Cairo yet, but I should text them and let them know where I was hiding. "There's no signal in here. I need to go out to the street for a second. I need to send a text message."

I slid off the dais and headed over to the sealed entryway, but then froze. A familiar buzz started tickling my head. I backed away from the door as if it was going to fly open any minute. "Oh, crap." My voice was a hoarse whisper. "They're here."

The buzzing stopped. Estelle dropped down off the dais and came to stand beside me, staring from the entryway to my face and back again. "Who are here? Where?"

"The Dopplegangers. I can feel them. They're nearby."

"What Dopplegangers? The creeps that you're hiding from? You think they're out there? How can you tell?"

I moved to the far side of the crypt, keeping the dais between me and the entrance. "I know it sounds mental, Estelle, but I can tell. Really."

The buzzing started again, so strong this time, I was absolutely certain that the Dopplegangers were on the other side of the closed slab. A breeze hit my face. The passageway that led deeper into the complex was my only hope. I grabbed the lantern with one hand and Estelle with the other and headed down it.

Chapter Thirty Five

"Misty! Hold on!" Estelle pulled back, dragging me to a stop. "Do you even know where you're going?"

It didn't matter, so long as it was away from that entrance. The buzzing had stopped but I wasn't relaxing. By my calculations, it would be another two or three hours at least before Danel and Cade landed. I turned on Estelle, frantic.

"Is there another exit out of here?" I clutched my signal-less phone like it was a loaded gun.

Estelle nodded, took the lantern out of my hand and led me wordlessly down the passage. The light only reached about ten feet, and beyond that, the tunnel was black. The ceiling was uncomfortably low, a little more than six feet high. I could walk straight, but it still felt claustrophobic. We could just barely walk side by side as the passage led downward. If I wasn't so panicked, I'd have been studying the glyphs and murals on the walls and ceiling. It was amazing how fresh and bright the colors were. A lifesize row of painted figures, each different, marched on either side of us, carrying gifts to some destination. I slowed as one caught my eye. I thought it looked a little like Danel. I remembered back to the first day of school when he said he was from Egypt. I would have stopped to look closer, but Estelle was moving and so was the light.

"Estelle, we're still heading down. I need to get back to the surface. I need to use my phone."

"Don't worry. We'll get to the Throne Chamber in a few minutes. Then we can take one of the other tunnels back up and out."

"Throne Chamber?"

"You'll see!"

We didn't speak for the next few minutes. I strained to sense any trace of the buzzing and began to relax when it didn't reoccur.

With the lantern shining around us, we were less than a hundred feet away before I noticed the glow coming from the end of the tunnel. I hesitated, hanging back.

"Estelle! Wait!" I hissed. "There are lights ahead." I stood still, trying to separate the swish of Estelle walking from the murmurs I thought I heard coming from up ahead.

"C'mon," Estelle turned to me. "It's just the Throne Chamber."

"Yeah, but I think there are people in there."

"It's alright. Come on." Estelle kept walking and disappeared into the chamber, taking the lantern with her.

The passage went dark. The only light came from the Throne Chamber. It sparkled with gold and jewel tones. I had a bad feeling about this. I toyed with the idea of heading back up the passage alone in the dark, but it was in the entry chamber where I'd felt the buzzing the most. There wasn't any buzzing coming from up ahead, so I swallowed my qualms and followed Estelle.

I stopped a couple of yards short of the opening, hoping that the shadows would mask my presence long enough to give me a moment to absorb everything I saw.

The Chamber was huge, maybe half the size of a football field. The ceiling was five stories high, supported by a forest of huge stone pillars, carved, painted and inlaid with gold, jewels and colored marble. The capitals at the top fluted out like glittering palm trees. In the center was a golden throne, its back so high that the seat seemed low and squat in comparison.

Sprawled on the throne was a man, his legs extended in front of him. He wore Arabian-style robes like I'd seen in the airport, but his were made of gold cloth, embroidered with silver and emblazoned with jewels. His hair was jet black and his skin was pale. Even though his face was handsome and chiseled, like an old time movie star, it was marred by a bored pout. He looked like a sulky male model.

It wasn't hard to see why he looked so jaded. On the ground at his feet were a dozen nearly naked women and a couple of boys of every race and body type. They were draped with swathes of pastel fabric that didn't even try to cover them. They grovelled and caressed his legs with a suppressed air of desperation, as if their very lives depended on pleasing the sulky man. From where I stood, I could see marble divans, positioned here and there with more lounging bodies. The loungers were all looking toward the sulky man. As I watched, some of the loungers detached themselves from their fawners and walked toward the throne.

I took this all in within a heartbeat. And that was long enough. I didn't care if the Dopplegangers were behind me, I wasn't sure what I was seeing, but there was no way I was going any further. I turned and ran back into the pitch black passageway.

I didn't get very far. A hand reached out and grabbed me by the back of my neck. I hadn't heard or seen anyone in the passage, but obviously someone was there. I was lifted off my feet and carried like a puppy back into the throne room.

It was a long walk to the throne. I tried thrashing myself free, but the rock hard grip on my neck tightened painfully, forcing me to hang like a wet rag. My eyes darted about as I tried to figure a plan.

I had heard only faint murmurs from the chamber when I was in the passage, but as soon as I was carried in, all sound stopped. There seemed to be two kinds of people in the room, the pitiful ones, boys and women who watched my entrance warily. Their averted eyes hid desperation and a slow depletion of the soul. Some were younger than me, but I felt that, in some way, all of them were old, sucked dry and done with life.

And then there were the strong ones. The ones that had risen and now stood in flanks as I was borne through the chamber. There were about two dozen of them, most were male, but there were a few females as well. They were all races and they all looked young and beautiful. I suppose if you can choose whatever body you want, you'd probably choose a perfect one, and they were all perfect.

At some signal that I didn't see or hear, all the fawners at the foot of the throne retreated, peeling away like fog in sunlight. I couldn't turn my head to see who was carrying me. He made no sound as he dropped me unceremoniously.

The man on the throne had straightened. He stared at me with ice green eyes but did not speak. A movement from behind the throne and Estelle skipped out.

"As you command, my lord, it has been done." She preened a moment before shooting me a grin that was tinged with regret, as if this was some harmless sorority prank.

My lord?

From the moment I had seen him from the passage, I had suspected the truth and now the sinking feeling in my gut had told me what I couldn't deny anymore. I had walked blithely and stupidly into the throne room of Sam Jaza, the Lord of the Fallen.

I shot Estelle a pissy glare, but I was angrier at myself for being such a moron to be so trusting of such a convenient stranger. I didn't speak. I didn't think anything I could say would possibly make this situation better. I figured my best chance was to delay the inevitable by making them do all the work. How many hours before Danel and Cade landed?

Could I stall that long? Even if I did, what could Danel and Cade do to stop Sam Jaza and his minions?

"This is it? The temptress that has lured two of my minions from my grace?" Sam Jaza's voice had a soft musical lilt to it, but I felt corruption and the lust for violence beneath the dulcet tones. He deigned to stand. "I had expected so much more."

I pulled myself to my feet. I didn't like being in a heap on the ground like one of his fawners. As I stood, I realized that even though I'd left my backpack up in the entry chamber, I still clutched my cell phone. I couldn't think what good it might do me, but I shoved it into my pocket and met Sam Jaza's stare.

I needed to come up with a plan to convince Sam Jaza to spare me, or at least to stall until Cade and Danel caught up. I had no idea what they could do against Sam Jaza and his minions, but I wasn't ready to give up and die that easy.

Would groveling work? I thought about that as I brushed the dust off my jeans. Faced with certain death, I could abandon all self-respect in a heartbeat and grovel as good as anyone, but when I looked in Sam Jaza's eyes, I saw my own death. He might toy with me for a while out of boredom, but he wanted me dead and I didn't think there was much I could do about it. So groveling: out.

"What a very boring little scrub you are." Sam Jaza scrutinized me with an intensity which completely contradicted his words. "Practically a nothing. Est, are you sure you've got the right human?"

Estelle didn't look put out by this question. She just shrugged and smirked. "She's the right one. I've been tracking them since Australia. Cade and Danel have been guarding her like she's a crystal grail."

At the term "crystal grail," Sam shot a look at Estelle with narrowed eyes. Estelle just beamed back, unfazed.

"What's your name, human?" Sam snapped at me.

"Franchesca Laticia Krutachia Esmeralda St. Colombard." I cracked. Maybe mouthing off wasn't very smart at the moment, but stalling was all I could think of at the moment. "You can call me Frankie."

A wave of heat and buzzing hit me like falling piano. I staggered for a moment, but caught my balance before I fell. This was a barrage twenty times stronger than Danel or the Dopplegangers ever hit me with.

Fake it. In my imagination, I heard Danel's voice whispering in my head. I knew he wasn't there, but I clung to the illusion. I let my eyes glaze over and my face go slack.

"Now, human. I will ask again." Sam Jaza crept up to me, stopping inches from my ear. I fought the instinct to cringe. "What is your name?"

"Misty Hill." I answered in a monotone. I hoped I wasn't overdoing it. "Melissa Elizabeth Hill, but everyone calls me Misty."

"She's lying." Estelle sounded like a ten year old tattletale snitching to the teacher. "She resists Persuasion."

I kept my face slack as Sam Jaza leaned in closer. His breath was hot on my neck. The buzzing was like the bass at a rock concert.

"Don't be ridiculous," he snapped.

I felt the breeze swirl my hair as he spun away from me, throwing himself back into his throne like a toddler taking a tantrum.

"No one can withstand Persuasion. What are you talking about?" Sam scowled at Estelle.

Estelle didn't speak. She smiled, keeping her eyes on my face as she pulled something out of her jeans pocket. A small blue folder embossed with gold. A flare of anger made its way past my fear and pain. It was a U.S. passport and I guessed it mine.

Sam snatched it from her fingers and snapped it open, his eyes narrowing with fury as he read it.

Mystery?" His voice was a deadly hiss. "Mystery Hill?"

The buzzing roared in my ears.

"My real name is Melissa." I said monotone, my eyes glazed. "They made a mistake on my passport and mixed up my birthplace with my name."

I thought that was a pretty good off-the-cuff lie and I bet he might have bought it if Estelle hadn't pulled something else from her pocket. It was thin, about eight inches long, silver and bejeweled. It cut a deep slash into my thigh before I realized that it was a dagger.

I screamed, clutched my leg and crumbled to the floor. Sam Jaza looked honestly appalled and for a fraction of a moment, I thought he was pissed at Estelle's attack on me.

"If she had been fully controlled, she wouldn't have felt that." Estelle smiled at me as if she said this for my benefit.

Sam Jaza didn't need that explanation. With a wordless roar of fury, he leapt up from his throne, grabbed me by the throat, shook me like a rag doll and then threw me thirty feet across the hall. I landed hard, sliding another twenty feet on the marble floor before slamming into one of the mammoth pillars. My blood smeared a trail behind me. I was beginning to feel light headed and I curled into a ball. Fear and adrenalin kept the pain at a dull throb and I ignored it as I instinctively pressing my thumb deep into my thigh, trying to stop the bleeding.

Sam Jaza roared like an angry lion as he paced around his throne. Everyone stared at him, for the moment ignoring me, but I could only wish I could try to escape. I would need something to use as a tourniquet but the only thing I could think of was my jacket and I would have to release the hold on my thigh in order to get it off.

"XERXI! YANI!" The walls throbbed as Sam Jaza bellowed these words. It sounded like he was calling someone and a moment later, two figures appeared from one of the far passages.

My breath caught as the silhouette of two figures appeared at the entrance of one of the tunnels leading out of the throne room and, for a moment, I thought it was Danel and Cade, but as they stepped into the light, I saw that, despite dressing like Danel and Cade, they looked nothing like them. They both had milky brown skin, lighter than African skin, like they were from India. The one that was dressed like Danel in tight black jeans and tee shirt with a leather bomber jacket had short thin black hair that was plastered tight against his head while the one dressed like Cade in flannel and denim had dark brown wavy hair. I guessed that these were Dopple Danel and Dopple Cade in their preferred bodies.

"Yes, my lord?" The denim demon groveled anxiously like some adolescent toady while the leather demon just slouched and leered at the more buxom women huddled in the corners.

"Xerxi!" Sam Jaza's question, directed at the leather demon, was more like an accusation. "Did you know that the human can resist Persuasion?"

This jarred Xerxi from his leering. "Nonsense!" he said abruptly, then, almost as an afterthought, "my lord."

"She has been submissive and under control since we picked her up in Shanghai," Yani, the denim demon, whined anxiously.

"And yet she escaped? She's been deceiving you!" Sam Jaza roared. "A human! Deceiving the pair of you! She resists Persuasion. She is named Mystery. And Danel and Cade have known this and have hidden her from me. Such treachery shall not go unpunished!"

"They didn't know!" I barely rasped the words. I couldn't save myself, but perhaps I could spare Caden and Danel from Sam Jaza's wrath. "I fooled them as well."

Sam Jaza stopped, mid-stride and spun toward me. I blinked and he was above me, grabbing me by my hair, lifting me from the ground until my face met his. The skin on his face was baby smooth and his scent was strong, like Eastern incense. The buzzing was so loud, I barely heard his exclamation of disgust.

"Bah!" He said at last tossing me aside like a used tissue. "It matters not. Find them! Bring them!"

My grip on my thigh had slipped when he had dropped and my fingers groped to fnd the artery before I lost consciousness. Xerxi stepped close to me, learing down.

"We shall be only too happy to assist you, my lord, but perhaps first, we should eliminate the human." Xerxi said with a smirk. "Then, Yani and I will track down Danel and Cade and return them for your justice."

Sam Jaza's fury began to ebb. He slumped back onto his throne and glared sulkily at the two demons. "Why do you still wear their clothes? To what end?"

With that, Xerxi morphed back into Dopple Danel. "With your permission, my lord, we wish a little time with the human before it is terminated. And we want to do it with these bodies. It will add so much to our conversation when we catch up with Danel and Cade."

"You want some time with her," Yani whined. "I just want her dead. And if you think I'm going to watch you while…"

Dopple Danel patted Yani's cheek playfully. "Oh, come on, Yani. You need to broaden your horizons a little. When was the last time you had a little fun with a human female?"

Yani slapped Dopple Danel's hand away angrily and glared at me as if this were my fault.

Sam Jaza turned to me, venom glinting in his smile. "Fine. Take her. You have a half hour. But don't kill her. If she can't be Persuaded, then perhaps, when she's been broken, she'll be a little more forthcoming." Sam Jaza smiled at me with anticipation. "One way or another we shall crack this little Mystery, eh?"

"A half an hour should be more than enough time." Dopple Danel said as he looked at me, his face hardening. "More than enough time."

Chapter Thirty Six

I tried to scramble away as Dopple Danel reached down for me, but when I took my hand from my thigh, blood surged out and my vision blurred. He frowned down at my leg as he pulled off his belt.

"Oh, no," he said quietly. "You don't get to die that quickly."

He knelt down to wrap the belt around my leg above the slash, and as he grabbed me, I picked up a familiar aroma. The warm scent of pine and leather. I looked at his face, shock making my features slack.

It wasn't Dopple Danel. It was Danel. Danel pretending to be Xerxi pretending to be Danel. I looked over at Yani who stood staring down at me, his face stone hard. I took a deep breath and tasted the sweet tang of the ocean. Yani was Cade. The real Cade. And Danel was Danel. Relief made my head spin even more.

"If you speak one word," Danel whispered harshly, "I will throttle you. Do you understand?"

I nodded. I understood. I pressed my lips together tightly as the belt tightened around my leg painfully, but I didn't make a sound. Danel pulled me roughly to my feet. I swayed and started to sink again, but he just grabbed me by the waist and tucked me under his arm.

"I'm not going to watch." Cade whined like Yani as the three of us moved out of the hall, back up the passage that led to the antechamber. "And if you think I'm going to join in, you're out of your mind. I don't even want to touch her unless it's to kill her."

We were in the passage and Cade's final words echoed back into the hall. I heard a distant snort of mirth from Sam Jaza and then the light and sounds from the hall faded.

It was pitch black in the passage but Danel and Cade didn't need light to find their way. Air whipped my face as we sped through the tunnel and in seconds we stood in the same antechamber that Estelle and I had entered earlier.

The entryway panel was drawn back, letting the faint light of the evening spill in. It was dim, but after the blind dark of the passage, it was enough. Danel set me down next to the dais. My hand reached out to lean against the sarcophagus, steadying me as I kept my weight off my wounded leg. But only for a moment. At some point in the darkness, Yani had turned back into Cade and now Cade's arms wrapped around me, lifting me up. I leaned into his chest, ignoring both my throbbing leg and my light-headedness. The energy that surged from his touch healed my heart and at that moment all I wanted to do was to melt into him and disappear.

"It's okay, Misty." Cade whispered into my hair. "We've got a plan."

I would have asked him about the plan, but evidently, there wasn't time. Danel pried us apart and handed me the paper cup still half full of lukewarm root beer.

"Drink this. You haven't lost enough blood for it to be fatal, but you need to get some fluids into you."

I took a little sip of the root beer and then discovered that Danel was right. I was very thirsty. As I chugged a large gulp, Danel pushed at the sarcophagus. The stone slab on the top grated angrily as it moved, revealing a coffin sized cavity. It was dusty and musty and I thought I saw something scurry into the corner. He reached in and tugged, freeing a long gray length of dusty fabric. He pulled it out and shook it, raising a musty cloud that made me cough.

Then the cup was out of my hand and I was hustled to one side of the antechamber.

"Get out of your clothes," Danel held the fabric up like a screen. "Both of you."

"What?" That was the last thing I expected but Cade was already peeling off his shirt and kicking off his shoes. As he stripped, he dropped his clothes into the sarcophagus.

"No time, Misty," he said as he pulled off his pants. "Just do it and give me your clothes."

I stopped breathing as my face burned. Cade didn't wear anything under his jeans. I never knew he went commando. I dragged my eyes away but the image was burned into my memory.

He was magnificent.

My fingers fumbled with Danel's belt around my thigh but Danel pushed my hands away and nimbly pulled it off. The room spun for a moment as the blood spilled out again, but Danel quickly tore a strip from his shirt. I was too dizzy to be stunned when he pulled down my pants and wrapped the strip tightly around the wound. With my pants around my ankles, I turned to the wall as I pulled off my shirt and wrapped the shroud around me. It was stiff and scratchy, filthy and smelly. I shuddered as it touched my skin and I tried not think about where it had come from and what it been touching for the past who-knew-how-many centuries.

As my clothes came off, Danel yanked them out of my hands. After I'd fastened the shroud around my torso enough for modesty, I turned back to find me looking at myself.

Cade had disappeared and in his place stood a disheveled and battered version of me. My mouth hung open. Cade had morphed into my twin. I looked taller than I thought I was, and with the cuts and bloodstains and crazy hair, I looked like hell.

"Get into the sarcophagus." Danel said curtly.

I dragged my eyes away from Misty/Cade as he dropped his discarded clothes into the vault.

I hobbled over to the dais and stared into the dark.

"Don't worry," Cade said my own voice. "There are ventilation slits in there. You'll be fine."

Creeped out, I thought I could make out something that looked like a body. "Wait, there's something in there!"

Danel wasn't in the mood to discuss. He lifted me up and dropped me into the cavity.

"Don't make a sound. Don't even move." Danel hissed at me.

Gingerly, I inched my hand over to touch something that pressed against my side. A gleam of light shone enough light for me to make out the leathery features of a mummified corpse, its grinning head inches from my face.

I tried to bite back a scream, but a tiny squeal escaped.

"Shh!" Danel hissed.

And then the lid scraped shut and I was sealed into the darkness.

It wasn't completely black. Light leaked in through a pair of long thin slits that ran along the sides of the sarcophagus. I squirmed my body closer to one of the cracks and away from my bunkmate. I pressed my nose against the crack, taking deep breaths, not only to fend off the feeling of suffocation and panic, but also the dank musk of a two thousand year old corpse.

I could see through the slit. It was a narrow view, but I could make out most of what was happening in the room beyond.

Misty/Cade was ripping my shirt to shreds, exposing my breasts. I bit my lip to keep from crying out. To see my own body exposed like that seemed like a violation. The pants were kicked off and as I watched, fresh bruises and scratches bloomed all over my body. I wanted to close my eyes and block it out. It was too graphic. Too real to what I would actually look like if the real Xerxi were to rape me. But I couldn't look away. I was trapped. A witness to my own defilement.

"More on the face," Danel whispered as he inspected Misty/Cade dispassionately. While I watched, my eyes turned bloody and my cheek was ripped.

"More," said Danel and my jaw dislocated and one eye bulged slightly out of a socket. It was horrible to watch and I clenched my jaw to keep from crying out.

Danel nodded as he ripped my jeans down the middle, then wiped it in my spilled blood from the ground. He then smeared it on Misty/Cade's naked leg before tossing the bloody fabric into a corner. When he stood up, he looked liked Xerxi again. He unzipped his jeans but from where I was, I could only see his back.

"Ready?" Xerxi/Danel asked.

Misty/Cade nodded and then started to scream. With my voice. I closed my eyes then, wrapping my arms around my head, trying to block out the sound. I didn't open my eyes or unbury my head until the screams faded to sobs and then to silence.

"I said not to kill her." Sam Jaza's voice was slightly annoyed.

I forced myself to peer through the crack. Misty/Cade was a lifeless pile on the stone floor and Sam Jaza stood glaring down grumpily.

"She's not dead," Xerxi/Danel answered with a shrug. "Yet."

"Where's Yani?" he asked as he reached down and lifted Misty/Cade by the hair.

"Sulking." A jerk of his head toward the chamber entrance was as much as Xerxi/Danel needed to explain. Sam Jaza sniffed.

"Well, I suppose there wasn't much I needed her to tell me. I'll get the details out of Danel and Cade when they arrive."

With that, Sam Jaza twisted Misty/Cade's neck. It made a sickening sound as the bones parted and I heard a gurgling death rattle. I watched my body fall lifelessly to the ground in a broken heap.

"So this is how the Mystery ends." Sam Jaza almost sounded disappointed. "Nothing. Not Enoch's Omen at all. She was, after all, just another useless human. A nothing." Sam Jaza nudged the corpse with one toe. "Get rid of the body. Take her out the Gharb Bab."

"The Eastern Gate?"

Sam glared at Xerxi/Danel. "I don't want you to be seen. Take it deep into the desert and bury it where it won't be found for at least a couple of centuries. And then find Danel and Cade. Don't waste time playing with them. I want them both here as soon as you can find them. They've been indiscreet. I need to know the details so we can cover her trail. Her disappearance isn't obscure enough to avoid comment. A girl vanishing is common as dirt, but I need to be sure that they have not exposed too much."

Sam Jaza had been muttering the last few sentences to himself, but then he cut off abruptly and spun on his heel. With robes sailing in his wake, he disappeared into the blackness of the passage that led back to his throne room.

The silence was static. Then, with a flurry of movement, both Xerxi/Danel and Misty/Cade disappeared from my sight. I twisted around to look out the other crack, but the sarcophagus lid grated open before I could fully turn around.

Cade reached down and grabbed his clothes a second or two before he reached in again to help me out. I clutched the shroud around me as he set me on my feet on the floor. He looked like himself again, shirtless, dressed in his jeans. I leaned into him, taking strength from his touch. Danel stared at us as he pushed closed the lid of the sarcophagus, his expression cold and blank.

"What next?" I asked Cade quietly.

Cade handed me my shoes without answering. As I slipped them back on my feet, I saw my shirt and jeans on the floor. They were unwearable, thrashed into shreds. Cade handed me his plaid flannel shirt and I gratefully put it on, letting the fetid linen drop to the ground. I still had my bra and underwear on, but my exposed legs pimpled with goose bumps, perhaps not just from the cold.

"We'll smuggle you out of here wrapped in a sheet like a corpse." Danel's voice was barely a whisper as he spread the old linen. "We'll put some miles between us and Sam before we figure out our next step."

I balked for a second about having to touch that shroud again, but Cade's hand, gentle on the small of my back, guided me forward. I grabbed my backpack and gingerly laid down, my arms clutching my pack to my chest.

Cade smiled encouragingly before lifting the ends of the shroud and hoisted me over his shoulder.

It was more cramped than cozy with my pack digging into me, and my leg throbbing with a dull pain, but I forced myself not to squirm.

"Comfortable?" Cade asked with a whisper.

"Mmmm," I grunted. I wasn't going to complain, but he was free to interpret that anyway he liked.

Carried on his back like a load of laundry, I could make out the shadows of dark and light through the sheet, but even that limited vision disappeared quickly as we moved into blackness.

I could tell from the cold dank air that we were heading back down the tunnel and not onto the street. I froze, then forced myself to go limp when the tunnel lightened, quickly building to brightness as we re-entered the throne chamber.

Voices called out laughingly to Danel and Cade as we passed through the chamber. I couldn't make out the words, but I could tell their comments were bawdy. Danel answered back with Xerxi's voice.

The darkness returned as we moved into another passage. It felt like we were moving very quickly, but downward. The blackness got blacker and the air got colder and danker. Despite my best efforts, I found myself shivering and moved to press even closer to Cade. I wondered whether he'd changed back into Cade as he sped through the passages. Cade still felt like Cade to me, no matter what he looked like.

There seemed to be several slight bends in the maze as we flew through the black tunnels but then we took a sharp right turn. I guessed we were headed east. Or maybe west. Or maybe somewhere else. Wrapped like a bag of trash in the pitch black doesn't do much for your sense of direction. Slowly, the air got warmer and less clammy. And then, like walking through an airlock, we were back on the surface. The blinding blackness eased only slightly. It was still dark, but in a gloomy-night, not-subterranean, kind of way. With a gentle swing, I was unloaded and set on a hard stone surface. The sheet fell away and I found myself blinking at a dark room, lit only by the faint moon and stars leaking through open windows.

It looked like a small ancient parlor made of chipped stone and cracked plaster. A half dozen obelisks, ranging from a foot high to one that nearly touched the ceiling were lined up along one side of the room. Centuries old carvings, damaged but still elegant, dotted the walls. Dust and litter settled over everything. I shot a questioning look at Cade, but it was Danel who answered.

"Welcome to the City of Dead."

Chapter Thirty Seven

There was something creepy about the place that made Danel's comment less than absurd. The silence was more muffled than soundless, as if everything that still lived around here tiptoed and whispered, not wanting to disturb sleeping spirits.

"Come again?" I asked, shivering as I wrapped the sheet tighter about me. The evening was cool, but I was trembling more than I could blame on the night air.

Cade ignored my question. "She needs warm clothes and blankets," he said to Danel as he squatted down beside me. He rubbed some warmth back into my arms. "And something to drink. She's lost a lot of blood and she's in shock."

Danel looked down at me with narrowed eyes. He pulled off his leather jacket and dropped it over my shoulders, the heat from his body still clinging to it. I hugged it close, letting the warmth sink into me along with his scent.

"I said, she needs clothes and food." There was an edge to Cade's voice as he stood and met Danel's eyes. I didn't understand his anger any more than I understood the long brittle silence that followed, but in the end, Danel gave a curt nod before turning quickly and leaving the room.

Cade didn't speak for a moment, nor did he sit back down beside me. My shivering seemed to be fading so I tried to stand, but it was too soon and I settled back down on the stone bench.

"The City of the Dead?" I asked at last.

Cade nodded, his back to me, looking out the window, into the gloom beyond. "In the past, Egyptians would build houses to bury their dead in. Mausoleums. There are acres and acres of these, packed in side by side. Think of it as an urban sprawl cemetery."

A distant voice echoing against the stones snapped my eyes to one of the windows.

"People live here." Cade knew my question without taking his eyes away from the blackness. "Some are poor. Some are not. Some have lived here for generations. Some just like living among the dead."

Cade was a million miles away. Not as bad as those times in North Carolina when he'd put up his walls to keep me out, but still, he was isolating himself from me and I didn't know why. I made myself stand and hobbled over to him.

I touched his back and he trembled in response. He didn't pull away, but he didn't turn back from the window either. The night air flowed past him like a sheet, heavy with the aroma of old stone and baking bread.

I waited for him to speak. I knew he would when he was ready. In the meantime, I would enjoy the current that ran between us. It was so hard to describe. It was warm, but it wasn't like heat. It didn't really vibrate or buzz, it was just flowing, more substantial than a breeze. The best way I can describe it was that his spirit poured like warm honey into my soul whenever we touched.

"He loves you, Misty." His voice was monotone, his body tense and his eyes still fixed on the night.

The air spilled from my lungs in relief. He was back on that again. He wasn't nervous about evading Sam Jaza and his horde of demons, he was worried about Danel again. I leaned into his back, breathing deep of his scent.

But he didn't relax. If anything, he tensed even more.

"He really does. He's in love with you. I've known him for eons and I've never seen him as enthralled with anyone like he is with you." He turned then and, taking me by my shoulders, he met my gaze. His eyes were wet and seemed as dark as the sky behind him. "And you love him, too."

"What?" I would have yelled at him, but his words had left me breathless. "That's ridiculous, Cade! I love you!"

"Yes," he said with a heavy sadness. "But you love him as well. Admit it."

I opened my mouth to argue, but words caught in my throat. I couldn't deny it. I did love Danel, but not the way I loved Cade. Couldn't he see that?

"Yes," I managed to whisper at last, "I do love Danel, but I'm not *in* love with him. I'm *in* love with you. You do know that, don't you?"

His hands moved gently up my arms until they cupped my face, his fingers like warm feathers against my cheeks.

"Yes," he said at last. The pain in his face faded to a melancholy confusion. "But he has taken part of your heart that you haven't given to me. Or perhaps that you can't give to me."

"No!" I grabbed his hands, pressing them firmly against my cheeks. "It's only that kiss. That one stupid kiss. But you could change all that. Every part of me belongs to you. Or it should. If you would only take it."

He made a move to free himself, but I wouldn't let him go. He was infinitely stronger than me, he could wrench himself away if he wanted to, but instead we just stood there, our faces inches apart, our spirits flowing as one.

"Now would be a good time." I whispered.

He laughed then. It didn't break the moment, but I felt some of his tension ebb away. I moved my face closer to his, my lips open slightly, but just before our lips should have met, he tilted my head down to place a chaste kiss on my forehead.

I sighed hugely. "That wasn't it."

"You don't understand, Misty." He rested his chin against my forehead, my face buried into his neck. "I'm not human.

I'm an angel. And I'm not even one of the good ones. I'm a fallen angel. There's a reason why they call us demons."

Firmly, he pulled back so our eyes could meet.

"We have no souls. Those small slices of God that makes each human both unique and precious. Angels don't have souls. Not even the good ones."

"I'm okay with that."

"You shouldn't be. If you truly understood what I was saying, you'd run out of this room, screaming in terror."

"I love you," I whispered. "I trust you."

"And you can. From the moment I first saw you on that beach, I was drawn to you in a way that I'd never experienced before. As soon as you would arrive in the morning, I felt alive. More alive than I'd felt in centuries. Perhaps more alive than I'd ever felt before. And when you'd pack up the kids and leave for the day, I felt as if I were dying. I wondered if that was what the end of life was like."

His eyes had wandered from my face, focused on the flickering light behind me, but then he brought himself back with an intensity that made me quiver.

"And then that day we first touched, I know you felt something, Misty, but for me, I felt as if, for that second, for that eternity, I had a soul."

"I felt it too. As if I had never been complete until I touched you. That I'll never be whole unless I'm with you."

That seemed to disturb him even more. He set me away from him, and dropped his arms, leaving me swaying unsteadily.

"No, you don't understand." His words were cold and biting. "I think I'm stealing your soul, Misty. Touching you is an addiction that I can't break, but I have to. Because every time you touch me, I feel as if a little more of your soul creeps into me and if we don't stop, you'll be soulless. I would have killed you."

"That's ridiculous!" I stepped toward him but he retreated. "How can you be taking my soul when every time we touch, I feel my soul expand? Whatever it is I'm giving you, it's not because I'm losing anything. The more you take, the more I have."

He turned back to the window and the night beyond. Addiction was the right word. The compulsion to touch him was as strong as the need to sleep and eat, but I respected his distance and stood back, swaying weakly, drained more by his pain then by my blood loss.

"I can't take that chance. I feel that if I kissed you, really kissed you the way that I want to, then I wouldn't stop until I'd drained every ounce of your essence," he paused and I opened my mouth to argue, but then he continued, barely audible, "or that I would pour what's left of myself into you and cease to exist."

That thought left me cold. A world without Cade. I'd rather be dead.

The light from the flickering lantern made our shadows jump and dance against the walls, but we didn't move. Frozen, I couldn't even sway from exhaustion, and that is where we stood for a very long time until Danel returned.

Chapter Thirty Eight

I couldn't meet Danel's eyes as he herded me back to the stone bench. Cade stayed a statue at the window, his back to us. Danel sat me down and laid a shawl over my lap. The clothes he'd brought were like the traditional clothes that I'd seen Egyptian women wear: a long black skirt, a loose, high collared, long sleeved blouse and a couple of scarves to cover my heads and shoulders. I didn't change into them right away. Instead I ate the food that Danel had brought: a bottle of water, flat bread that was still warm and some spicy meat that might have been chicken. I ate quickly, barely tasting it.

"Feel better?" Danel asked, his voice deceptively neutral.

I nodded. I wasn't as woozy, but a big part of me still ached because Cade was hurting.

"Good." Danel handed me the stack of clothing he'd brought with him. With a jerk of his head, he gestured to the space behind the obelisks. "Get changed. We'll move out as soon as you're ready."

I took the clothes and headed for the corner while Danel stood beside Cade, staring out into the night, matching him stillness for stillness. I watched them as I changed, trying to sort out my feelings. Cade was right. Of course. I felt something for Danel. I'd thought it was just friendship. Friendship tainted by the kiss that had changed me. I hadn't thought it was more than that, but now that Cade made me see it, I had to admit. I loved Danel. In a deep and meaningful way. And in a physical way as well. I couldn't deny that to myself. But Cade was... Cade. He completed me. If ever a person could be called your soulmate, Cade qualified. I pulled the shirt over my head and stepped back into the center of the room.

"Cade," the words rushed out of me as fast as the realization hit me, "you can't steal my soul, because it's yours. We share a soul and when you claim your part, it's better for both of us."

Cade didn't turn back to look at me, but Danel did and the blood fell from his face, leaving him looking like a death mask.

"Put the scarf over your head and wrap it around your shoulders." Danel's voice was brittle and harsh. "We're moving now."

The night was a murky pitch. Buildings loomed on either side of us as we hurried down alleys barely wide enough for a car. Mini-mausoleums were sandwiched between adobe hovels. Everything was derelict, but while some of the buildings were boarded up and obviously vacant, light and music and laughing voices poured out of others. We squeezed by cars parked in front of the occupied cottages and I peeked through tattered drapes to see people merrily cohabitating with their ancestors.

I had lost track of time. It was night, but it could have been eight o'clock or it could have been two in the morning. I would have pulled out my cell phone to check, but I was being hustled through the streets, bounded on either side by Cade and Danel. This would normally be a pleasant place to be, but the silence was crushing. Without meaning to, I was hurting both of them, and I didn't know how to fix it.

We finally reached the gate and we broke into the bright lights and clamor of Cairo like passing through a curtain. Without missing a beat, Cade and Danel guided me to a battered light brown sedan that was parked near the entrance.

Danel dropped my pack onto the back seat before getting behind the wheel. Cade opened the front door to let me in. It was a small car, but the front seat was a bench seat and I slid over so that Cade could fit beside me. Doors slammed and the car purred to life as Danel pulled out into traffic without even a glance. Tires screeched and horns honked but it seemed that I was the only one in the car that noticed.

The silence lasted another twenty seconds before I broke.

"So, where are we going?" I asked, trying to force a chipperness that I didn't feel. "What's the plan?"

Cade didn't actually glance over at Danel, but I got the feeling that he was passing this baton to him.

"No plan, really." Danel said. "We're on the run. It'll be a challenge, but we need to keep you out of Sam Jaza's way for the next sixty or seventy years. It helps that he thinks you're dead, but he's suspicious by nature, so he'll probably send someone up to Wicassett to follow up and make sure your disappearance doesn't lead them to search in the right direction."

My throat was dry and I swallowed hard. "You mean, I can never go home?"

Cade reached for my hand in sympathy. I didn't move, I just stared out the windshield as Danel took us out of the surface streets and onto a highway.

"You have to go back to Sam Jaza." I said at last, the beginning of an idea forming.

Cade squeezed my hand gently. "It's okay, Misty. Don't worry about us."

That wasn't what I meant. I mean, I *was* worried about them, about what would happen to them if and when Sam Jaza found out I was still alive. Would they get shredded like Rojo? I shelved that thought as a new question hit me. "What happened to the Dopplegangers? I think he called them Xerxi and Yani? What will happen when they show up and Sam finds out that it wasn't them?"

"Don't worry about Xerxi and Yani." Cade said with a shrug. "We just need to keep them on ice for the next century or so. We've got it covered."

I straightened. "Did they get shredded?"

Cade nodded.

"When?" I ran by the time line in my head. "When did you have the time? How did you find them? And how did you get to Cairo so fast?"

"We found a military base outside of Nanjing and commandeered a fighter jet." I could hear a little cocky pride in Danel's voice. "It was a little tricky navigating international airspace, but we got into Cairo about a half an hour after you. We found Xerxi and Yani looking like us so we changed our appearance so we looked like another pair of Sam's stooges. We agreed to help them find you, but the first chance we had, we jumped them and shredded them."

"Where are they now?" I asked, wishing I didn't need to know.

"At the moment, most of their parts are buried under some vacant lots around the airport," Danel answered. "We'll move them to a more secure location some time in the next couple of years."

"Most of their parts?"

"We've got their heads in the trunk." Danel gave me a wicked wink.

The time would come when the idea of dismembered demon heads rattling around in the trunk wouldn't freak me out.

I think I was just about there.

"But Sam thinks they're looking for you. If they don't show up and you don't show up, he'll know something's wrong."

Danel shrugged.

"No, listen to me. I've got a plan." I stared out the windshield as I gathered my thoughts. "What if you both went back and act just the way Sam's going to expect you to act. Sam said he was worried about you leaving loose ends in Wicassett. What if, in order to get back into Sam's good graces, you agree to have one of you impersonate me and go back to New Hampshire, let everyone think I made it back okay. This way, I can go home, pretending to be you pretending to be me."

It sounded a lot more convoluted in words than in my head. I waited, barely breathing, while Danel and Cade thought about it. Finally Danel shot Cade a twisted grin.

"Could work." Danel seemed a little reluctant to admit that I could have a good idea. "It needs a little tweaking. But it would cover everyone's tracks and give you a little more time at home before we have to 'disappear' you."

I let that pass. I didn't want to have to disappear from my home in a year or two, but I figure I could cross that bridge when I got to it. For the moment, I was happy for the chance to get home.

"We'll head up to Alexandria to check you into a hotel." Danel continued, both hands gripped the wheel, his eyes hyper-alert. "We'll need to pick up a burka for you, because you're going to be on your own in Alexandria for a few days. We'll tell them you're from Saudi Arabia. They'll understand that you won't be able to leave the room since you'll have no escort. Stay in the room until we get back. They'll either send a woman up with Room Service, or leave it outside your door. Since you don't speak Arabic, don't speak to anyone."

"Saudi women can never walk around by themselves?" I asked, thinking about Pinky and her posse. "That must get old real fast."

"Saudis are very protective of their women," Danel answered. "They never let them out without a male escort and when they do go out, they need to be covered head to toe. A woman's face can't be seen by any man other than her husband or a family member."

"Still?" Cade was idly curious.

Danel snorted. "It's worse now than it was four hundred years ago."

"And then what?" I asked. "You guys go back and face Sam while I watch the news and take naps?"

"Exactly." Cade shot me what he thought was a reassuring smile, but I could tell he didn't like the idea of leaving me alone in an Egyptian hotel for a couple of days any more than I did. "Then we need to get you back to that cruise ship."

"What cruise ship?"

"The Semester Aboard program. That cruise ship that you're supposed to be on will be docking in Alexandria in eleven days." Cade said. "It's nearly perfect timing."

"When it gets to Alexandria, we'll sabotage the engines," Danel continued. "Bad enough that they'll have to send all the students home. Then you can fly home like the rest of the students and we should be able to fix it that no one will ever know that you weren't on the ship the entire time."

"You're just making this up as you go, aren't you?" I asked.

Danel's lips tightened into a tiny smirk as he nodded. I leaned back against the seat and stared out at the night. We were out of the city and clusters of dark buildings could be seen huddled up against the highway, breaking up the monotony of the flat endless fields. Lights were sparse out here but the stars glowed bright and a half moon lit the world dimly.

It was a good plan. For the first time in weeks, I felt good about tomorrow. Well maybe not about tomorrow when I'd be left alone in a hotel while Cade and Danel went off to do battle with the lord of all demons, but certainly about the future. My head nodded with the rhythm of the car as the tension in my gut loosened. I leaned against Cade's shoulder and with my eyes nearly shut, I stared, unfocused at the dashboard lights.

The clock read 23:59. I waited for the minute, wondering if it would next read 24:00 or 0:00.

0:00.

Happy birthday to me, I thought wistfully before falling into an uneasy doze.

Chapter Thirty Nine

I woke to a nightmare. Chaos mangled the line between sleep and reality.

We were tumbling through the air. We were still in the car, Cade's arms tightly wrapped around me, but we were spinning. Up was down and then up again.

And then up became down with a shriek of flayed metal and exploding glass. The car was flipped, sliding sideways over a field of foot high crops. Cade's body shielded me from most of the shards of glass and metal and I could see Danel's arm pressing against the roof of car, preventing it from collapsing and crushing us.

Before the car could slide to a halt, Cade kicked out with one leg and what was left of the door flew off. Even before the wreck stopped skidding, we rolled out onto the ground. With me caged within his arms, Cade was on his feet and running.

We moved even faster than when he'd taken me home in New Hampshire. That time he'd been practically flying, his feet only touching every couple of hundred feet and then only to push back to glide. This time, his feet beat like machine gun fire and we sped like a missile over the fields. I was disoriented, terrified, and I began to add nausea to the list.

From the way that Cade held me, I could see back over his shoulder. Something was gaining on us. I gripped Cade tighter, too breathless to call out as I watched the pursuer close the gap, but then I recognized Danel's silhouette emerging from the blackness. He ran ahead, and once more I had nothing to focus on except the dark, blurring landscape screaming past.

Something hurled at us from the blackness. A figure on a path to intercept. Cade leaped and we were airborne. The figure turned on a dime and shot up to follow, but a second figure soared from the dark to intercept him. Danel. They crashed into each other with a sound like two freight trains exploding and then they both disappeared into the shadows. Cade landed on his feet running and we sped on.

The landscaped changed. The green fields ended abruptly and white desert took over. The moonlight reflected more strongly off the pale sand and it grew easier to see, but my eyes were no way near as good as Cade's, so when he turned sharply and veered off in a new direction, I had no idea what it was that he had seen.

Until he stopped. Then I could see them. A line of figures etched black against the glowing sand. They were on all sides, thirty or forty of them creating a ring around us, a couple of hundred yards away. They weren't moving forward, they just stood there, waiting.

A figure fell from the sky and landed with a thud beside us. I gasped as a fountain of sand shot up, but then I saw it was Danel, half-crouched and tensed for battle.

Cade set me down on the sand and the two of them turned their backs to me, focusing on the ring of demons on the horizon.

"Plan?" Cade asked with a whisper.

"Fight," Danel answered, even quieter.

"Thirty eight against two," said Cade, dropping into a crouch.

"Yes," Danel nodded. "They won't be expecting it. It's the only thing we've got in our favor."

Danel and Cade poised motionless. The demons around us stood as well, although not as still. Everyone seemed to be waiting for something. Or somebody.

Then, with no warning, Danel pounced. He covered a hundred yards in a single bound and then leaped again. Those demons near his target moved to engage, but on his second leap, he shot up, disappeared into the dark sky and didn't come down. The sounds of a scuffle in the other direction made me turn around to see that he had managed to veer in mid-air, coming down on the demons at the other side of the circle. In the pale starlight, I could barely make out the details of the struggle, but it was ferocious, with angry gasps and dismembered limbs flying in all directions.

The breath was knocked out of me as Cade's arm gripped my waist. In the same millisecond that Danel had bounded, Cade was airborne, sailing high into the air. The fighters on the battlefield below turned toy-size as Cade carried me above and away from the melee below. I opened my mouth to protest leaving Danel behind, but the wind pulled the breath from me and I could barely make a sound.

Our descent landed us outside the ring. Cade wasted no time. He hit the ground running and again we were tearing across the desert sand.

I couldn't see behind us, but I was aware that the cloud of sand trailing behind us was bigger than could be attributed to Cade's running. The demons were in pursuit. The entire Sahara Desert lay before us, and while Cade wouldn't tire, neither would our hunters. The desert would run out first.

Cade faltered. Not from exhaustion, but he had caught sight of something on the horizon that made him hesitate. A stripe of darkness rose up along the edge of the landscape, black against the glittering starlit sky. Cade veered to the north, but the ribbon stretched there as well. We both turned to look south. No escape there.

The demons behind us slowed, blocking our retreat, but not approaching us. Whatever the black mass was, the demons didn't seem to want to mess with it either.

The strip rose taller as it approached. I could hear it now, roaring and throbbing like a jet engine. But this wasn't just a windstorm. It stood like a solid mass, impenetrable, sweeping along with a will of its own. As it closed in, the sand whipped my hair and bit at my skin. When it finally slowed to a stop, one hundred yards away, it curved to wrap a semi circle in front of us, a screaming and black wall of rage.

My feet touched the sand as I slid out of Cade's arms. I had lost one of my sneakers in flight. The sand was was fine and warm and slid like a living thing between my toes. I kicked off the other shoe and crouched, my fingers and feet vibrating in sync with the energy that surged through the shifting dunes.

Cade's voice was cold and gritty as he crouched beside me. "I've got one more card to play."

I looked at the set of Cade's jaw and a choking foreboding rose in me. Whatever his plan was, I knew I wouldn't like it.

"Cade, wait," I started, but he waved me silent and straightened, staring at the wall. I stood as well, pulling my hands from the pulsing sand with a strange reluctance.

The barrage roared and reared, but kept its distance. Cade focused on one point and it was there that the wall parted and a figure emerged.

Sam Jaza. His robes glittered brighter than the starlight could take credit for. He glided toward us with a disdainful pout, but I could sense the anger throbbing beneath his nonchalance.

"It's over, Cade." Sam Jaza stood about a hundred feet away from us, but his voice carried easily over the din of the storm. "Give her up."

I edged closer to Cade, our elbows and thighs touching while I looked around for Danel. There were only about twenty demons behind us, so maybe Danel was still dealing with the rest of them. I didn't want to think about what the alternative might be.

"Why do you care, Sam?" Cade's casual shrug might have fooled Sam, but I could feel his tension flowing into me like boiling water. "As you said, she's just a human. She'll die on her own eventually. Why are you bothering?"

"Ah, Cade," Sam Jaza smiled and tapped his fingertips together. "I could ask you the same question." Sam looked directly at me and I met his eyes, puzzled by the hint of paranoia and fear that I thought I saw beneath his amuzed façade. "Why do you bother? Why have you and Danel kept her hidden from me? Why wouldn't you immediately report that you'd found a deviant human? A human that defies Persuasion? What are your motives in this?"

"Nothing that need worry you." Cade met Sam Jaza smile for smile. "She amuses me."

Cade gave me hand a meaningful squeeze, but it wasn't necessary. I knew his feelings for me, but if denying them at this moment kept me alive and him in one piece, I was fine with that. I squeezed back, but my eyes stayed locked on Sam Jaza's.

"Amuses you?" Sam's smile turned brittle. "Or is she a tool? What were you and Danel planning to do with a human that defies Persuasion? A human named Mystery?"

"You're paranoid, Sam." Cade tensed. "You have to know that the last thing that I'm interested in is usurping your position. You know there is nothing on this planet that I want less."

"True." Sam Jaza spat out the word like it was an insult. "I don't accuse *you* of ambition. But what of Danel? What drove him to defy me? Do you honestly believe that it was mere infatuation that motivated him to risk insubordination?"

I could sense that his words shook Cade. He had barely seen Danel for centuries before they'd crossed paths in Wicassett. I didn't understand what Sam Jaza was accusing Danel of, but I believed in him. The same way that I believed in Cade. He could not, would not betray us. I gripped Cade's hand, willing him to understand. After a moment's hesitation, Cade squeezed back.

"Love, lust, greed or ambition," Cade answered. "Danel's motives are irrelevant. Misty is not the catalyst of the prophesy. We all heard Enoch's words. Our final judgment, the Year of Mystery, would be in ten thousand years. It's too soon. She is not the Mystery of the Enoch's Prophesy. There is no reason for her to die."

"And yet, I cannot take that risk. Perhaps it was not ten thousand years after the fall, but ten thousand years since we first descended. Prophesies are always ambiguous, just to confound us."

Cade opened his mouth to argue, but Sam Jaza held up one hand to silence him.

"It matters not. I have never trusted Danel, not since the Fall, and now, with this current treason, I have taken steps to ensure that he never has the opportunity to betray me again."

Sam Jaza extended his arm higher as something whistled over our heads. With a stab, he grabbed it and held it up for us to see.

A stifled scream escaped from my chest. My knees went weak and I clutched at Cade so I wouldn't sink to the ground.

Sam Jaza held Danel's head, his fingers grasping Danel's hair.

Danel's face was still alive, though. His jaw clenched with impotent rage. He did not try to speak, I knew he could not without a chest, but his eyes said what his mouth could not.

290

Fury. Revenge. And despair. He looked at me and I couldn't break away from his stare. He would help me if he could, but there was nothing he could do. His greatest misery was the hopelessness of my situation. I nodded my acceptance. I would die tonight and even greater than my own fear of death was the regret of the pain that it would cause Danel and Cade.

Sam Jaza was speaking. I barely heard him.

"Right now, Danel's body is being scattered all over the globe. And even if his body is ever able to reassemble itself, I will keep his head close to me." Sam raised Danel's head to speak into his face. "From now until the end of creation, your head will be in a cage, suspended above my throne. And from there, you will witness my greatness and my final victory."

Death. Or as near to death as a Fallen Angel could experience. I let out a small sob, more for Danel's fate than my own. My death would be relatively fast and my end, clean. Whatever exists for us beyond this mortal dimension, that would be my future. Unknown and unknowable, my chances were still better than Danel's destiny.

My sob turned Sam Jaza's attention to me, his face pinched with vicious mirth. "You weep for Danel, stupid girl? And not for yourself? Trust me, your fate is far more dire than his."

Fear and grief made me mute, but I shook my head.

Sam Jaza glared at me, and through tears, I met his eyes. Something in him snapped and he let out a feral roar, hurling Danel's head high into the air. It soared over us and was caught by one of the demons behind us.

"Hold it tight!" Sam bellowed. "When we are done here, put it into the cage, but first, make sure he watches while I destroy the omen wench."

He turned his full attention on me now. I stepped to the side, away from Cade and crouched back down, gripping handfuls of sand, tensing every muscle in my body. I fought

291

back the impulse to flee, knowing it would be useless, but I couldn't fight down the instinct to fight. It was just as futile, but maybe if it couldn't delay the inevitable, it might make it quicker and less painful.

"Wait!" Cade stepped in front of me, a desperate edge in his voice making it crack. "I offer you a trade, Sam. An exchange for the girl's life."

Real amusement made Sam pause. "And what, Cade, could you offer to me that I don't already possess?"

"Consumption." Cade spoke calmly, but it was an eye of a hurricane. Dread throbbed from him and vibrated through me.

I could feel a wave of shock from the demons behind us. Sam Jaza looked stunned too. Behind him, the tempest wall fell to the desert floor like a curtain, the fine sand settling in a murky haze.

Sam Jaza's amazement quickly shifted to a voracious greed. Whatever "Consumption" was, it was obviously something that he wanted. I grabbed at Cade's sleeve, my fingers digging into this arm.

"What?" I hissed into ear. "What is Consumption? What are you offering?"

Cade turned to me and cupped my face in his hands, the tingling of our souls stronger than ever before. "Consumption," he whispered back. "I offer myself as a sacrifice. My existence for yours."

"And what happens to you? Do you die? Can you die?" Dread made my voice wispy.

"As close to death as one of us can achieve. I will cease to have my own body. I will exist only as a subjugation within Sam Jaza."

"No!" I didn't fully understand what he meant, but every cell within me knew that this was wrong. "Why does Sam want it so badly?"

292

"It is a sacrifice that must be given voluntarily. He cannot ask for it, nor can he coerce it."

My mind reeled, fighting to absorb all that Cade had told me. He turned from me to face the demon lord, who had kept his distance, avarice holding him at bay.

"Sam Jaza." Cade's voice rang strong and loud over the desert sands. "I offer you my consumption in exchange for the life of this human. You must agree that neither you, nor any of your minions, shall ever raise a hand against her and that she will be allowed to live out her mortal existence free from your malice."

Sam nodded his head eagerly "Agreed."

"No!" I yelled, loud enough to be heard by the demons behind us. I grabbed Cade's face with both hands, dragging it back until we were nose to nose. I dropped my voice to an urgent whisper. "Your soul, your being, whatever your essence is, will be added to Sam's, won't it?"

Cade gave me the briefest nod.

"Your sacrifice will increase his power? He will become stronger, feeding on you?"

Again, Cade's nod was barely perceptible.

"I can't let you do this, Cade. I will die. Maybe tonight, maybe in a hundred years, we can't avoid that, but you will have sacrificed yourself to empower something that is evil. That's so wrong."

Cade dug his fingers into my hair, pressing our foreheads together. "I can't live without you, Misty. I have no soul except yours. If you are gone, I cannot exist. If there is any way I can extend your time here on earth, I must take that path."

"Cade!" The grip I had on his wrists would have caused a mortal to wince, but to Cade, it was a caress. "Your soul is my soul and my soul is yours. If you do this thing, this great evil, then it's my soul that will pay the price. Our soul."

Cade's eyes bored into mine as my words bled into his mind. He knew I was right. He might be immortal, he might be inhumanly powerful, but in this, he was weak. He could see no future without me.

But then a glimmer lit his face. I couldn't know what he thought, but it strengthened him. He bent his head to whisper into my ear.

"I bequeath my essence to you, my sweetest soul. To you, I bequeath my spirit."

His lips brushed my ear and then my cheek before finding my lips.

And then he kissed me.

The memory of Danel's kiss scurried into the furthest corner of my mind. Danel's kiss has stirred my body in a way I'd never felt before, but Cade's kiss found my soul. My body arched against his as the storm within me threatened to shake me into splinters. I clutched at his neck, his head, his back, clinging to him like an anchor in a tsunami. His lips fast on mine, Cade poured into me like a stream of molten lava, seeping into every corner of my body, embossing his essence into every cell like living stone. The fear that I was being swamped, losing my mind, only made me cling to Cade more tightly. I would have cried out but my mouth was still bound to his.

I was drowning in his kiss.

And then, like the surf receding, I found myself. Cade was still there but so was I, but even more so. My feet were moored to the earth but my mind filled the universe.

My gut clenched as I pulled myself back to reality. It was if we had been holding that kiss for months, but I knew it had been only seconds and I dreaded the moment when it would break.

He pulled away slowly, reluctantly. His hands still cupped my face, his eyes on mine. I could feel the electricity

294

that I'd always felt when we touched, but now, the elation wasn't only where our skin met, it filled me. I felt dizzy and I clenched at his arms to keep on my feet.

He bowed his head and his cheek brushed mine, his breath, hot and soft in my ear.

"I will always be with you, Misty. Don't ever forget that."

He stepped back then, and I braced myself for the vacuum.

It didn't come.

Confusion made my legs weak and I sunk to my knees. I looked up at Cade, but he was turning away from me, stepping toward Sam Jaza and his own destruction.

I hugged myself, but not from grief. I was embracing the essence of Cade that still lived within me like an unborn child.

Chapter Forty

Cade didn't look back. Maybe he didn't have to. But I watched him walk away. He walked stiffly, almost clumsily, his normal grace abandoning him at his final moment. Even with the turmoil inside me, I needed to watch, to see him surrender his body forever.

Sam Jaza was greed manifest. He drew himself up as Cade approached, avarice drooling from every pore of his body. As Cade stood there, I once again realized how beautiful he was. Not just his appearance, but something within him. He wasn't like the others, not now. If he'd been as one of them before, then he had changed. I couldn't see how someone as good as Cade could be condemned for all eternity. If there could be redemption for humans, why not Cade as well?

Sam Jaza stretched his arms out and let out an inhuman scream that pierced the desert night. As I watched, his body stretched upward, his skin darkened and he turned into a black filmy sheet, almost like an inky fog, but more substantial. His arms and legs and head distended out to form wing-like appendages and his face dissolved into the mist. The wings folded and unfolded with scalding hisses.

Cade's body stood tall and unflinching while Sam Jaza flexed in a frenzy like a massive demonic starfish. A foul wind blasted sand all around us. I couldn't tell if those wings were causing it or if it was surging off the desert. I shielded my face but didn't look away.

The end was painfully quick. Sam's wings rose above Cade and then came down, enfolding him like a cocoon, pressing him into the void. Cade didn't make a sound or even twitch. One moment he stood there and the next, he was gone.

The winds died down and the desert grew deathly silent. The stars reappeared but the wings didn't open again. Instead they bound together more tightly and reformed back into the human form of Sam Jaza. He raised his head and screamed his elation to the heavens. It sounded like an animal dying. Painfully.

And then he turned toward me.

I was still kneeling on the ground. My body felt alien to me. I couldn't seem to make it move. I wanted to mourn Cade, but something within me wouldn't let me. Instead, I just watched as Sam stepped closer to me. He stopped in front of me and, looking down, started to laugh.

I was trying to rise to my feet when he reached down and grabbed me by the collar, lifting me off the ground. Maybe it was fear or adrenalin, but even though my body was trembling with violent spasms, my disorientation seemed to decrease. I looked directly into his face and didn't blink.

His laugh died and a brooding fury twisted his grin. "Stupid human," he spat. "Almost as stupid as Cade."

With a movement as if he were flicking away a bug, he threw me. I flew over the desert floor, landing in a dune a hundred feet away. The fall should have killed me, or at least broken some bones, but the sand gave way like a feather mattress and I rolled to my feet. Part of my mind was amazed that it hadn't hurt at all, but most of me was wavering between fear and anger. I forced myself to focus on the rage because it was easier to act out of anger than cower in terror.

Sam Jaza strode toward me across the sands. If he was surprised to see me standing, he didn't show it.

"You, of course, could not have known how stupid it is to try to bargain with me. Cade should have, but somehow, you have managed to bewitch him, to delude him into believing that by sacrificing himself, I would spare you. Such folly is laughable in a human, but disgusting in an angel. He deserved to be consumed."

Fury flared within me, giving me a false courage. Maybe I would die tonight, but I was tired of being frightened. I could try to face the end with some shred of dignity, but that Cade should have perished in vain made me shake with rage.

"You are not an angel," I screamed. "I don't know if Cade was or wasn't, but you definitely are not. You are twisted parody of an angel. A disgusting corruption. A demon."

I spat the last word at him like acid. The grin fell from his face and reared above me, hissing as he pounced.

I dove to one side and a laugh escaped me as Sam landed on the dune where I had stood, his fingers clawing impotently at the sand.

"You laugh at me, human?" Rage was making Sam clumsy. He sprung at me again but I stepped to one side, grinning as he missed. "You nasty splotch of mud and filth! I was going to kill you swiftly, as a courtesy to Cade, but now you shall die so horrifically, that in the end you will plead for death, but I will not show you even that small mercy."

I was a little insane. I should have been paralyzed with fear, but, having resigned myself to death, I couldn't fear it anymore. Whether I lived another minute or another century, I wasn't going to live it as a cringing coward.

Sam Jaza pounced again, and again I scampered easily out of his reach. He was moving so slowly, at first I thought he was playing with me, but a lurking trace of alarm in his face made me realize that he was in earnest. There was something wrong with him. Perhaps my defiance was triggering a reaction. If it was, I wasn't going to stop now.

"So, all those eons ago, when the Fallen pledged themselves to you, they all had to keep that oath, but you? You can break your vows? Why is that Sam Jaza? Why?"

I was openly taunting him now and I could feel a wave of uneasiness coming from the demons behind us. Were they wondering why Sam hadn't finished me off yet? I know I was. I caught the glimpse of a movement behind me and I turned to see if any of the others were sneaking up on me. They weren't, but I was distracted and when Sam jumped again, I didn't move away in time.

The force of his strike slammed me onto my back. Sand flew up on both sides of me as his fingers locked around my throat.

"This is my planet, you piece of mud." Sam Jaza's breath was foul in my face. "I make the rules."

I grabbed at his wrists in a feeble attempt to pull him off my neck. I managed to push back enough to give myself enough breath to speak.

"So the rules have changed?" My chest strained to push the air through my throat and my words came out in a hiss. "The vows of the Fallen are no longer binding? Is that what you are saying?"

He screeched as he pressed again. I didn't know why he was toying with me, why he didn't just rip my head off. Instead he snarled down at me as he slowly crushed my throat.

I was going to die now. Now would be a good time to feel fear. But I didn't. I don't know why. Perhaps because I could still feel Cade within me. Or perhaps this lack of fear was a side effect of hysteria. Whatever the reason, I glared up at Sam Jaza .

That's the first time that I realized that something had seriously changed. I wasn't dead. I wasn't dying. I couldn't breath, but I wasn't suffocating. I could feel Sam Jaza's death grip on my neck. It hurt, but I didn't feel like I was dying. For a moment I thought that maybe I was already dead. It was a bit liking having an in-body/out-of-body experience. But if I was confused, it was chicken scratchings compared to what I saw on Sam's face. He wasn't just baffled, he was terrified.

Sam Jaza hadn't grown weak or slow or clumsy. Somehow, I had become strong and agile. Inhumanly strong. Angelically strong. In taking on Cade's essence, I had somehow inherited his powers as well. I reached up and grabbed Sam Jaza by the neck.

For a very long moment, we both froze, holding each others throats. Disorientation gave way to realization. Whatever had changed, neither one of us fully understood it.

I moved first.

I rocked Sam forward and then, with a quick jerk, flung him back over my head. I didn't let go, but allowed the momentum to carry me and I found myself straddling him, pinning him to the ground with one hand.

"Release Cade," I barked. "Release him now."

I don't know why I said that. I didn't even know if releasing Cade were possible, but things were being so crazy, I had stopped rationalizing. I was working on instinct. And instinct told me that I wanted Cade back.

Sam squirmed like a speared trout but didn't speak. Maybe with my hand on his neck, he couldn't, but I wasn't about to let up. His jaw trembled as he clenched his lips tight.

Then he opened his mouth. If he was trying to say something, he never got the chance. As soon as his lips parted, a beam of white light poured out of it, bright enough to pierce the night sky, seeming to reach all the way to heaven.

I released him then, and jumped back as his body arched in convulsions. The beam of light shot up like comet, flaring like a quasar in the sky above. The night was as bright as day, but with a pure colorless luminescence, like moonlight. Times twenty. I stared up, it was bright enough to be blinding, but my eyes didn't even squint. The light was so beautiful, it couldn't hurt me.

Mesmerized, I barely noticed Sam Jaza roll to his feet and into a feral crouch. He launched himself and was airborne before the movement caught the corner of my eye. I spun instinctively and grabbed his wrists, turning on the spot, twirling him away like a dance partner. When I let go he sailed halfway to the cadre of demons that still stood, confused and spell-bound.

But not for long.

"Kill her!" Sam Jaza's screech sounded like a panther. "Kill her now!"

The demons flinched into action, leaping and screaming toward me. Fear came flooding back. There was no way I could fend off dozens of demons attacking at once. I would be shredded. I faced them, every muscle tensed for battle and death.

The flare in the sky started to ebb and sink. It gained speed and landed like a fiery asteroid between me and the demons. I threw myself on the ground and curled up as the molten sand splashed up in a liquid glass fountain, spraying like crystal droplets, arcing over my head to land in a perfect circle. The light condensed into a pillar and then the pillar condensed into Cade.

If Cade had been beautiful in his human form, he was glorious now. He glowed with a brilliant white light that pulsed back at the advancing demons. They balked, rearing back from the ring of his glow like it burned them.

"The Metatron has spoken." Cade's voice rang like the brass section of an orchestra, chiming across a dozen octaves. "The vows of the Fallen are no longer binding."

At the edge of the circle, Sam Jaza's face paled even more than the colorless light could account for. His eyes blazed red as he stabbed a glare at me before turning back to Cade, straightening with a brittle bravado.

"Metatron? What Metatron? There is no Metatron here." Sam sneered as he spat out the words. "She is no Metatron, She is just a human! A smelly, mewling, useless human!"

I had no idea what a Metatron was, but it was obvious that it was really freaking Sam out. I looked over at the horde of demons, still at bay, hovering in the shadows of Cade's glow. They muttered as they stared at me, edging away. A few broke and ran, disappearing into the pitch of the night, which only unnerved the others all the more.

"You know it to be true." Cade spoke to Sam but he was looking at me, his expression warm, his voice, soft. "I should have noticed it sooner. Danel saw it, but he never said a word. It was so obvious. The signs were all there. But then, everything is so obvious now."

With that, Cade threw back his head and let out a symphony of sound like the entire universe was an orchestra ringing a single chord over a thousand octaves. It was a sound of pure joy and the hair buzzed on my arms and my spine shivered in response.

The notes slowly faded, the tingling slowed, and when Cade looked down at me again, we were alone. Sam Jaza and his demons were gone, banished from sight.

I was still crouched on the sand. The urge to leap at Cade and wrap myself around him was almost overpowering, but something in Cade's stance held me back. It wasn't the cold wall that he used to throw up when he was hurt or wary. It was more like a big part of him wasn't there.

How long we stared at each other, I can't say. It seemed like years, but finally I spoke, anxious to create a bridge.

"Where'd they go?" My breath was an achy whisper.

"Not far." Cade's voice still tinkled like silver bells. I shivered.

"Will they be back?"

"In time."

It was like talking to a magic eight-ball. *Ask again later.*

I stood slowly.

"Why did they go?" I asked, brushing the sand from my clothes and my hair.

"It was time for them to leave."

Normally, these kind of non-answers would tick me off, but this time, I was just creeped out. Cade wasn't being evasive, it was like he was speaking to me from another dimension.

"Okay, if you're going to be like that." My hands went to my hips. "What is a Metatron?"

Cade's face softened as he looked at me, like a father talking to a favorite daughter. "Literally, it's a mediator chosen by God to communicate."

"Like a prophet or something?"

Cade nodded. "Or something."

"But you told Sam that I was a Metatron!"

Cade nodded again.

"Well that's wrong then. I'm not even religious!"

"Prophets rarely are." It was a bit disturbing the way Cade didn't blink when he looked at me. "And Metatrons shouldn't be."

"What's the difference between a Metatron and a prophet?"

"A prophet is just a human, but a Metatron is a human that's been granted special powers to do good works."

"Special powers?" My stomach felt sick. "Like some kind of superhero?"

Cade chuckled. It was a real Cade laugh and I warmed at the sound of it. I had hated the fatherly smile. "Something like that. More like the powers of an angel than a superhero."

I scrubbed my fingers into my scalp. There were too many questions in my head.

"Why?" I asked at last. "Why me?"

"Oh, Misty," Cade was sounding more and more like his old self. "There is so much I can see now. I am the Fallen Redeemed, no longer bound by time and space. And while there is much that I know, it is not for me to tell you. You are still bound by earthly constraints and you must learn all things in your own time."

"I can't begin to tell you how helpful that is," I said dryly.

He laughed out loud at that. It was so familiar, so much like the old him, that I started to approach. He didn't push me back, but he didn't welcome me forward either. I stopped when I was inches from him. Hesitantly, almost fearfully, I reached out my hand to touch him, my fingers barely resting against his chest.

Something had changed.

The energy that I'd always felt whenever I'd touched Cade was no longer there.

I trembled. A vacuum opened up inside me and I suddenly felt more alone than I could ever remember. I must have been this empty before I'd met him, all those months ago, but if I had, I hadn't been aware of it.

"Where are you?" Maybe that was a stupid question, but he seemed to know what I meant.

"I'm everywhere, Misty." He raised his hand to lightly brush away the hair from my face. "Everywhere and everywhen."

"But you're not here?" I know I wasn't making sense, but suddenly everything seemed so wrong. "You're not here with me. Now."

"Misty." Cade cupped my face in his hands and stared unblinking into my eyes. "The love I felt for you when I was bound to earth is just a grain of sand compared to my love for you now, and that love is not quantifiable. Human love is so limited, bound by space and time, but now my love for you is infinite, beyond human comprehension."

I fell against him, clinging to him, searching for that connection. In spite of his words, I still couldn't find him. I pressed against his body closer, yet I felt nothing but his skin against mine. Slowly, painfully, I pulled back from him until only my hands held his shoulders. His arms dropped to his sides and he met my eyes.

"I don't like this." The breath stuttered in my chest. "I want it to go back to the way it was before. To the way you were before."

"There is no going back for me, Misty. There is no before and no tomorrow. There is only what is, which is everything."

I stepped back, the sight of him blurred by my tears.

"I need you, Cade." I whispered. "I need you to be with me, the way you were before. I need you to *be*. Now."

He smiled as he gleamed brightly, his body blurring now as light and energy replaced his human body.

"I will always be with you, Misty. I will be your angel. Your guardian angel. But I cannot maintain human form. It's too corruptible. All too soon you will understand what I mean, but until that time, you must trust me. You may be alone, but I will always be with you."

He raised his hand to stroke my face as his gleam grew bright, turning the desert night to day and then to a blinding white. I could feel his fingers on my skin. I grabbed his wrist, pressing his hand tighter against my cheek, but his hand faded into a silky mist. Then the mist began to dissolve as the light flared nova. When the light disappeared, so had Cade.

I was alone.

Chapter Forty One

I sat curled in a ball on the sand. I don't know how long I sat there. I didn't care. Cade was gone. Danel was gone. I must have been this alone before, but I couldn't remember. Now there was nothing but an aching void. Cade may say that he was still with me, but he wasn't. Not really. And Danel. I realized now how much I had come to love Danel, but he had been shredded and his limbs carried off. Who knew how long it would be before he could locate his parts from where they'd be scattered? Even if he could get his head back from Sam Jaza, it would probably take centuries, or at least decades. I'd be dead by then. Or old.

Misery took me. I forgot all about my Metatronism... whatever that was, and focused on willing myself to die. I couldn't find one reason to take another breath. And the fact that stopping breathing wouldn't be enough to kill me was irrelevant. There was nothing left to live for. I wondered if I sat here on the desert sand, how long it would take me to die.

The sky was beginning to lighten. The night, which had already seemed to last for two lifetimes, was finally over. The sunrise was magnificent. Typical. I don't suppose they often get overcast skies in the desert. I sat watching the sky turn from black to purple to pink. And then the sun crested. I stared at it as it turned from a sliver to a half circle. I wondered if I could damage my Metatron eyes by staring at it for too long. I didn't care. I was just curious in a detached way. Probably not, since I didn't blink and it hadn't hurt at all.

I searched for a trace of the stars, but the desert sun bleached them from view. I wanted to see the stars. To study them. To pick one that I could believe was a physical manifestation of Cade. To be able to focus on it, talk to it and be able to say, *There. There is Cade.There he is.*

But a star can't talk to you. A star can't hold you in his arms and make a cold day warm and a lovely day even lovlier. A star can't chuckle and laugh and make you smile even when you were determined to keep a straight face. A star is really no good at all.

The sun was resting on the horizon and I was still curled up, my arms cradling my head, when I noticed a fleck silhouetted against the sun. I watched it approach, not caring what it was. It was moving quickly and the part of my mind that still cared about such things noticed that it was a human. No, I take that back. It was human shaped. There was no way a human on foot could move that fast.

So deep was my funk, that I couldn't rouse myself to care. It might be Sam Jaza, or perhaps one of his flunkies, but I was too far gone to get alarmed. I wondered what this demon could do to me now. I wondered if I didn't put up a fight, if it could kill me. I'd let it. I might even thank it.

The demon slowed as he approached. With the sun behind it, I couldn't make out its features, but I could see it wore long layered robes, the same as Sam Jaza and his stooges. It stopped in front of me, and then stepped to its left so I could see its face.

Danel.

But not Danel.

It looked like Danel, but I wouldn't be fooled. Danel was scattered to the four corners of the earth. Sam Jaza must not have figured out that I can tell the difference.

"Stand, Metatron," said the Dopple Danel quietly.

For no good reason, I stood. This Dopple Danel had been sent to me for a reason and I supposed I would have to confront my demons at some point. I brushed the sand from the shreds of my skirt, straightened my spine and looked at the demon, eye to eye.

"Well?" I was impatient to meet my doom. "What is it? What do you want?"

The demon smiled.

"You."

I tensed for battle. Maybe this is what I needed. A vicious, bloody fight that would shred us both to splinters. My fingers curled into claws as I waited for its next move.

Yet the move, when it came, surprised me. Its left arm whipped out, grasping me behind the neck before I had a chance to react. It dragged me forward, pulling our faces together.

I clutched at its hair, ripping its head back, away from me, but it was relentless and its mouth latched onto mine. A handful of its hair came free. I flung it away.

And then I froze. The kiss was familiar. Not just the kiss, but the response within me. I took a deep breath. Leather and evergreen with a hint of cinnamon.

It was Danel.

The real Danel.

I pushed away from him. Hard. My grief for Cade still ached like a hundred bleeding gashes. But curiosity warred with despair and I spat out a broken question. "How?"

Danel's chuckle rumbled in his chest. "The demons that Sam had ordered to scatter me didn't leave right away. They wanted to see what happened to you and Cade. When Cade declared you a Metatron, they fled, dropping my parts as they ran. It didn't take me much time at all to pull myself back together."

"Where's your other arm?" I could see where the robe fell slackly off his shoulder his right arm should be.

Danel shrugged as well as he could with one arm. "It'll catch up."

There was a warm gleam in Danel's normally stoic expression and anger flared in my chest.

"Cade is gone!" I snapped. "He was your friend and you just stand there grinning."

Technically, Danel hadn't been grinning before, but he did now. That one sided smirk that made me long to strike him.

"If you only knew, Misty," Danel said softly. "You will understand someday, but for now, all I can say is don't grieve for Cade. You've given him a gift that he's been craving for centuries; a gift that many of us have sought and despaired of every achieving."

My arms folded across my chest, pressing to fill the void that his words did nothing to ease. "And what would that be?" I asked.

"Humanity."

It wasn't the answer I was expecting and my fists unclenched. I hadn't even been aware that I'd been gripping them. "Why? Why would he want humanity? Why would any of you want it?"

"Because with humanity comes redemption and that has been denied to us since the last Metatron refused to mediate for us all those centuries ago."

His mention of the Metatron brought my fists to my hips. I glared at him. "Did you know? About me? Being a, you know, Metatron?"

It was still too weird of a concept. I didn't know what it meant, but a whole lot of weird had happened last night and I was still trying to wrap my brain around it.

"I wondered," he admitted. "From the very start, I wondered what had drawn Cade to you. Even at the beginning, Cade had been the most reluctant of the Fallen. And then his centuries of self-imposed isolation, rather than hardening him, had given him a sensitivity to humanity that Sam and the rest hadn't noticed. But I had. And then there was your ability to block persuasion, to detect the true nature of the Fallen despite their illusions. This and other clues led me to hope."

Hope. Hope that I was a Metatron. Hope that I could be the key to his redemption. That's why he was so interested in me. Didn't I feel sexy. Bile twisted my stomach.

"So all that crap about Sam not wanting Cade to love, that was crap?"

"I did not lie. That was Sam's initial motivation for wanting you dead. But that was just a passing fancy. Now, he's got a real reason to eliminate you."

"Wait a minute! Did you miss what happened last night? I didn't just survive! I whipped his butt! I didn't just whip his butt! I owned that boyscout! There is no way he'll be coming back for more." My words faltered at the pitying look in Danel's eyes. "Will he?" I added weakly.

"You're not immortal, Misty. At least, your body's not. Nor are you the first Metatron since Enoch."

"Enoch? The guy who wrote all that stuff? Enoch was a Metatron? He could whip demon butt? You would think with all the blathering he'd written, he'd have mentioned that."

"Those scrolls have long since been lost. Mostly destroyed by Sam Jaza and his minions."

"So, if there are other Metatrons, where are they?"

"None survive."

The bile in my stomach had turned to stone. "Gee thanks. I was feeling a little depressed, what with losing Cade and all, but you've made me feel so much better."

I stood my ground as Danel stepped toward me, that warm light glittering in his eyes again. He raised his one hand to brush back the curls that blew into my face. His fingers sketched a trail across my cheek before reaching behind my neck and pulling my face towards him.

"I've waited Misty. I've been so patient. And now, at last Cade is gone."

My body, the traitor, trembled in response and he smiled as he felt it.That crooked, one-cheek half smile that made me long to hit him.

So I did.

Sucker punched him right in the gut and sent him flying a couple of hundred feet over the dunes. I heard him land with a thud and a grunt on the sand.

I turned and headed north. As the breeze blew my hair back off my face with the softest carress, I heard Cade's chuckle in the wind.

I smiled as I walked to Alexandria.

www.ingramcontent.com/pod-product-compliance
Lightning Source LLC
Chambersburg PA
CBHW071246170626
46809CB00001B/98